# Also by Alex Day

*The Missing Twin*

# The Best of Friends

## Alex Day

One More Chapter
an imprint of HarperCollins*Publishers* Ltd
1 London Bridge Street
London SE1 9GF

HarperCollins*Publishers*
1st Floor, Watermarque Building, Ringsend Road
Dublin 4, Ireland

www.harpercollins.co.uk

This paperback edition 2021

First published in Great Britain in ebook format by
HarperCollinsPublishers 2021

A catalogue record for this book
is available from the British Library

ISBN: 978-0-00-845513-2

Set in Birka by Palimpsest Book Production Ltd,
Falkirk Stirlingshire

Printed and bound by CPI Group (UK) Ltd, Croydon, CR0 4YY

# PART 1

*Whether we fall by ambition, blood or lust,*
*Like diamonds we are cut with our own dust.*

— *The Duchess of Malfi,* John Webster

# *Prologue*

'Y o'u were jealous, weren't you? Angry that you had been usurped by the man you thought belonged to you.'

The QC's voice is calm and contained as always, though the steel beneath its surface is barely concealed.

'Of course I was jealous. Anyone would be.' The defendant cannot keep the anger out of her voice. 'But not enough to ...'

She falters, finds herself unable to say the words out loud, perhaps mindful of the jury, twelve pairs of eyes intently fixed upon her, or of the journalists watching from the public gallery, wolves waiting to fall upon their prey.

'Not jealous enough to do what I'm accused of,' she continues, her voice little more than a whisper now, her gaze cast demurely – but still somehow defiantly – down.

She's doing well and seems to have – at least temporarily – won the sympathy of the court, convincing the jury of her innocence, her blamelessness. But the QC has more – much more – up the sombre black sleeve of his capacious gown.

'And you had secrets, did you not. Things that you'd done that you needed to make sure no one ever found out about.' It is a statement, not a question.

3

The woman's face blanches visibly.

There is a long pause. It's pin-drop quiet. The QC is playing it for effect, making sure he has everyone on the edges of their seats in this, the greatest theatre in the land. In the silence, the white noise of the building seems deafening. Somebody coughs, and the sound echoes out like a death knell.

'Didn't you?' The QC repeats himself, and now it is a question, prompting her to respond.

'Yes.'

An audible murmur, like a far-off earthquake or explosion, vibrates around the room. The atmosphere changes in an instant. It's as if everyone knows that something big is coming, that a hand grenade is going to be launched into the respectful arena of the courtroom. It had been insane for her to ever think it could remain hidden. The truth will out, as the saying goes. But far from setting her free, it may well prove to be the final nail in her metaphorical coffin, the evidence that puts her behind bars.

'There were things you'd hidden from even your closest friends, weren't there?'

Silence.

'One thing in particular, wouldn't you agree?'

He's going to reveal it and very soon everyone will know her history. She wills it over and done with. The jackals wait with bated breath, eager for the next titbit to feast upon. The QC inhales deeply before continuing, as if believing that oxygen will be in short supply once he has made the revelation.

The collective gasp that follows seems to prove him right. It emits forth with such force it might have come from the walls themselves. The woman's blonde hair falls across her face as she drops her head in despair.

The case that has hitherto slithered back and forth has turned on a sixpence. The entire courtroom can see that the defendant has no way back from this.

The QC turns to the judge. 'No more, m'lord.'

He sits, and his black gown balloons and then descends around him like the darkening sky before a thunderstorm.

# Chapter 1

## Susannah

A gust of March wind blows across the emerald grass and sends the torn paper pieces whirling into the air in bright swirls of colour – orange, pink, yellow, and blue. I shiver and pull my insubstantial coat tighter around me, wishing I had something warmer to wear. Living in the city for so long has made me soft and I've forgotten how to cope in the country, without buildings and pollution and warm tarmac to keep the elements at bay. Now the cold is creeping into my bones and lodging there, insidious and immoveable, joining the pain of my newly single existence, the anxiety that is inherent in knowing that I bear sole responsibility for the day-to-day upbringing of my two young children.

I look over to them, my precious boys, eight-year-old Luke and eleven-year-old Jamie, who are waiting with a bunch of other kids for the paper chase to start, a cacophony of over-excited shouts and cheers emanating from the group. My heart leaps with love and hope at the sight of them, so intent on being part of it all, wanting desperately to join in, to belong. Poor lambs, they've been through the mill over the past year, what with their dad's business collapsing, the money drying up, their family home being sold from over their heads, and all of this culminating in a messy and protracted divorce and a house move which has meant new schools and new everything.

I've tried not to let them see me cry but of course it's been impossible to completely hide my distress. Despite this, they've been stoic throughout and I'm so proud of the way they've coped. Through it all, they've never complained, not once.

They're not complaining now, not about the bitter weather, nor the fact that, unlike most of the other kids they're with, they don't have a father here to cheer them on, to wave their flag. Nor any long-standing friends, either. Along with all the material things we lost when Justin went bankrupt, our social circle deserted us en masse, as if we'd become toxic, liable to infect anyone who came too close with the malaise of failure. Without the status that coupledom conveys, and the outward indicators that everything is perfectly fine – a nice house, good clothes, food from farmers' markets, foreign holidays – I became a nobody overnight. Being persona non grata myself was one thing, and hard enough to take. But to see my boys similarly ostracised, through no fault of their own, was much, much tougher.

At least right here, right now, that is not the case. The boys, judging by the excitable chatter that surrounds them, seem to have been accepted without question into this new milieu.

For me, things are somewhat different. All around me are gaggles of parents, all of whom seem to know each other, all of whom are already invested in this community in some way or other. I hear snatches of conversations, enquiries as to levels of school satisfaction, decisions on holiday destinations, proclamations about the weather or the political situation. Nobody else is alone, and none of them look like they are currently freezing their balls off as I am. They are all perfectly attuned to their environment, apparently evolutionarily adapted to the countryside in a way that I am not, and sporting the kind of practical, sensible outerwear that would not be found in the department store under the 'coats' sign but in 'outdoor pursuits', categorised by function and purpose.

Loud laughs waft towards me from one of the jolly groups. Despite how much I stand out in my inappropriate attire – a totally unsuitable lightweight trench coat in a particularly brilliant shade of pillar box red – none of them has so much as spared me a glance. The carapaces of belonging protect them, making their togetherness impenetrable. Even if this weren't the case it probably wouldn't change anything because I am utterly lacking in networking skills and too shy to make friends easily. The longest conversation I've had with anyone over the age of twelve in the last three months was with the removal men, and that was only to give them instructions – put this box there, that bed in that room, and so on.

A whistle blows and Jamie looks over at me, waves, then takes off his coat and drops it to the ground. He steps into place amidst a long row of boys and girls of similar height. Luke likewise casts aside his anorak without a care. He will be with the second younger group of runners. Smiling despite the bitter wind, I walk over to them and pick up the discarded garments.

'Good luck, boys,' I call, receiving a nod of acknowledgement from Jamie and nothing at all from Luke.

Cool and calm as ever, Jamie then turns his attention to quietly scrutinising the competition, sizing them up, whereas Luke, always effervescent, is jumping around wasting energy for the run on by playing the clown. I laugh despite myself. They are cute and funny and infuriating in equal measure but above all, they are mine and they seem to be doing OK, and that's the only thing that really matters.

The whistle goes again, a different tone this time, signalling that the race has begun. The runners stream past, clouds of vapour hanging in their wake, thrumming footsteps shaking the ground beneath.

As I follow their progress, I catch the eye of a woman standing nearby. She smiles at me. Relief, combined with a profound gratitude, floods through my veins. Someone has noticed me, is ready to welcome me into the fold. I beam back over-enthusiastically, ridiculously and embarrassingly pleased by the attention. I grasp the mettle, determined to overcome my natural timidity, and walk towards the friendly woman, my lips parted ready to introduce myself, my mind working hard on what kind of greeting would be appropriate.

'Hi, my name's Susannah, what's yours?' or, 'Hello, I'm Susannah, I'm new in the village. Have you lived here long?' Unlike the children in the paper chase, I've had little chance to limber up for this challenge but, nevertheless, I'm going to go for it.

I open my mouth to speak.

But there's someone else in front of me, almost, but not quite, elbowing me to one side, and shrieking, 'Hattie! So lovely to see you,' and throwing her arms around my erstwhile friend and I realise, with a searing stab of disappointment, that she had not been acknowledging me at all but this other person, the person she already knows and who is already part of her social circle.

Stumbling awkwardly, I march on, having to suddenly veer to my right to avoid careering straight into this Hattie person who is still being vociferously embraced, my smile fixed on my face as if it hadn't been for her in the first place, but for someone else entirely. The wind whips up anew, seizing a handful of the paper pieces that mark the trail and turning them into a feverish whirlpool of kaleidoscope colours.

How I wish there was something similar to this paper chase in the adult world of social interactions, a designated route to follow, carefully signposted, guaranteed to lead to the desired endpoint.

But of course there isn't.

I'm suddenly acutely conscious of standing alone on the village green with an armful of coats and a heartful of loneliness. I clutch the garments tighter and trudge towards the finish line. The twenty or so minutes until the first runners return seems like an eternity. During the wait, the mantra 'fake it until you make it' runs through my head like an irritating radio jingle, and then changes to a refrain of 'things can only get better', and all the while I keep a welcoming and optimistic faux-smile plastered onto my face.

But deep inside, I long for Justin, or perhaps not even for him but for *someone* ... a friend, lover, husband, anyone – just so as not to be always on my own.

# Chapter 2

## *Charlotte*

R ed.
Bright, eye-catching harlot-red, poison-red, blood-red. Red that spells danger.

You stand out like a sore thumb in that unsuitable coat, which is why I notice you as soon as I arrive on the green. My imagination runs wild, thinking of all the – overwhelmingly negative – things that red symbolises. It must be tiredness, hallucinations brought on by having all my four boys home for the Easter holidays, eating non-stop, playing computer games until the small hours and fighting with an assiduity that would be admirable if it weren't so exhausting.

I've been intrigued by you since Toby first came home with stories of a new family in the village – two boys the same age as him and Sam, and an absent dad. You've bought the terraced house at the less fashionable end of the village that was on the market for quite a while. It seems faintly ridiculous that such a small backwater as this should have such a thing as a 'less fashionable end' but there's no doubt that the area has become markedly less desirable since the massive housing estate was built right in the middle of it, providing homes for commuters into the M3 corridor.

Toby, of course, has no idea of such subtleties as the 'right' postcode or the 'wrong' one, and he's particularly taken with your Jamie in a way I've not seen in him before. So of course I'm interested in Jamie, too. Every mother wants their child to have friends, to be popular. And it's useful for me to have some inside info on you, brought to me from the innocent mouths of my own children. Of course, like most pre-teen boys, when pressed for details about someone's appearance or character, Toby has almost nothing to say beyond 'I dunno' and 'just, like, normal' but I got a little more from Sam and my imagination had already created a picture of you as a devastatingly attractive divorcee with an undertone of beguiling vulnerability.

Exactly the kind of woman I need to worry about. To keep tabs on.

Seeing you for real, though, I observe that, though you are undoubtedly good-looking, you don't look like the guileful type, the type who preys on other people's husbands. You look altogether more innocent than that, more ingenue than femme fatale: sweet, self-effacing, hopeful and above all, cold. It will take a bit of time for you to get used to our country weather if you're a townie. There's so much I'll need to tell you, when we get to know each other, when we become friends. Which we will, without doubt. I'm sure of that already.

For a start, you should know that this is a cold place.

Our village nestles in what is known as a frost pocket and winter temperatures fall below what you'd expect for the south of England. A powdery dusting of hoarfrost coats cars, trees, and lawns in the mornings from November right through to May. As if to prove my point, the runners stream by, cheeks reddened not only by exertion but also by the chill north wind.

Spring is a long time coming this year, even longer than usual. Thank goodness for the only two things that have got the boys out of the house this Easter: football on the green and Miriam. I'll tell you all about her, for sure, although she'll probably seek you out before I have the chance. She likes to be at the centre of everything, to know all the comings and goings in the village. Miriam truly is Biglow's uber-mother, always looking after everyone and everything, organising events from the fete to the flower show – and of course, the paper chases.

It's her raison d'être to spend her time recreating a bygone age, bringing back to life the childhood pastimes of a distant halcyon era, one in which children befriend strangers on trains without fear that they might be child molesters, where obesity and ruinously overpriced, sugar-coated breakfast cereals are unknown and healthy outdoor pursuits eagerly partaken in by all. And whilst they do entail hours of chilly hanging around and making small talk with people I have no particular interest in, I always turn up to her events.

I like to show my appreciation of all she does, and to play my part in a way which befits the owner of the manor house. Feudalism may be long gone but people still like to know the pecking order and to have someone to kowtow to and look up to. How else do you think the royal family survives? But of course the main reason why I'm always there on the sidelines, however inclement the weather, is to support my boys, to cheer them on, to laud them whenever and however I can.

I had so little of that when I was a child; no one ever came to sports day and praised me for my hundred-metre sprint or my discus throw, and told me I was wonderful and they were proud of me (even though I was rubbish and came last every time). It's such a cliché but I want everything to be different for my children. I want them to have all the things I didn't have: love and devotion and adulation, a stable family life with a mum and dad and everything just as it should be.

Dan and I fall in and out of love – that's normal, in long-term relationships, isn't it? No doubt you and I will discuss this at some point. Right now, the brutal truth is that he gets on my nerves most of the time, and mostly I'm glad he spends such long hours at work so he's not hanging round the house irritating me. But one thing is certain. We'll always be together, a unit.

I would never let anything get in the way of that.

# Chapter 3

## Susannah

There's something bewildering about drinking tea in the deliciously warm kitchen that throbs with people and voices and the clinking of numerous glasses and not having spoken a word to Charlotte, the hostess, yet. She's busy distributing trays of elaborate nibbles and pouring liberal quantities of prosecco into outstretched champagne flutes. Brunette hair rippling and gleaming like a TV shampoo ad, she looks amazing. Dressed casually but immaculately in skinny jeans and an oversized, extremely stylish but still cosy cashmere sweater, she's as pristine and perfect as her house. I've only seen the kitchen so far, but it's to die for – opulent and enormous, white units and marble worktops that glitter under the artfully mismatched copper domes of designer lighting. All the glistening appliances look brand new and the central island must be about five metres long.

Once I've finished gazing nervously around me, I start to feel conspicuously alone again. It's like the first day at my new school, which I joined at fourteen when the money for

17

my private education had run out because my dad had lost his job and his savings were all used up. Everyone else was already in their friendship groups and all the other girls wandered around in tight little cliques with entwined arms and matching hair styles and speech patterns and I knew, just knew, I'd never be able to penetrate their armour-plated solidarity.

My hands grip tighter around my mug. I force myself to remember that I did, eventually, settle in and make friends and although it was never as if I'd been there from the beginning, at least I stopped being the odd one out. I raise my eyes and search the room. There must be people here, other women, other mothers, who I might get to know. Of course it doesn't happen quickly; it's not an overnight thing. I need to give it time.

As my gaze strays across the crowds, it falls on Charlotte and our eyes lock. She gives me the smallest, briefest, sweetest smile. There's a moment when I recall the Hattie incident of earlier, but then my heart leaps and I smile back, a huge grin like that of an over-friendly dog ecstatic at being patted. Quickly, I modify it to something less undignified. Almost immediately, Charlotte's attention is taken by someone else, another guest congratulating her on the food, the ambience, the decor, the general wonderfulness of everything about her, her house, and her hospitality. But just before she looks away, she smiles again and winks.

The gesture of complicity is so unexpected, and makes me feel so special, that I'm momentarily too stunned to respond. By the time I've come to my senses, Charlotte has moved off, snaffled by a red-haired woman with super-long legs, deep in conversation already. I bask for a few moments in the warm glow of her attention, even if so briefly and fleetingly caught. I allow myself the luxury of believing that it's all going to work out, that this move to the country on which so much depends will prove to have been a good thing after all.

A rush of air at my side announces the rapid arrival of Jamie. He leans in and plants a kiss on my neck that I think was intended for my cheek but missed.

'The party bus is awesome,' he says, breathlessly. 'It's got more games than you could ever imagine. I'm going back. See you later.' He turns to leave as precipitously as he arrived, only pausing for a fleeting second to call back over his shoulder, 'Love you, Mum.'

I have no idea what they are actually playing – apart from the ubiquitous Fortnite, I'm woefully ignorant of any of these online games, and I have to trust that Charlotte will only have booked those that are age-appropriate. The main thing is that the boys appear to have been well and truly accepted. Jamie's triumph in the paper chase – he won by some margin – far from provoking jealousy, seems to have elevated him to the status of some kind of hero. At the finish line, the other boys clustered around him to heap praise upon him and claim the prime place as his best friend whilst Luke, as is often the case, basked in his reflected glory.

'Well done!' The words are boomed into my ear at such volume that I jump out of my skin. 'Excellent effort!' the voice goes on.

I turn to see a stout, determined-looking woman with a

double chin and bushy eyebrows looming over me. I recognise her as the large lady who was mustering all the children on the green and who I took to be the organiser of the event.

'That boy of yours!' Everything she says seems to end with an exclamation mark. 'He put the rest of them to shame, won the paper chase hands down. Good show!'

I smile modestly. I'm proud of Jamie, though I'd never boast or crow about his attributes. He's everything a mother could want in a boy: clever and handsome, tall and sporty. He always wins everything, every spelling bee and times-table competition, all the athletics prizes plus the football and rugby tournaments – the latter not single-handed, obviously, but he takes a lot of the credit as he is usually captain as well as star player. This is what I try to focus on, when times are bad – how lucky I am to have my sons, that things can always be worse.

'I'm Miriam, by the way,' the hearty woman continues. 'Miriam Whitehead. Nice to meet you.' She proffers a large, unkempt hand, fingers unadorned by rings of any type, finger-nails bitten and misshapen.

I take it and we shake, awkwardly. At least, I feel awkward. She seems oblivious. Her skin is rough and her palms slightly sweaty. It is more than warm in the kitchen now; in fact it's decidedly hot, the Aga pumping out heat while the doors and windows are shut tight against the wind. I was frozen earlier, but now I wish I could take off my jumper, something that is not possible as all I have underneath is a faded and tatty old camisole that could not possibly be shown the light of day. I shift uneasily on the stool I'm perched on. Miriam hauls herself laboriously up onto the one next to me.

'Lovely do, isn't it?'

I nod. She's a little odd, but I could forgive her anything because I'm so grateful not to be sitting here like Billy-no-mates anymore. And if I want to become a part of this community, I've got to start somewhere.

'Charlotte's children's parties are always the most sought after!' Miriam's words explode forth in staccato bursts like anti-aircraft fire. 'No expense spared. Party bags that cost more than I would spend on a present!'

'Gosh,' I reply. 'That does sound extravagant. But lovely,' I add hurriedly, in case Miriam should take what I have said the wrong way and think I'm being critical or judgemental.

'Well, they can afford it. Dan is rich.' Miriam purses her lips and nods, then lowers her voice to a conspiratorial tone as she leans closer to me. 'I mean, stinking rich. Absolutely loaded. All four of the boys down to attend Rugby – it's where Dan himself went, of course. Oldest two, Jonny and Angus – they're twins you know – are already there.'

'Oh.' I'm at risk of coming across as mentally incapacitated if I keep on answering in monosyllables. But Miriam doesn't seem to have noticed and it certainly isn't inhibiting her. There's an air of adulation in the way she talks about Charlotte and Dan, mingled with a tinge of subservience. There are people who like looking up to others, glorifying them, who admire and lionise the rich and privileged. She appears to be one of them.

'They have a beautiful home,' I say. I know so little about the couple, the host and hostess, that I don't have a lot to contribute to this conversation. I want to show willing but

I'm acutely aware of the difference in our circumstances. I'm penniless, skint. It's only the generosity – dished out with tight lips – of my parents (long since restored to full financial wellbeing, thanks to a new career for Dad and a couple of handy inheritances) that has kept the boys and me from dependence on the welfare state.

'Oh, isn't it just?' shouts Miriam. And then she lowers her voice to a conspiratorial stage whisper that would be clearly audible to anyone within a radius of about five feet, if they were inclined to listen in, 'I think they're going through a bit of a bad patch in their marriage at the moment though. Problem is, Dan does nothing to help Charlotte around the house or with the children! She's positively downtrodden in that respect. Although on the other side of the coin, when he's out earning millions, how much laundry can he really be expected to do?'

The rhetorical question hangs in the air. I look across the room. Charlotte's handing a bin bag to a young woman, presumably a hired help whose job it currently is to collect rubbish. OK, I think, so she's in charge of domestic arrangements, which she may or may not be happy about, but 'downtrodden' and 'rich as Croesus' are hardly concepts that fit seamlessly together. Miriam is possibly prone to a bit of exaggeration – not to mention the fact that she's obviously an incorrigible gossip.

'No kids myself, of course,' she proceeds, well into her flow now, 'but I am the scout leader and I run weekend sporting activities for the local young people. So important to keep them active, I always think.'

I'm glad she's not telling tales about Charlotte's marriage anymore. It's really none of my business and tittle-tattle always makes me feel uncomfortable. I've been the subject of enough of it over the last year or so.

'I couldn't agree more,' I respond, pleased the conversation is moving onto safer ground. 'My experience of boys is that, like puppies, they need plenty of exercise to keep them out of trouble.'

Miriam laughs.

'So, you're new to the village?' she asks and then, without a pause, continues straight on, answering her own question with another one before I have a chance to say anything.

'Of course you are. And you will want to join the Food for Free club, won't you? Membership is gratis, it gets you out and about, and the bonus is that you reduce your shopping bill.'

'Well,' I answer, hesitantly. 'That sounds ... interesting.'

I've got absolutely no idea what she's talking about. Perhaps it's a reference to a foodbank – in which case I must look even more impoverished and desperate than I think I do. Though this comfortable – some might say complacent – community hardly seems the spot for such a charitable enterprise. Whatever it is, I'm pretty sure that I don't want to be involved in this particular club.

No further enlightenment is forthcoming, however, as Miriam carries on regardless, onto yet another subject already.

'The end-of-terrace in the street that leads off the far end of the recreation ground, isn't it? It's not a bad place, though I heard when it went on the market that it had a bit of a problem with damp.'

She seems to know a lot about me. I keep quiet, wanting and simultaneously not wanting to know how the village of Biglow has categorised me.

'Well, did it?' Miriam demands, interrupting my thoughts. 'Have a problem with damp? I mean, you hear so many rumours but you don't know if any of it is true or not. It looks like a nice house to me. Small, obviously – but people seem to want so much these days – en suite bathrooms, open-plan kitchen-diners, you name it. What's wrong with walls, I ask you? Anyway, your little place is, in my opinion, quite ample for a family of four, I'm sure.'

Finally, she dries up. She takes a big swig of her glass of fizz and looks at me expectantly. I'm not sure which misconception to address first.

'The damp is really nothing serious,' I say, deciding on the least personal, 'and the seller sorted it as a condition of completion.'

I finish my cup of tea, deliberately place it back on the counter and look at my watch. 'And there are only three of us – me and my two children. I'm divorced.'

It seems ridiculous that, in this day and age, it should still be so difficult to say the 'd' word. But it is. Far from symbolising freedom and opportunity, it conjures up an image of someone unwanted, cast aside. There's such comfort in coupledom, such cosiness. Two people, standing side-by-side, against the world is such a beguiling prospect, and it hurts when I think that I might have lost that feeling forever, might never know it again.

But the reality is that I can't imagine how, where, or when I could ever meet someone new, find another partner. I know that lots of women – and men – find their partners online. But I've heard so many scare stories, of terrible dates, scary dates, boring dates, cringeworthy dates, not to mention the horrendous attempts at extortion that women – especially women – suffer, or the ghosting, or the revenge porn. I'm full of admiration for those who take the plunge and for whom it works out well. But I'm nowhere near brave or self-confident enough for that right now, and I'm not sure I ever will be. Which leaves me exactly where I am, focusing on doing the best for my amazing boys but knowing that, one day, they'll have grown up and left home.

And then it'll be just me and my solitude forevermore.

A phone rings, its piercing bell cutting through the chattering voices, clinking glasses, and setting down of crockery. My heart skips a beat. All of a sudden I'm reminded of all the calls from Justin's creditors that presaged disaster, the demands for money that he could not pay. Charlotte's phone rings and rings and no one answers, just like I, too, stopped answering for fear of who might be on the other end.

'I–I really ought to be making a move,' I say, flustered. 'It was lovely to meet you, Miriam. I'm sure we'll see more of each other, round and about.'

Miriam looks momentarily nonplussed that I'm not about to divulge any more secrets about myself, but quickly changes her expression to one of regret.

'That's a shame, going so soon,' she exclaims. 'I'll drop by sometime soon though, see how you're doing!'

'I'll look forward to it,' I dissemble. I can't see Miriam and me becoming soulmates but I'm grateful to her for reaching out to me. Even if her motive does seem to have been gleaning as much information about me and my family as possible.

I slide off the high stool and onto the tiled floor, my heels click-clacking against the stone and leaving behind a trail of mud specks, a legacy of the wet field earlier. As I make my way through the enormous room, ducking and diving between the groups of guests, I see Charlotte standing by the door, gazing distractedly out into the walled garden. She looks troubled and I wonder what could possibly be amiss in her apparently perfect life. I want to say goodbye to her, and thank you, but something stops me. It's as if, right now, a magnetic forcefield surrounds her, preventing anyone getting close.

Then I remember the wink that she gave me earlier, that indicated alliance, allegiance. My footsteps lighten and I sigh with relief.

Perhaps she and I will become friends, like our boys are friends, and I'll fit into this community in a way I never felt I truly did in Barnes. I leave the kitchen in search of the boys with the sudden, heady, and totally unexpected feeling of hope.

# Chapter 4

## *Charlotte*

Steamy, sultry heat. Sweat beading on my back and my forehead. Concentration furrowing my brow. The weight of a wordless silence, the low flutter of rifled notes, my breathing forcibly steady and even.

The envelope pushed under the door, a note inside it comprising one single word.

I press my forehead against the sliding door that separates inside from out, desperate for the feel of the cool glass against my skin. The phone's ring was klaxon loud, cutting across the noise of the prattling horde in the kitchen as if it were no louder than whispers, rocking the house to its very foundations.

I thought, when I heard it, what I always think. That this is it. That this time, it is them. Oh God, please don't let it be them.

I didn't answer it. I didn't dare to. I ignored it and it rang out.

The house is full of people and I should be tending to their every need. But right now, in the aftermath, I just need a moment. A moment to compose myself. I was majorly pissed off with Dan for being late. Now I'm almost grateful. He might have noticed my agitation, questioned me. Answered the phone himself, God forbid. Even though he never, ever does that, there's no knowing that he won't, one day. And then my dirty, guilty secret would be out – and what the consequence of that would be I don't dare imagine.

In the reflection, I see you making your way out, pausing as if wondering whether to approach me, then thinking better of it and proceeding on your way to retrieve your boys and go home. I appreciate that you actually read the party invite and know what time it ends. Rousing myself to action, I hand out more black bags and instructions to the agency girls; there are plates and wrappers and napkins that need clearing. I hate mess. And the process of tidying, of sweeping detritus into trash sacks, is a good signal to guests that it's time to start thinking about leaving. Nevertheless, there are people in this room I know I'll be – politely – throwing out hours after the end time stated on the invitations. It's as if they haven't got homes to go to, nor anything better to do.

There's another shrill, piercing ring and my heart stops – and then I realise it was just a clanging glass, not the phone.

When I've calmed down again, I make my way around the room, collecting discarded mugs of tea and half-empty glasses of prosecco. To take my mind off the unanswered phone call, I think of you, imagining your life and what has brought you here to this sleepy backwater. I wonder if you work, if you have a job. I suspect not. You seem to be just like me: someone who's put their own career to one side in order to facilitate that of their husband. Dan didn't bat an eyelid when he asked me to go on his first posting to Hong Kong, even though he knew it would mean me having to kiss goodbye to my TV job, the career I was so intent on, that I'd worked so hard to wheedle my way into. I was moving up the ladder, about to take on my first assistant-producer role. But it was either go with Dan or lose him so I did what countless women have done through the ages and gave it all up.

The thing is that it was obvious from the very start that Dan was going places. Literally. We must have lived in a dozen countries in our first fifteen years together. But of course I don't just mean geographical moves, I mean that Dan was headed for the top from the beginning. He only has one default setting and that's himself as a major success story, acing everything, outplaying everyone. Dan always has Dan in the number one slot and everyone else fitting into the adulatory queue behind him.

I very soon realised that if I wanted to keep him – and I did, I really, really did – I had to fall in line.

In Hong Kong, we lived on The Hill along with every other overpaid ex-pat. The apartment was beautiful, all sparkling glass, stainless steel, and polished tiles. There was a swimming pool in the complex, and a gym, and the majority of the wives just hung around there most of the day. There wasn't much else to do while the men were at work and it was so hot, so relentlessly, hideously humid, that often I joined them, feeling sapped of all energy, stripped of the inclination to do anything constructive.

My idea that I'd find work once we'd settled in fizzled away, burnt out like the whizz-bang fireworks the Chinese love so much. Any job available locally was paid at local wages which were laughably low and anyway they weren't appropriate for women like me. I'd have had to speak Cantonese, for a start. Plus Dan had a constant round of client entertaining and evening dos that I needed to accompany him to and preparing for those so I that I lived up to his high standards and expectations – tailor-made dresses, haircuts, spray tan – took up a huge amount of time.

As the weeks and months passed, I gave up on even pretending I was ever going to get gainful employment. And anyway, Dan poured scorn on any such suggestion. He simply couldn't understand why I would want to work when he made more than enough money for both of us. He constantly urged me to relax, to enjoy myself.

'All I want is you here waiting for me at the end of a long day. What's the point of both of us being stressed at work when there's no need?'

He didn't understand that I required more than that. Perhaps I didn't understand it, either. If I had, surely I'd never have got involved, never have done the things that, unbeknownst to anyone but me, blight my life to this day.

Sometimes, I even manage to convince myself of that.

# Chapter 5

## Susannah

I have to literally drag the boys out of the bus but I insist we're leaving despite all their protestations; I'm weary and I need to go home. And anyway, the party invitation clearly stated 4-6pm and I don't want to outstay my welcome. Retracing my footsteps back through the house towards the front door, I pop into the kitchen where a group of immaculately groomed women are clustered around the Aga. I ask them if they know where Charlotte is so that I can say goodbye. As one, they exchange knowing looks before the blondest of them all says, 'She's just gone to see if that was Dan pulling up in the drive.'

There's a pause when it seems that none of us knows what to say next.

'He's just a little bit late, you see,' continues the woman, with a strange expression that is half grin, half grimace. 'I think he's in the doghouse.'

And then, with what is clearly now a smirk, she concludes with, 'He often is.'

'Charlotte'll be tongue-lashing him as we speak,' laughs another. 'You know how strict she is with him.'

That sets them all chortling insincerely away. And I thought these people were her friends.

'Oh, right,' I reply, with a nervous half-smile. There's certainly no shortage of people wanting to pass comment on the state of Charlotte and Dan's marriage, that's for sure, or on Charlotte herself. Poor woman, under such constant surveillance. It must put her under a lot of pressure. I guess living in the manor house and being loaded makes her an object of envy – and animosity. People always hate it when someone else is blatantly richer and more successful than they are. And forgive me for mentioning the patriarchy so early, but it's always the woman who's judged the most negatively. Charlotte's frustration with her husband's tardiness is perfectly understandable and yet here she is, being accused of nagging, of fishwifery of the highest order.

'Well, I must be off,' I say breezily, as if I really don't have time to hang around any longer. As if I have somewhere exciting and interesting to go, and my busy little life doesn't allow time for idle chit-chat. When, of course, nothing could be further from the truth.

'Lovely to meet you all,' I add, wondering why I insist on following convention, even if it means blatantly lying.

'And you,' the bitches – sorry, women – chorus, in varying tones of insincerity.

*Well, I don't like you either*, I say to myself, petulantly, childishly. Poor Charlotte. With friends like those, who needs enemies?

'Why do we have to go now?' remonstrates Jamie, as I purposefully take the boys' hands and pull them with me towards the door. 'It was just getting wicked in there. I got to the highest level I've ever been on.'

'And what about our party bags?' whines Luke, tired now and liable to have a meltdown. 'I want a party bag!'

'Because we do, Jamie,' I say, unequivocally, to one side. 'And don't be so ill-mannered, Luke,' I say to the other.

Before either boy can come back with a rejoinder, the subtle scent of expensive perfume heralds Charlotte, standing on the threshold of the huge, wide-open front door.

'What on earth time do you call this?'

Her voice is sharp and cold, her icy words clearly carried towards me on the chill breeze that's blowing in from outside.

She sounds angry, and critical. But, I reason to myself in the face of the glamour-puss's recent comments, she has every right to be. Dan should have been back for his son's party.

Charlotte edges outside without seeming to have noticed me and the boys. All her attention is focused in one direction. I hesitate, not sure whether to go on. I don't want to interrupt. But I don't really have an option; I can hardly retreat to the phalanx of terrifying women in the kitchen.

As I'm dithering, I see a huge box by the door, overflowing with bright, tempting packages. The famous party bags. Great. Somehow, as well as navigating around Charlotte and her errant husband, I've got to get Luke past them without a tantrum.

'Look, just get yourself inside. Everyone's been asking where you are; it's so embarrassing.' Charlotte's voice is impatient, biting – a result, I assume, of weariness as well as irritation – because she must be tired after organising and running this whole shebang by herself.

'Not to mention how you've let Toby down,' Charlotte continues. 'All he asked for was his dad to be at his party – and you weren't.'

This might have gone on for some time, I suppose, but it's interrupted by the phone on the hall table ringing once more, loudly and uncompromisingly, demanding to be answered. Scolding abandoned, Charlotte is there like a shot, snatching the receiver from its cradle, turning her face away and muttering a few words so quietly I cannot hear what she says. She opens a door and disappears behind it, as if the conversation she will have is private and mustn't be overheard. As she slips through I catch sight of her face, which carries an expression that is a strange mix of underlying anxiety tinged with welcome relief.

I'm feeling really in the way now, so I hurry to the front door, trying to put my body between Luke and the treasure trove.

'Party bags,' shouts Luke, my efforts to avoid him spotting them proving futile.

'No,' I say, not without a tinge of regret; I'd love to see what's inside them after Miriam's tantalising descriptions. I step outside, slap bang into a tall, athletically built man who's poised on the top step, sleekly dressed in a work suit and designer sunglasses and incongruously clutching in one hand an enormous bunch of helium balloons in a range of garish colours.

'Whoa, watch out for yourself,' he says. His voice is rich

and deep with a suave transatlantic twang that speaks of money and sophistication.

'Sorry, so sorry,' I stutter, utterly mortified. 'Um, we were just going. It's been great. A super party, thank you so much ...'

My mouth is on autopilot but after a frantic search, I manage to find the off button and, in the hiatus that follows, I take in every detail of the infamous Dan's appearance. He pushes the sunglasses up onto his head and I see that he has a longish face, with eyes that slant sexily downwards and a high forehead with thick dark hair that is greying slightly at the temples. His mouth is strong and determined and extends now into a slow and inviting smile.

There is no denying that he is absolutely gorgeous, but he looks like a nice person, too, his bearing confident but not arrogant. I instantaneously reassess what I've been thinking of him, and of Charlotte. Perhaps she is being unfair, after all.

'I'm pleased you enjoyed it.' Dan glances briefly through the open door and then at the balloons as if wondering how he's going to get them inside. 'Here,' he says, pulling out two from the bunch and handing them to Luke and Jamie.

'What do you say, boys?' I demand, in that way that parents have that we are aware must be so annoying to our offspring but we do it anyway, to show those we don't know well our dedication to good manners and correct behaviour.

'Thank you,' says Jamie, always obedient.

'I want a party bag,' wails Luke, 'not a stupid balloon.'

'Luke!' I can't believe he's letting me down like this. 'I am so sorry,' I say to Dan, and then, tugging angrily at Luke's arm, chide him. 'Luke, don't be so rude.'

I don't know what to do to cover my mortification, so I just look down and try to make my way past Dan. But he and the balloons together make an impassable barrier, so I have to stop.

'Don't worry about it!' he exclaims, 'and I'm the one who should be sorry. I got stuck with clients waiting for a delayed flight. I couldn't just dump them at the airport and leave them so ...' Dan tails off, as if realising that it's not me he needs to explain himself to. Although, having heard his excuse, it seems eminently understandable. I hope Charlotte can see reason, for Dan's sake.

'Of course he must have a party bag,' Dan resumes, equanimity quickly restored. 'They both must have one. I'll fetch them now. Please wait.'

He thrusts the bundle of balloon strings towards me. 'Hold these for a moment, please.'

He disappears inside whilst I stand there feeling like Mary Poppins and wondering whether I should start to sing. I'm just about to launch into 'A spoonful of sugar' when Dan reappears and, with a flourish, gives each boy an enormous party bag.

'Thank you,' they both chorus in unison, no prompting necessary this time.

'It was a super party,' I say again. 'They had so much fun. Please do thank Charlotte for me – I didn't quite get the chance. The phone, you know ...' I gesture back into the hall, to where the phone cradle still stands empty on the table.

Dan nods and holds out his hand. It is strong and lightly tanned, with long, elegant fingers. On his other wrist I notice, as we're shaking, is the most beautiful man's watch I've ever seen; it's clearly worth thousands.

'Glad you came, er ...' his voice trails off as he realises he doesn't know who I am, has no idea what my name is.

'Susannah,' I fill in hastily. 'And of course you're Dan,' I add, in case he wonders why I don't ask.

'Susannah.' He says it slowly, rolling it around his tongue as if savouring it. 'What a pretty name.'

I blush. It's so long since anyone paid me a compliment that I don't know how to react.

'Thank you,' I mumble. Charlotte must be off the phone now as I can hear her voice calling from inside the house, but not what she's saying.

'We must see you again sometime,' Dan continues, and he's about to say more when Charlotte obviously calls something from inside, inaudible to me, before she appears on the threshold. She seems tense, on edge but not, right now, with Dan. Instead, she has that look in her eye of someone who's been distracted by something they can't quite get their head around. I wonder what it could be – perhaps the phone call contained unexpected news of some sort. Her eyes flicker absentmindedly over me and the boys and then she addresses Dan again, as if she's already forgotten that we are there.

'Hurry up and come in, you're letting all the cold air in,' she says. Her voice is softer, her manner more subdued.

Mutely, I hold the balloons out so that Dan can reclaim them. He smiles, says goodbye and then follows Charlotte back into the house, wedging the balloons with some difficulty through the door despite its opulent width. The boys and I descend the steps.

'Bye and thank you again,' I call back over my shoulder,

and as I do so, Dan turns. He gives me a conspiratorial shrug that says 'I have to do as I'm told' before the huge, heavy door closes and he and the multicoloured balloons are gone.

All the way home, as the boys chatter excitedly about their exploits of the afternoon, my thoughts are fixed on Charlotte and Dan, Dan and Charlotte. Little quarrels and disagreements aside, their lifestyle is enviable, their wealth and glamour all-pervasive, the opportunities and advantages they can offer their children too numerous to mention. Oh, may God strike me down for my shallowness, but I would love just a little bit of what Charlotte has.

In all honesty, who wouldn't?

# *Chapter 6*

## *Charlotte*

Forgetting all about Dan, his tardiness, his ridiculous gesture of reconciliation that is the heaving mass of helium balloons, as soon as the phone starts to ring once more I rush to answer it, grabbing the handset from the cradle, resisting the urge to smash it to the ground. Out of the corner of my eye I see you, cowering in the doorway, your boys clutched in your hands. You cannot be witness to my humiliation. Muttering my habitual greeting, 'Biglow 601017', I slip into the butler's pantry, shutting and locking the door behind me. I do all of this before I've even registered that there's no one there, no one on the other end of the line.

It's another drop down. I dial 1471. Number withheld.

I turn around, lean against the solid wood of the door, and concentrate on steadying my breathing, bringing my heart rate down to its usual pace. One ... two ... three ... One ... two ... three ... I count slowly in my head to slow my racing pulse.

It feels like an age has passed before I am fit to re-enter the hallway. Running my fingers through my hair to smooth it

39

down, I emerge from the pantry, assuming a nonchalant gait and trying to look normal – whatever that is. The handset is clutched in my sweaty palm and I replace it, slowly and deliberately. Then I turn towards the front door which is swinging wide open, no longer a barrier to the cold grey outside.

'Are you still out there?' I call to Dan. And then, as I feel the rush of frigid air billowing in, I urge him to get himself inside. I'm not mad with him anymore, not the way I was, not since the phone call. How can I be, when the sin I've committed is so great, so shaming, so unconscionable? If it ever came out, I'd need to garner every ounce of his forgiveness – and I'm not sure I could, or even that it would be enough. Oh, but it's hard, pretending all the time that nothing's wrong, that I am exactly who I seem to be. Sometimes I forget what, exactly, I'm pretending about. Confusion befuddles everything. All I can be really certain about is this. Dan can't find out.

Ever.

All our marriage, I've been subordinate to him. He has made the decisions and I have fallen in line. I guess both of us had our reasons for liking it that way in the beginning. I saw the life of luxury that Dan could offer me and I thought that would make up for losing my independence. I loved him, for God's sake. And I was young enough to believe, completely and utterly, that love is enough.

He saw a young, mouldable trophy wife who'd look good on his arm and always be there for him, the buttress behind the facade. And he loved me, I'm sure of it. Still does, quite probably. It's just that he's been so rich and so successful for so long that he believes himself to have risen above the standards – moral or otherwise – by which the mere mortals amongst us must abide.

Thinking back to the beginning though, it was always going to come unstuck at some stage. People have to kick back, don't they? Everyone needs some autonomy. The more I found mine in the kind of way that other, saner people would look down upon, the more I felt I had to take a backseat in all other matters.

A kind of quid pro quo of unremitting acquiescence in return for my underhand exploits.

The crunch point came, though, when we were living in Kuala Lumpur and it was time to start thinking about preparatory schooling for the boys. Before I met Dan, I had no experience of the kind of life where you leave home to go to school whilst still in single figures and effectively never return. It's a miracle he ever met someone like me, whose background couldn't have been more different. Our meeting was a chance encounter at a party held by a friend of a friend of mine who just happened to be Dan's cousin. I still can't imagine why I was there, how I got invited. The truth is that I probably wasn't. My friends and I were fairly adept at gatecrashing.

But I digress. Dan only understands one type of education. The exact same one he had: boarding prep school followed by boarding public school followed by Oxford. I didn't understand it then and I'm not sure I'm any the wiser now. I put up so many arguments against following this route for my own children. The idea of the twins going off to England alone at such a young age appalled me. But Dan insisted and this insistence was unrelenting. He kept on and on and on at me until I gave in. And so it was that Jonny and Angus found themselves on a Heathrow-bound plane at the age of nine. Nine! The only concession Dan made to my sensibilities was allowing me to fly with them rather than handing them over to the school escort service at KL international airport.

But perhaps that only made the parting harder. It broke my heart to leave them. Hampshire was cold and rainy; though born in New York, we'd left before they were two so all they'd ever known was the steamy heat of the Far East – Hong Kong, Singapore, KL – and the riotous, relentless sunshine of Rio, Delhi, and Lima. When I said goodbye to them, I don't think they had any concept of how long it was going to be before they saw me again. I did, and I hated it. I cried all the way back to Malaysia.

How long they cried for I've never asked because I couldn't bear to know.

Thank God I managed to keep hold of Toby and Sam, but that was only because when Toby hit seven, we were on our way back to England anyway. I put my foot down and both the younger ones attend prep school as day boys. That was one of the many reasons I was so determined to buy this house; it is close enough to drive them to school (the one that Dan and all his family have attended since time immemorial) and back every day. But Toby will be starting at Rugby in September, and three years later, Sam will follow. I'm dreading it.

The result of losing my older boys so young is that I overdo it with them all. I mean, they're absolutely not spoilt, not at all. But I shower them with love and attention and days out and specially cooked favourite foods, most of which they probably don't appreciate, wearing myself out in the process. That's not the point, though. The point is both assuaging my guilt and getting my fill of them in the time that I have, as if I can store up the contact with them so that it lasts when they're gone.

This small rebellion over schooling is the only time I've insisted on getting my own way. In all other matters, I do what Dan wants. I argue with him about the little things – punctuality, for instance, apropos the party – but never, since the school debacle, about the things that really matter. And when push comes to shove, I value our partnership more than I dislike the compromises. A marriage is a buffer to the world, providing safety and security. People can understand it, can't they? A divorced woman is always liable to be looked on with pity, don't you think?

I shiver when I contemplate ... but no, I'm not going there. He would never be able to understand why I did what I did nor to accept it. Which is why it has to stay secret forever. The worst didn't happen, and hasn't yet, though that doesn't stop me from always looking over my shoulder. I'm constantly waiting for the past to catch up with me, half knowing that one day, it will, and half hopeful that I'll make sure it never can.

People envy me, I know. I'm sure you do. Dan and I appear to be the perfect couple: beautiful, gilded, rich, and powerful, a pair of shining stars in a rich, exclusive, and opulent galaxy.

But you should always remember that appearances can be deceptive.

# *Chapter 7*

## *Susannah*

The pavement is slick underfoot, but the rain has stopped now, and the wind has dropped. Magnolias are poised to burst into bloom, waxy pink flower buds standing erect on bare branches as if waiting for the command to open. In London, before we left, some were already out but it's colder here, everything several weeks behind.

Spring comes early in London, I think. I feel a pang of deep regret, of sorrow for what I've left behind – its familiarity that gave it an illusion of safety – and what lies ahead. But I banish the self-pity before it can begin to take root, quickening my pace, my feet hitting the tarmac evenly and lightly, the hedges, lampposts and trees flying by, as if I am trying to run the past out of me. I'm a good runner, and a fast one; Jamie inherited my sporty genes, I always think. Let's just hope they do more for him than they've ever done for me.

Passing the green, I cast a glance over the stone wall that fronts Charlotte's house – the prize of the village, a stunning Queen Anne manor house restored to perfection. The

45

sweeping circular drive is empty of cars and the house stands silent, a beguiling combination of homely and majestic, creamy stone mellow and inviting despite the unappealing weather. Since the party, I now know that it's as beautiful and stylish inside as it is out.

I marvel that, despite the gaping chasm in their circumstances, the huge disparities in their lifestyles, the four boys – mine and her two youngest – get on so well together. Jamie and Luke have had several playdates with them, though never at our house; they always go to Charlotte's, which has everything a child could want in terms of entertainment: table tennis, games consoles, and a hand-built adventure playground, not to mention an indoor swimming pool. In all truth, I do find Toby and Sam a little spoilt – but perhaps that's inevitable when you have so much and never want for anything. If money is no object, it makes no sense to deny your children what their hearts desire. Though even when I was a great deal better off than I am now, I still took care not give my boys too much and to make sure that they understand the value of money.

Anyway, my two are going round to Charlotte's this afternoon after school. Having buddies just down the road is definitely making the transition here so much easier for them. And where they have forged ahead, I am determined to follow.

If they can make it, so can I.

I run on, a new determination in my steps, turning into the road that leads to the recreation ground where there is a short cut back to my house. On the right-hand side lies the Biglow Tennis Club. Its notice board stands proudly out front, advertising events, competitions, and opening times. I pause, glancing through the crunchy brown leaves of the beech hedge to the grass courts where a groundsman is checking the condition of the bright-green sward, systematically pacing forward a few metres and then bending low before standing straight once more.

There's a poster about the Biglow tennis championship which I stop to read, rocking back and forth on my toes and holding my hands up to my mouth and blowing on them to keep them warm. I wish I could take part in the competition, but I've already looked the club up online and found that the membership fees, though not extravagant, are far too high for me to justify with things the way they are. I'll try to scrape together enough to allow the boys to do a holiday scheme in the summer because I think they'd really enjoy it, and I want them to be able to play the sport that I once excelled in. But a few lessons or a short course here and there are likely to be the sum total of their involvement with Biglow's tennis fraternity.

Just as I am turning away, a man emerges from the club's automatic doors, his bag hastily packed with the racket handle emerging from the zip. He's walking briskly, tall and upright, and he has an indefinable presence about him of ownership and assuredness. I watch him without much interest; I hardly know anyone here yet, least of all anyone male. But as he draws nearer, he flashes me a brisk smile of recognition and I realise who it is.

Dan.

I falter for a moment, instantly self-conscious. I'm not

dressed or made-up for meeting people, my face bare, my hair pulled back into a tight ponytail. The last person I want to come across while looking like this is the cool, debonair (my judgement) and stinking rich (Miriam's words) Dan. But it's too late. I can't get away now.

'Susannah!' He's holding out his hand to shake mine and I have no option but to reciprocate. The shake is as pleasant as the first one, his palm cool and dry, his grip firm.

'That's right. Clever of you to remember!' I'm conscious that my voice is unnecessarily high.

'I never forget a name.' Dan's clear-eyed gaze is disconcerting. I'm not sure how to respond so I don't.

'What are you up to?' he enquires nonchalantly, then looks around him and back at me, as if wandering why I'm loitering there. 'Were you ... waiting for someone?'

'Oh no!' I exclaim, laughing over-enthusiastically. 'No, no. Absolutely not. No, I don't know anyone to wait for.' I pull a doleful face. 'Still settling in, you know, trying to meet people. I was just finding out what's going on locally.'

I gesture towards the noticeboard to explain the latter comment. 'And then you came along,' I conclude.

Dan bursts out laughing. 'You make me sound like a nasty rash!' He pauses and regards me as I feel the blush of embarrassment after saying something stupid creep over my cheeks.

'But anyway ... do you play?' he asks, his face suddenly serious again.

'Er, yes.' I shrug as if my playing were nothing, dismissing instantly the idea of telling him that I was once my county's under-18 champion. Nobody likes a boaster.

'Great,' replies Dan, his attention now elsewhere, searching for a phone that he can obviously feel vibrating in a pocket somewhere. 'We must have a game sometime.'

'Oh, I'm not sure that will be possible. I'm not a member.' I try to make it sound like a mere administrative error. It's stupid, I know – having no money is nothing to be ashamed of – but nevertheless, I don't want him to know that I can't afford to join the tennis club. The last thing I want to evoke is his pity.

Dan's missed the call but one glance at the screen sends him marching off towards his car.

'Doesn't matter,' he calls back over his shoulder. His long stride means he's halfway down the path to the car park already. 'I can sign you in. I'll look forward to it.'

And then he's making a call and lodging the phone between his chin and his shoulder whilst he pulls his car key out of another pocket. He disappears out of sight behind the hedge and in the distance I hear the sound of a car door opening and clunking expensively shut and then the noise of a six-cylinder engine starting up. The swish of tyres on tarmac and the roar of acceleration come next, followed by silence.

It has begun to drizzle, ice-cold globules dotting my face and hands, soaking into my hair and my running jacket. Turning determinedly for home, I set off down the footpath, my pace faster now because of the wet but also because of my need to shake off my despondency. Damn the financial crisis, damn my ex-husband Justin, and most of all, damn the fact that I was so dependent on him and put such misplaced faith in the fact that he would always be able to provide for me.

And then again, damn myself and all the mistakes I've made.

I reach my house and give an involuntary shudder as I am confronted once more by how tawdry it is, with its pebble-dashed facade and weed-strewn pocket-handkerchief front garden. As I struggle with the uncooperative lock, trying to avoid looking at everything I dislike about my home, I hear a car approaching and sliding to a halt right behind me. I freeze. Unexpected callers have freaked me out since the bailiffs came.

My hands are shaking as I abandon the lock and, slowly and with my heart in my mouth, turn around.

# Chapter 8

## Susannah

For the second time in a matter of a few minutes, the person I am confronted with is Dan.

I exhale loudly in relief, unaware that I've been holding my breath. Only Dan. Nobody threatening.

He is waiting at the end of the path, standing by his car, looking like a promotional picture from an upmarket lifestyle magazine.

'Hey!' he calls, his voice sonorous and commanding. 'I forgot to take your number.'

My stomach flips over. I really shouldn't go out without eating anything. Ignoring the grumblings coming from my innards, I walk towards him, just avoiding an embarrassing stumble at the broken paving stone halfway down my front path.

'So we can book up that game,' he says, proffering a notebook and pen towards me. 'Give me your mobile and I'll set something up – maybe doubles with my mates Tom and Lucy?'

'Of course, absolutely,' I stutter, still getting over my surprise.

I scribble down my number on the notepad and hand it back to him. 'Whatever you prefer.' Doubles would at least mean it's not just me and him, which might be tricky in a way I can't quite define. Too intense? Too exposing?

'But isn't Charlotte your doubles partner?' I ask him. I had them down as the archetypal tennis-playing couple, burnished by their existence under a perpetual metaphorical sun. 'Who would I play with?'

The sardonic snort that greets these questions takes me by surprise.

'She hasn't played for years,' he replies. 'Bad back, she says, but really she's just not interested – in tennis or in m—' He pauses as if aware that he has said – or is about to say – too much. 'She prefers other things – yoga, swimming, that kind of thing. A while back it was dressage – lessons, courses, practice etc,' he continues in a more measured tone.

'Gosh.' There doesn't seem to be anything to say to this; I have no intelligent conversation I can offer up on the subject. I don't know anyone for whom dressage is a hobby, not even when I lived in Barnes, which is the kind of place where many expensive and unusual pastimes are undertaken.

'And her personal trainer comes to the house most days to do Pilates with her, of course,' Dan adds as an afterthought. 'Plus, she quite often disappears off to have mysterious beauty treatments – I'm not too sure of the details of those.'

'That explains her amazing figure,' I say, unable to keep from my voice the wistful envy that I feel, 'and her perfect complexion. Whatever she's doing, it's definitely worth it.'

Neither of us speaks for a moment.

Dan seems to remember something important. 'And of course there's her foraging club.' He emits a short burst of mirth, quickly turning it into an appreciative smile. 'That's her latest fad – finding food for free in the fields and hedgerows, living like she's in the eighteenth century.' He pauses and then, as if afraid of sounding disloyal, hastily adds, 'I mean, it's quite amazing what she dishes up. She's even writing a book about it.'

'Wow,' I say, inadequately. There seems to be nothing that Charlotte isn't involved in, nothing that falls outside her sphere of interest or expertise. It occurs to me that this must have been what Miriam meant when she told me about the Food for Free club – not a foodbank at all but a way of living off nature's bounty.

'I think Miriam alluded to it at the party,' I muse, 'but I wasn't quite sure what she was on about. I'm glad to have got to the root of it.'

There's a tense and awkward moment when I'm not sure if my joke has landed wide of the mark. But then Dan's face lights up and he laughs, real laughter this time rather than the ironic type from earlier.

'The root of it!' he laughs. 'Very good, very clever.'

'Pardon the pun,' I say, grinning broadly, chuffed at how funny he seems to have found it. Humour brings down barriers – as long as it's actually funny, or at least cheesy. Not like Justin's speciality of mother-in-law and fat-wife jokes. I read in a women's magazine once that it's essential to have a store of one-liners and quips up your sleeve for those awkward moments on a date when no one can think of what to say. I didn't take it too seriously at the time, being married to Justin and having no intention of ever being single again. Even now that I am, here in the cold chill of a barren Biglow morning, the idea of ever going on a date seems more unlikely than the Pope not being Catholic. But I've made Dan laugh and that gives me a warm, fuzzy feeling inside.

'You must ask her about it, get involved,' Dan is saying about the foraging club. 'She and the girls have a whale of a time out in the countryside.'

'Oh, I will.' And I mean it. I'd love to be in Charlotte's club; of course I would. 'Is it just in Biglow, or are there other branches?' I add, innocently.

'No, just Big—' Dan pauses and starts to chuckle again. 'Very clever, I see what you did there. You're too good at this!' He thinks for a moment before speaking again. 'Perhaps I should plant the seed of an idea in her head for an expansion ...'

'From little acorns and all that,' I contribute. 'I recommend a root and branch approach.'

We're both chortling away now, enjoying our silly little word game.

'As long as she's not barking up the wrong tree,' he concludes, giving me a cheeky wink.

In the spirit of always quitting whilst you're ahead, I put forth my final sally. 'You should take your leaf now,' I rejoin. 'I don't want you being late on my account.'

Dan shakes his head, still laughing. 'I'll remember this conversation.' He pauses, and then thinks of something that brings a frown to his handsome face. 'You have to be a bit careful, though. In the foraging club, I mean. Some of the plants out there are poisonous.'

My grip tightens on the roof of the car where rain drops have balled and separated. 'Yes,' I agree slowly. 'I always remember my mother telling me about deadly nightshade, and never to eat berries of any kind. It's the sort of warning you remember all your life.'

Dan nods, the humour of our earlier exchange having disappeared from his voice. 'I'm talking about mushrooms. We had an unfortunate episode once with some that Charlotte inadvertently gathered.' He pauses, sighing ruefully. 'There are all kinds of dodgy ones, some really quite nasty.'

His voice, with its suave and soothing cadences, continues but I'm feeling dizzy and finding it hard to concentrate.

All of a sudden, Dan stops talking. 'Are you all right?'

His question is tinged with anxiety, my sudden silence after so much jollity causing him to break off from his chatting. 'You look like you're about to faint.'

He's at my side, his hand on my elbow.

'I'm sorry,' I stutter. 'Just a sudden head rush. Low-sugar blip – I haven't eaten anything yet today.'

'So get yourself indoors and get something hot inside you,' he says commandingly, shaking his head disapprovingly as if I've broken a rule and let him down. I almost titter at the double entendre, but stop myself just in time as Dan is clearly oblivious and I don't want him to think me crude. 'And don't go out running on an empty stomach again.'

'No.' I smile at him gratefully. 'I won't. You're right. Silly. Silly thing to do, silly me.'

Dan's forehead creases with concern. 'Would you like me to come in with you? To make sure you're all right?'

I shake my head.

'I'm fine,' I say, 'really.' I rub my fingers across my forehead as if that will erase the headache that's gathering there. 'Before you go, though, can I take Charlotte's number? I don't actually have it. I'd like to invite her over for a coffee. Get to know her better, you know.'

'Of course. She'd love that.'

Dan writes down the number, tears off the piece of paper and hands it to me.

'I must fly now; I'm due in the office in an hour. Take care of yourself, won't you? Eat something!'

He speeds away, my 'goodbye' floating feebly in the Porsche's slipstream.

After a renewed tussle with the lock, I manage to get the front door open. The house is gloomy and dank, the curtains still drawn, the heating off. There's a permanently fusty airless smell about the place that makes me think that perhaps the damp hasn't been adequately dealt with, despite what I told Miriam so confidently. Either that or we've got mice.

I perch on a chair in the kitchen as I create a new contact in my phone and add the number Dan gave me. Then I get up and stash the piece of paper carefully in one of the dresser drawers, just in case my ancient and outdated mobile packs up, which gets more and more likely as each day passes.

I force myself to eat a banana, shower and change, and then go up to the boys' bedroom to do a bit of ineffectual unpacking of yet another box of toys – Lego, Playmobil, and some weird orange remote control thing with wheels and claws. I have no idea where it came from and nor do I ever recollect either of the boys playing with it. I want to throw it in the trash – after all, if they ask about it, I can always say that it got lost in the move. But somehow I lose heart. Maybe it's something really important and they've lost so much else that it would be cruel to wrest it away from them.

I look around at all the rest. I should probably try to sell it on eBay – someone told me that you can get a fair bit for Lego, even incomplete sets and all mixed up. I sit back on my heels and consider this. I actually have no idea how to sell things on eBay; it's just one of those terms that people bandy about but probably half of them don't actually do it, either. I half-heartedly put some potentially saleable bits of Lego in an empty box and then ponder the mess anew, despairing of ever sorting it and knowing that, even when the boxes are all unpacked and the toys binned or stowed away in cupboards or under beds, the metaphorical mess which is my tattered life will still surround me.

A rapping at the front door jerks me forcibly from my reverie. I'm immediately on high alert, my body tensed for the next noise. When the bailiffs called, all those months ago, I unwittingly opened the door without using the chain because I lived in Barnes and didn't think about danger on the doorstep. And certainly hadn't ever envisaged six-foot bully boys coming to call.

A size eleven shoe was immediately placed on the door jamb, and a letter from the local authority thrust towards me saying that the bailiffs were authorised to collect money and/ or goods from the house in payment of substantial council tax arrears. After that, everything descended into a horrific blur; I didn't have any money to pay them off and whilst I tried to call Justin to find out what the hell was going on, the two large and intimidating men made themselves busy carting away the flatscreen TV, the Bose sound system, and the Gaggia coffee machine that were his pride and joy.

That was how I found out that my world had fallen apart and that we were going to lose everything. Talk about a rude awakening.

I get up nervously and peer over the banister and down the stairs. A bundle of post lies on the doormat. The noise was just the postman, after all. His visit also terrifies me, albeit for different reasons. I go downstairs to pick up the sheaf of envelopes, flicking quickly through them. My eyes are pierced for the franking stamp I've come to dread but don't see it.

In fact, most of the letters are addressed to the previous owner who obviously hasn't bothered to set up a forwarding service with the Royal Mail. I've already marked her as a cheapskate; she took every lightbulb, every loo roll, every curtain pole from the house, leaving it ripped bare, an empty shell. She also hasn't left her new address so I dump all her post in the bin. It'll serve her right if one's about her win on the premium bonds or an inheritance she needs to claim.

All the remaining letters are bills. Nothing unexpected, not today. Just bills, bills, and more bills. There's an electricity red notice, demanding instant payment, which I can't understand given that I've only just moved in. And a council tax bill, the very thing that Justin neglected for years, resulting in the bailiff's visit. It's for a huge sum, much more than I expected. I had harboured the notion that it was cheaper to live in the country; that was half the reason for the move to the sticks, the hope that I would be able to eke out the little I have a bit further if my expenses are less and all we eat is budget-range pasta and tinned tomatoes. I laugh bitterly to myself. As if. Everything costs just as much here as in London, if not more: a longer drive using more petrol to get to the supermarket, a colder climate so higher heating bills.

Opening my bank statement does nothing to alleviate my black mood. I need a job and I need it fast but it's been so long since I was in gainful employment outside the home that I can hardly remember how to go about it and, having dropped out of uni without finishing my Pharmacy and Toxicology degree, I'm not really qualified to do anything. All I have to my name are a few GCSEs and A-levels; zilch recent or relevant experience. I'm not a pharmacist and never will be, nor can be.

I ran a gift shop for the ten years between the aborted degree and marrying Justin and that kept me going, but there's no point in setting up something similar now. Nobody goes to shops for presents anymore. Or at least, if they do it's only to do research before they buy it cheaper online. And anything I find has to be something that can be done during school hours because if I have to pay for childcare it won't be worth it, and it also needs to be local as I can barely afford to fill the car up these days. That doesn't seem to leave many options.

A loud buzzing noise echoes out into the silence around me and I start. But it's just my mobile; none of Justin's creditors ever had that number, and anyway, it's all over and done with now so I shouldn't be letting it worry me anymore. I should be able to forget it.

I pick up the phone from the pile of debris on the table and read the message.

*Tennis, 11am Sunday. And do contact Charlotte. She'll be expecting to hear from you. Dan x*

I read it carefully several times, a smile spreading slowly across my face, before putting the phone back down and continuing with the tidying up. At last I have something to look forward to.

# Chapter 9

## Charlotte

The black car is here. Again.

It cruises past me as I walk along the high street on my way back from the church, blacked-out windows making invisible ghosts of those inside, side lights shimmering eerily in the dusk. My pulse soars, my mouth is dry with fear, my clenched palms damp with sweat. The car pulls into the petrol station. Quickening my pace, I try to see out of the corner of my eye if it has emerged yet, and in which direction.

It is right behind me.

I suppress a scream. My breathing is laboured, and my legs feel weak. I can't face this now; I can't do it. I've done everything they've asked – nearly everything, anyway. Why are they chasing me, hunting me down? What else do they want from me?

The tone of the car's engine changes as the driver moves up the gears. It purrs as it passes me, as sleek and smooth and quiet as a cat. It's an expensive model, a top of the range BMW. It disappears around the bend at the end of the high street and soon I can't hear it anymore. I'm just aware of the sounds of televisions issuing forth from the living rooms of the cottages that sit right on the road here, and of a blackbird singing on the telegraph wire above.

Perhaps it wasn't them. How do I know? How can I tell? How can something so evil be stalking me in the quiet tranquillity of an idyllic English country village in the springtime? But the reality is that although they may be based on another continent, their reach is long, infinite. They can seek out whoever they are looking for with ease. They can definitely find me if they want to. This much I have always known.

I turn off the road and across the green where the wide, sympathetic front of my beautiful house awaits, calm and serene as always. I can't wait to get inside, to shut the door behind me and hope that I am safe.

I used to dream, whilst living in a series of soulless modern apartments in foreign cities, of a house just like this. It was something I held onto, a lifeline that kept me going through the worst of times. That one day our peripatetic existence would end, and I would have a permanent base where Dan and I and the boys could grow and flourish. I let myself believe that when that time came, everything would be perfect.

That I would break my habit.

That Dan's affairs would end.

Which came first, the chicken or the egg? That's what I often ask myself. If Dan didn't play away from home, would I have fallen prey to the predilection that has all but sucked the life-blood out of me? Did he play away because I was so preoccupied?

Was it his fault or mine?

I shiver and remember the heat, the steamy, enervating mugginess of the Far East that I associate most clearly with my folly. Even now, after so many years back in England, if I step into our sauna I will be immediately transported back there. Not to plush, high-security, over-air-conditioned suites, but to seedy, oven-like bunkers where condensation ran down the walls. Two different environments. Two different types of punter. Apart from me, who frequented both.

I don't tend to use the sauna if I can avoid it.

The humidity was extreme, the boredom of day-to-day life intense. Moving to Singapore from Hong Kong at least brought a change of scene – and legal situation – and at first the city state's cleanliness was a welcome relief from the crowded chaos of the enclave. After a while, though, the sterile atmosphere became as cloying as Hong Kong's had been febrile. At least there, if you could summon the energy to brave the heat, you could wander the vibrant streets and there would always be something new and strange to see, from the jade merchants' stalls in the market, to whole pigs roasting on spits, to the gentle offerings of neon-bright flowers, flickering candles, or burning incense sticks outside Buddhist temples. In Singapore, the main entertainment was the luxurious shopping malls with their opulent window displays and immaculate customers, seemingly untouched by the sweat and tears of the real world's travails.

My dabblings alleviated the tedium of it all. But they turned into obsession and obsession leads only in one direction. When we left the east and headed west, to America, that continental shift should have been the opportunity to start again. In San Francisco, I swore that would be the end of it. And for a while, it was. My relationship with Dan got back on track. In fact, if anything it was better than before. It was so much easier to live in San Fran, to enjoy life, away from the stultifying surroundings and relentless, unmitigated pursuit of material gain that seems to be the ultimate goal of every single person in the places we had come from. And in America I could legitimately hope to get a job, to be something in my own right rather than just existing as Dan's wife. We moved to New York and I began work as an assistant in a film company.

I enjoyed it.

Then I fell pregnant.

We were delighted, obviously. I was still young by my peers' standards – only twenty-six – but having been with Dan for so long by then, it seemed the obvious next step. Secretly, I hoped that the arrival of children would fill the gaps of my isolation and force me to curb my bad habit forever. But the pregnancy was a difficult one, as is often the way when expecting twins. The weather was awful: bone-cold and grey, day after day. Having grown to hate the heat, now I missed it like one of my own limbs. I dreamt of the sunshine, of the constant feeling, when outside, of being just a bit too hot for comfort, that had characterised the last few years. The glacial conditions were accompanied by ever-worsening morning sickness, which soon developed into hyperemesis gravidarum. At its worst, I was vomiting up to twenty times a day. I spent a week in hospital on a drip.

After that, Dan refused to let me go back to my job. He told me that the only thing that mattered was my health and that of the babies. Which was good, really, as I no longer had a job to go back to. I'd been sacked, caught 'misusing' the company phones and computers for personal matters. Pregnancy turned out to be the perfect cover story. Dan never knew. It was a close shave but I got away with it. Perhaps it was that lucky escape that gave me the courage to believe that I always would. Though right now I'm not so sure.

It's not just the car. The phone calls are more frequent than ever.

They come at odd hours, always number withheld, and when I pick up, there's a slight pause – just enough to set my heart racing – and then silence, before the long, flat tone of disconnection. Two in one afternoon during the party is some sort of a record, but since then there's been at least one every five days or so. Which makes me wonder if they are watching me, if they know my routines, have access to my calendar.

If they know my children's routines.

That latter thought is too chilling. I will stop asking the au pair to do the school run for Toby and Sam and I'll do it myself. I need to be alert, to know if we're being followed. That black car gets everywhere. Purring down the main street, past the post office and the greengrocer's. Slowing down outside the general store as if I might be about to step out onto the pavement.

When we're friends, if I tell you about it, about any of this, you'll probably say I'm overreacting, that I'm being paranoid. That I have an over-active imagination. That's the way people like you, who are somewhat staid and uninventive, think.

You might even be right. But in any case, I'm not planning on divulging.

No matter how well we get to know each other, I can't share this with anyone.

The house is quiet when I enter. I go through to the kitchen. Opening the huge glass windows, I step onto the terrace. I can hear shouts and cries drifting towards me from the adventure playground. We had it constructed not long after we bought the house. It's custom-designed and hand-built and fits perfectly into the back of what was once the walled vegetable and flower garden. These days, Toby and Sam rarely play on it when they're alone, but your boys are with them today.

Now that the weather is improving and the evenings are getting lighter, they often go out onto the green for a football match after school and it's not uncommon for various village boys to drift back here with them afterwards. I don't mind; in fact, I love that they all congregate here. I like the house and garden to be full of laughter and happiness. I like having my children around me, knowing they are near. Especially in the current circumstances, where fear lingers, ever-present, in the outside world.

Walking along the terrace, I make out four little figures clambering over the wooden structure. They're supposed to be supervised when playing here. However safely it's been built, there's enormous potential for accidents. I'm absolutely against our risk-averse society but, were someone to fall, I'd want there to be an adult around to deal with it. I look for the au pair and see her sitting at a picnic table that the gardener uses for potting plants, huddled into her winter coat even though it's now May. She's not only too far away, but she's also on her phone, which is strictly forbidden when on duty.

She jumps when she sees me approaching and hurriedly shoves the phone in her pocket, starting to explain in her broken English that she needed to make a call and came to get a better signal nearer the house. But she falters halfway through as she realises she's landing herself in it even further.

I wave her excuses away and tell her she can knock off work now that I'm back. She's fairly stupid and inclined to be truculent, but the boys quite like her and the main thing is that she's monumentally unattractive. No temptation for Dan there. She's also always available for extra babysitting by dint of the fact that she doesn't ever go out or do anything other than watch YouTube videos in her room in her free time.

Tramping onwards over the grass towards the fortress structure, I soon make out Jamie and Luke with Toby and Sam. They're cute, your kids. Somewhat over-indulged, I must say – you don't seem to do discipline in the way that I understand it – but nevertheless, they're still cute. Little Luke with his spiky hair and cheeky smile. Dan told me how piteously he begged for his party bag, poor lamb. He probably doesn't get lovely treats very often. And Jamie, so tall and handsome, with that shrewd, intelligent look in his eye. I can't help feeling sorry for him, condemned to attending the local primary and then the comp.

I suppose he'll come out with a clutch of GCSEs – I mean, schools are held to account for things like that these days, aren't they? Not like in my day when it was perfectly acceptable to consign pupils to the rubbish heap. Back then, society didn't need everyone to be uber-educated; in fact, for some it was better not to be. There were jobs specifically for people with no qualifications, the kinds of jobs in factories and workshops and Royal Mail sorting offices that you wouldn't get if you had so much as a grade 3 CSE to your name. Somehow, despite everything, I managed to scrape some decent results together but it was because of my own efforts, nothing to do with the apology for an educational institution that I attended.

I'm glad things are different now, that league tables reveal to everyone what schools are achieving for those in their care. But it's all the other things Jamie – and all kids like him – will miss out on. Now I've had so much experience of public school through my own children, I just know that attending somewhere good would really bring out the best in little Jamie, and in sporting terms, with his innate ability, perhaps catapult him to county or even national level. Rugby, football, cricket – any of these could be his big talent, if he got the chance.

But when I mentioned to Dan that you would more than likely never think about the possibilities and that perhaps I should make some enquiries about bursaries or scholarships on Jamie's behalf, he told me not to be ridiculous, saying that it's nothing to do with me and you'd probably be insulted at the implication that you're not capable of acting in your own children's best interests. He told me that I can't single-handedly take care of all of life's woes, can't rescue all the lame ducks. So I dropped it.

I stride onwards towards the first of the big towers that form the corner pieces of the fortress. The boys have raided the dressing-up box – another thing that these days remains untouched unless friends are here – and all four of them are brandishing swords and wearing helmets and imitation chain mail tabards. As I approach, Jamie is performing a daredevil trick that involves throwing himself bodily off a wall, catching a knotted rope and swinging vigorously on it so that he arrives at the next set of battlements. He really is remarkably agile. But I still worry. It would be so easy to slip and fall, even for the most adept, the one with the best balance.

Toby watches from a distance, clearly in awe of Jamie's ability to find new ways to use this old toy. Luke, the adoring younger brother, is less circumspect. He's not foolish enough to attempt what Jamie has just done but he's observing how he is now tightrope walking across one of the crossbeams that tie in the castle walls. Though I don't think it's really meant for this purpose, I'm not worried that it won't hold his weight, but that he surely cannot have good enough balance to get across. But he does it, and thus emboldened, he makes his way up to a similar beam on an even higher level. I'm starting to get really nervous now. For any mother, her children are the most important thing in the world. For you, since your divorce, they're all you've got.

Jamie tentatively steps onto the highest cross beam.

'Careful! Jamie, watch out!'

My warning shout is out before I've properly thought it through. Shouting at a child in a dangerous situation is the worst thing to do; it makes them jump, breaks their concentration, causes them to turn around to look at you – all things that can lead to disaster.

Jamie, steady as a rock, does not falter. But, outside of my field of vision to the left, I hear a sharp, anguished cry. I turn with lightning speed to catch sight of Luke struggling to keep his footing, his arms flailing wildly but futilely in the air, his mouth open in a wide circle of shock and fear, his eyes full of panic. As I look on, unable to help in any way, he slips and plummets to the ground like a stone.

There's a pause, that pause that all mothers dread, before the howl of pain emanates forth from the depth of his lungs.

I rush over to him. He's lying motionless, one leg twisted beneath him. I kneel down beside him on grass that's wet from the earlier rain. The wood must have been damp and slippery – enough to cause his fall, nothing to do with my cry of alarm after all.

Shushing and soothing the boy with my voice, I reach out my hands to feel for broken bones. I touch his leg. He screams.

'Fetch Hana,' I shout to Toby, 'quickly!'

Hana has first aid training. She did a year of nursing in Bulgaria or Rumania or wherever it is she's from before she came here. She'll know what to do. This hasn't gone quite according to plan; I'm not completely in control which always unnerves me.

Whilst I wait for Hana to arrive, I cradle Luke's head in my arms and tell him that everything is going to be all right. Even though I have no way of knowing that it will be.

# Chapter 10

## *Susannah*

Lying on the sofa with a blanket pulled up to his ears, Luke looks pitifully pale and wan. As I tuck him in even tighter, I bend to kiss him. He manages a little smile, and then a bigger one.

'Can I have hot chocolate, Mum?' he asks. 'And watch telly?'

This indicates the extent to which Luke feels he should be rewarded for surviving his accident as the boys are not usually allowed to eat and drink in the living room. It also indicates that he's already feeling rather better.

When the doorbell rang half an hour before, I assumed it was the boys coming back from Charlotte's house earlier than expected. I opened the door to be confronted by Charlotte's au pair carrying Luke like a baby in her muscular arms. Charlotte was right behind her, a look of such utter anguish on her face that I was momentarily more concerned about her than about my own son. And then it registered that Luke was injured and the panic that engulfed me rendered me speechless.

'It's all OK,' said Charlotte, hastily, 'he's fine. Let's get him

71

inside and then I'll tell you what happened. Where shall we put him?'

Helplessly, I gestured Hana into the sitting room and pointed at the sofa.

'No broken,' pronounced Hana, plonking Luke rather unceremoniously onto the pale blue cushions. 'No head hurt and no leg broken.'

I crouched down beside Luke, my precious boy, kissing him, smothering him with love.

'My poor baby,' I spluttered, as I started to cry. 'What's happened to you?'

Charlotte explained all, telling me that the boys had been taking rather too many risks on the adventure playground. She was about to stop them but didn't get there in time before Luke slipped. That was it, that was all that had happened. No great drama, nothing too terrible, just a simple childhood fall.

Now Charlotte and I are sitting in my dilapidated kitchen, sipping tea. Hana has gone home to get Toby and Sam their supper and Jamie's keeping Luke company in front of the TV. I've put frozen pizzas in the oven for them; I'm too stressed to think about proper food, exhausted after so much intense emotion.

'Thank you so much,' I say, for about the fiftieth time. 'I can't thank you enough. Thank goodness you were there to help him, thank goodness you're so vigilant.'

Charlotte waves her hand dismissively. 'No, honestly, I didn't do anything special. And I'm just so sorry it happened at my house. I mean, of course I have a policy that they don't play unsupervised and I always make sure my au pairs are first aid trained, but …'

I rub my hands across my face, conscious that my mascara is probably streaked all over my cheeks from crying. 'I mean it, Charlotte. You were there for Luke when he was in trouble and I'm honestly so grateful.'

I generally take a rather laissez faire attitude towards parenting, whereas I get the feeling that Charlotte is quite an anxious mum, always looking for danger. But when it comes to potentially serious accidents, all mothers are the same; nothing is more important than our children's health and wellbeing.

The oven timer beeps and I pull the boys' pizzas out, put them on plates and cut them up. I deliver them to the sitting room – another ban broken, as pizza is normally for Saturday nights only. Both of them beam delightedly and I can see Luke's mind working overtime.

'Don't get any ideas,' I say sternly, frowning in a mock-strict way. 'This will not happen again so don't even think about feigning future injuries in the hope of the treats you've had tonight.'

Luke smiles cheekily and I leave them to it, relief suffusing my body. He's had a shock and a nasty fall but it seems that no serious harm has been done.

When I get back to the kitchen, I open a packet of almond slices and place them on the table. I'm feeling very strange still, detached, as if I've had an out-of-body experience, and I'm conscious of being a less than perfect hostess. This wasn't the coffee morning I had hoped to invite Charlotte to, when I would have had fresh flowers on the table and homemade delicacies to proffer rather than Mr Kipling. I push the plate towards her anyway.

'Please do help yourself.'

'Not for me,' Charlotte says, suppressing what seems to be a slight shudder. 'I never eat anything sweet.'

Bemused, I take one of the cakes for myself. I need some sugar for the shock, plus I haven't eaten since lunchtime. I'm just about sentient enough for it to cross my mind that it's a good thing I didn't spend hours baking seeing as Charlotte wouldn't have eaten it anyway. But then I look at my almond slice and realise that I can hardly start scoffing it if she's not having anything.

'Can I get you something else?' I ask. 'Fruit?'

I leap out of my chair again and fumble in the fridge for some blueberries, hastily removing the film with the tell-tale half-price sticker before putting them on the table.

'Lovely,' says Charlotte unconvincingly. She pops a blueberry somewhat reluctantly into her mouth as I nibble at my cake, attempting to be as parsimonious with my food as she is.

'You are good,' I say, and then immediately wish I hadn't. I hate the female thing of congratulating anyone who eats like a bird and flagellating those who have a healthy enjoyment of their food.

'I try,' sighs Charlotte, 'but it gets more and more of an effort as one gets older, doesn't it?' Without giving me time to reply she continues. 'I have to be so careful not to put on weight and Dan really doesn't help. I mean, sometimes ...' she pauses as if to brace herself for the enormity of what she is about to say, 'he wants potatoes for supper.'

There's a silence.

'Gosh,' I say, eventually. 'So what do you do then?'

'Well,' she responds, 'obviously I ask Agnes to do some for him, if that's what he wants. But I don't eat them.' She says this with utter finality.

I scrutinise my almond slice. I want to greedily consume what's left of it, all of it, stuffing it into my mouth, the whole sweet, sticky, sickly mass of it, but force myself to slow down. Charlotte takes another blueberry, places it delicately into her mouth, and chews it slowly, two calories to my two hundred.

*She asks Agnes to cook potatoes*, I think. I can't decide if I'm more jealous of having a housekeeper to prepare these fabled spuds or a husband to share them with. There goes my feminism, again, right out the window along with my willpower. I finish the almond slice.

'I've got a crate of wine in the boot of the car,' Charlotte is saying, interrupting my thoughts. 'I was waiting for Dan to unload it because it's too heavy for my back. But I could manage the weight of a single bottle.' She smiles at me, a smile that entreats me to agree but says she'll do what she wants anyway. 'I'll go and get one, shall I? Or two. I think we could both do with a drink.'

I hardly touch alcohol these days. Apart from not wanting to be a desperate, lonely old soak, I simply can't afford it. But a drink suddenly seems extremely attractive.

'I'd love one,' I agree, trying not to sound too keen. 'For medicinal purposes, obviously. Better than a potato, any day.'

I don't know what makes me say it, and as soon as the words are out, I clasp my hand over my mouth, convinced Charlotte will think I'm making fun of her.

Her head snaps towards me, and I see that she is frowning.

Oh no, I inwardly groan, I've totally blown it. There goes that friendship.

But then, as I ferret around in my mind for some words with which to apologise and make amends, the frown turns into a grin and then a broad smile and then she is laughing and as soon as she laughs, I laugh and we are both rolling around on our chairs emitting such hearty gales of laughter that Luke shouts through from the sitting room to tell us to be quiet because he can't hear the TV.

'Potato ...' splutters Charlotte, 'what on earth am I telling you about potatoes for?'

'I don't know,' I gasp, trying to catch enough breath to speak properly. 'But it was quite funny ... and I didn't like to tell you that I love potatoes.'

'Roast ...' she responds.

'Baked, chipped, sautéed ...' I continue.

'Boiled, mashed, medallioned ...'

'Medallioned ... ha ha ha! What about confit?'

'Yes, confit ...'

'What even is a confit potato anyway?'

'No idea.'

This last is so hilarious that we laugh and laugh and laugh and when we finally calm down, Charlotte pronounces herself thirstier than ever and heads off to the car. She returns with an expensive-looking bottle of wine under each arm.

'Corkscrew?' she asks.

'Oh,' I reply, surprised. I haven't had wine with anything other than a screw top for a long time. 'Somewhere.'

I delve into a drawer and eventually withdraw a battered

corkscrew, one of the most basic kind, the sort you get free with a card full of filling station points.

Despite the substandard tool, Charlotte makes light work of opening a bottle and pours us a generous glass each, once I've located the wine glasses at the back of one of the cupboards.

'I know it's a horrible way for it to have happened,' Charlotte muses, after she's taken a lengthy swig of her wine, 'but it's so nice to have this opportunity to talk to you, to get to know you better.'

I nod eagerly. 'Oh yes,' I say, 'absolutely.' I drink a slug of wine and feel it surge down my throat in a warming rush. 'I don't know if he told you,' I continue, 'but I bumped into Dan outside the tennis club the other day and he invited me for a game.' I grimace apologetically at Charlotte. I hope she won't be annoyed that I'm taking up his time, taking him away from her and the children. Although, she seems well able to stand up for herself, to tell him if that is the case; she's so strong, so independent and confident.

'I said yes. I hope that's OK,' I continue, drinking more wine. 'And I asked him for your number so I could invite you over. I just hadn't quite got round to it,' I add hastily, gesturing humbly around me, at the messy kitchen with unpacked boxes piled in the corner, and back towards the living room where removal company crates still litter the floor.

Charlotte shrugs. 'Dan loves his tennis and he's always looking for new partners. Watch him, though, because he's a seriously bad loser.' She finishes her glass and then tops it up. There's a dribble left in the bottle that she pours into mine.

'Oh,' I giggle, feeling a bit tipsy already with the unaccustomed alcohol, 'like most men, then. I'll make sure I let him win.'

Charlotte raises her eyebrows. 'No, don't do that. That'll make him worse than ever! I was looking at you and those sturdy arms and thinking you'll be able to give him a thrashing.'

I laugh, though less heartily than before. Sturdy arms. Right. Of course she doesn't mean to be insulting – it's only the truth. It's my fault for being so insecure about myself that I wish it wasn't accurate. That I care that I don't have the svelte and perfect physique that Charlotte has. Jealousy has always been one of my worst traits and I suppress it angrily now; I don't want anything to get in the way of this friendship.

'But honestly,' Charlotte continues, 'joking apart, I'm really happy for you to be playing with him. He's the kind of person who needs constant stimulation, newness, excitement. It gets rather exhausting sometimes. So if you can wear him out on the court, I'll be eternally grateful.'

I swallow another gulp of wine. 'We'll be equal then,' I smile. 'You've looked after my son and I'll have taken your demanding husband off your hands for a bit. We can call it quits.'

'Absolutely.' Charlotte reaches over and gives my hand a quick squeeze. 'God, I'm glad you've turned up in the village. People here are so small-minded and provincial. It's great to have someone fresh from London, with a wider outlook on life.'

We talk and talk and I end up telling her all about Justin

and his disastrous business affairs, the divorce, the whole song and dance of it all. She's patient and polite enough to listen carefully to every word and I realise how I've missed having a female friend I can really confide in. When I've finally exhausted the topic, she smiles sympathetically.

'Oh dear,' she says. 'You have been through the wringer, haven't you? But hopefully the only way is up from here on in.'

She looks around her, and then at her watch. 'It's only nine,' she says, 'and it's Friday. Let's open that other bottle. I feel like we've only just got started.'

# *Chapter 11*

## *Charlotte*

I pull the cork on the second bottle just as you arrive back in the kitchen from a trip to the living room to check up on Luke.

'Sorry,' you say.

I've already noticed your habit of giving unsolicited apologies for everything and anything. It's endearing, as if you are always anxious that you are not quite good enough. I know that feeling only too well – it took me years of gut-wrenchingly awful evenings and weekends and holidays with Dan's posh friends before some of their in-built, genetically programmed superiority complexes started to rub off on me. You are far more to the manor born than me, but you seem to have a similar habit of self-deprecation. Perhaps it's something to do with having fallen on hard times.

Or maybe there's something else, a dark secret in your past.

I laugh to myself at that thought. I vacillate between believing that I'm the only person in the world with so much to hide, to imagining that everyone else is guilty of the same levels of deception that I am. Who knows which is the truth?

'How is the invalid?' I ask.

'Fine,' you reply, 'absolutely fine. He must have nine lives, like a cat. So,' you add, giggling, 'let's drink to a happy ending,'

I refill the glasses and we chink. 'And to the start of a beautiful friendship,' I say.

You giggle again, and I realise you're a little bit tipsy. 'Thank fuck for that,' you sigh, uncharacteristically swearing, and referring, I assume, to Luke's remarkable recovery rather than to us being mates. I've noticed before that you are a bit of a helicopter parent; I hope your boys don't suffer too much from it – and that this unfortunate incident doesn't make you even worse. It's a shame when excessive caution curbs a young child's naturally adventurous spirit, I always think.

'So when are you meeting up with Dan for this match, did you say?' I ask.

'I can't remember if I did say or not, but it's on Sunday, 11am,' you reply. And then you add anxiously, 'is that OK? It doesn't interfere with any of your plans?'

'Oh no,' I respond. 'We've got people coming for a late lunch tomorrow, but nothing planned for Sunday.'

There's a pause for a moment as we both drink.

'When you go to the club, you'll probably meet Naomi,' I muse, rubbing a spilt streak of wine into the table top with my index finger, 'and you'll be able to tell me if you think Dan's shagging her.'

Your mouthful of wine explodes over the table, obliterating the tiny drop I'd been preoccupied with.

'Wh-wh-what do you mean?' you stutter, clearly flabber-gasted, your eyes wide with astonishment.

'Naomi is the manageress of the tennis club cafe,' I explain. 'She's obsessed with Dan, and he doesn't exactly do anything to dissuade her in this adoration. I don't think they're sleeping together. But you never know.'

If it's possible, your eyes widen even further. I didn't mean to upset you, but I suddenly felt the need to tell someone. Though I know practically everyone in this village and have numerous acquaintances, there's no one I feel I can really trust. I could never let on about Naomi to anyone else around here; half would delight in the information and spread it like wildfire and the other half, already waiting to pounce on Dan themselves, would see it as their cue to go in for the kill. I'm only too aware, frankly, of how many women are ready and waiting to snatch my husband from under my nose. You're too new here to have anyone to gossip with and I instinctively feel that you're someone I can be sure of. Even with the news that my husband is a philanderer.

'You shouldn't let him treat you like that!' you exclaim indignantly. 'If you really think he's cheating on you, you should do something. I'm sure if you spoke to him about it ...'

But this isn't a situation that's easily fixed. In those immortal words, it's complicated. I've taken the decision, like thousands of women before me and thousands still to come, to turn a blind eye to Dan's indiscretions. What's different about Naomi is that she's a little bit too close to home for comfort. Too firmly ensconced in the tennis club where she's able to see Dan on an almost daily basis and keep track of his every move. Too utterly shameless to let propriety or decorum get in her way.

I shrug. 'To be honest, it's my fault. I started it. I invited her to dinner when she first arrived as the club manageress. All I was trying to do was be nice, show an interest in Dan's hobby, welcome someone new into the fold. And Dan loves playing lord of the manor, taking the serfs under his wing, ingratiating himself with everyone, spreading his largesse far and wide.'

You are listening, bug-eyed and stunned into silence.

'I'd picked mushrooms from the fields specially for the meal but she was so picky, going on and on about whether they were safe or not. As if I were trying to poison her or something!'

You drink a big slug of your wine. 'P-p-poison?' your voice is suddenly shaky and uncertain, and I begin to worry about how much you've drunk, whether you're going to be too incapacitated to take care of Luke tonight. 'Of course, that would be absurd. Absolutely absurd.'

'Precisely,' I say, placing my glass decisively onto the table. 'Who in their right mind would attempt to poison someone?'

You don't reply. I continue.

'I didn't know that Naomi fancied Dan at this point, obviously,' I explain. 'I didn't know anything about her at all. As soon as I saw them together I could see what she was up to – and I knew it was a case of "keep your friends close and your enemies closer". The problem was that the mushrooms did make her a tad unwell – dicey stomach, you know. But she made such a fuss about what was just a simple mistake!'

You seem nonplussed, at a loss as to what to say. I'm

suddenly conscious of having overshared, of having burdened you with problems of mine that you shouldn't have to be involved in.

But then you speak and it all feels all right again.

'I'm sorry, Charlotte,' you say, slightly slurring your words. 'You extended the hand of friendship to Naomi and she slammed it back in your face. It clearly wasn't your fault about the mushrooms.'

You're so right. I knew you'd understand. Stupid Naomi, with her 'local' accent and guttural man's laugh and her tits that are the size of cantaloupe melons, is completely out of order. And it's so galling to see how generously sized she is all over; it's the thing about her that especially maddens me. Since the post-twin battle of the bulge, I have always gone to so much time and trouble and effort to stay a size eight and here Dan is, only too happy at the prospect of being eaten alive by a ten-ton temptress. And one who is always available by dint of living just around the corner. What do they say about low-hanging fruit? Naomi is certainly that and I'm not just referring to her over-large bosoms. The thing that probably annoys me most is that she's just so damn cheap and common, so blowsy, with her huge hoop earrings and orange tan. How can Dan not see how far beneath him she is?

My thoughts are rambling, running away with me. I pull myself together.

'I should go,' I say. 'It's getting late.'

After a few obligatory exhortations for me to stay, to have a coffee or a cup of tea, which I refuse, you escort me down the short and narrow hallway to your front door.

'It's been so lovely to spend time with you.'

'And you,' you say, as we air kiss. 'Thanks for providing the wine – and for gifting me your evening.'

I smile. 'It was my pleasure.' I even mean it.

I almost trip on the uneven path to your front gate. Once again, you apologise for something that isn't your fault, namely the loose paving stone. It's clear you don't have the money to fix anything about the house, which is a bit run-down all over, if I'm honest, and with a slightly strange smell. But homely. Definitely homely.

'Um, are you OK to drive?' you ask as you see me retrieving my car keys from my bag.

'Oh yes, fine,' I reply, zapping the car doors unlocked. 'It's only round the corner.' I turn and give you a short wave. 'See you soon. I'll be in touch.'

In the dusky evening light I see your face blanch as I open the car door. But, unlike many women, I can hold my drink and I'm actually not the least the worse for wear. And you'll soon learn that everyone pushes the alcohol limit in the country – there's only one police traffic patrol car in the whole county, so the chances of being caught are practically nil.

Climbing in, I stow my handbag on the passenger seat. I start the engine and fasten my seatbelt, looking around me warily. You have disappeared back inside your gloomy house and there's no one else around. I'm so edgy these days, always tense. If I see the black car I'll just ram it, I tell myself, full of alcohol-induced boldness. That'll teach them.

Immediately, I feel sick. If I see the black car, I don't know what I'll do.

But I don't encounter a single other vehicle on the short journey home. As I enter my driveway, I nick the wing mirror on the gatepost, but it's nothing serious. After checking the boys, I climb into bed. Dan's left me a message to say he'll be late home. I'm exhausted but, despite Dan's unexpected absence, less desolate than usual.

It's always good to make a new friend. Someone who can pledge to my good character in court, I think to myself with a hollow laugh. If it were ever to get that far. Something tells me that the people I'm dealing with don't bother with the small matter of the rule of law.

They are a law unto themselves.

# Chapter 12

## Susannah

As soon as Charlotte's gone, I rush to the sitting room to check on Luke again. He should have been in bed hours ago but I wanted to keep him near me so I would hear him if he called. Curled up on the sofa, he's fast asleep, his expression relaxed, serene, and peaceful. I can't believe he got away with nothing more than bruises from a fall that sounded quite serious; I know Charlotte was playing it down to stop me getting hysterical.

Even though he's eight, and I'm half the size of Hana the au pair – notwithstanding my 'sturdy' arms – I manage to lift him and haul him up the stairs to his bed. As soon as I put him down, he turns and wraps himself around his bear, but he doesn't stir. I thank God again that he's all right, and then ponder that every cloud has a silver lining. In this case, it was the chance to get to know Charlotte better and much more quickly than would have occurred under normal circumstances; there's nothing like a crisis to pull people together.

Once I've checked on Jamie, who's also asleep, but fortunately in his own bed as there's no way I could carry all 5ft of him, I go back downstairs. I'm too tipsy to sleep right now – I'll have head spin if I so much as try to lie down. And anyway, there's a TV drama I want to watch. I settle into the warm dent in the cushions where Luke had been lying and fiddle with the remote until I've got the channel I want. The opening credits of *Look Back in Anger* roll, and I concentrate on the unfolding drama.

When I finally crawl upstairs to bed, it's well after midnight. Setting my alarm for the morning, I have to contemplate the real reason why I've been so reluctant for this day to be over and the new one to start. Because tomorrow my parents are coming to lunch and I'll have to face their quiet disappointment in me, with no escape until they choose to leave. I bury my face in my pillow and fall into a fitful sleep, in which tennis-playing mushrooms loom large.

I wake in the morning feeling groggy from the alcohol and do what everyone does the day after drinking too much, namely swear to myself never to do it again. I start to prepare the lunch, peeling potatoes for the pot roast (cheaper than a joint and anyway, it's Saturday, not Sunday) and apples for the crumble. Peering in the fridge, I realise I forgot to buy cream and, shouting to the boys that I'll be back in ten minutes, I put my coat on and head out to the shop. Luke has woken up as right as rain and I'm not worried about him at all anymore, just bemused by his apparent indestructibility.

The only cream in the village shop is UHT single, which isn't what I want but will have to do. I reach out my hand to take my change whilst tucking the pot into my bag. In a hurry to get back and get on with the cooking, I turn hastily towards the door and walk straight into a previously unseen customer waiting to pay, knocking what he's carrying out of his hands.

'I'm so sorry,' I exclaim, taking in the mess I have caused. On the shop's uneven linoleum floor lie the remains of a box of eggs, shells, whites and yolks liberally distributed across a wide area – including halfway up the trouser legs of the person who had been trying to buy them.

Who, I see now, is Dan.

'Oh, hello Dan, gosh, how embarrassing,' I stutter, and then without pausing for breath, 'I'll buy you another box – and pay for these,' this last addressed to the shopkeeper who is bustling around under the counter, looking for something with which to clear up the mess. I grab the kitchen roll he emerges with and kneel down to start wiping up the egg, which is slimy and slippery and resistant to my efforts. Humiliation suffuses me and I know my face is bright red, making me unable to look anywhere but down at the floor, whilst ineffectually trying to cover my mortification by a stream of apologies and exclamations.

'Dan, your jeans are filthy, they're … well, they look rather terrible …'

I'm on my hands and knees, right in front of him, but still incapable of raising my gaze to where it might meet his. 'Can I take them home and wash them or something?'

There's a pause, broken only by the sound of egg being slopped about as I continue to chase it ineffectually with my wad of paper. Eventually, the pause has gone on for so long that I simply have to look up. There's nothing further to lose; whatever impressions he may previously have had of me as a reasonably articulate and together person will be as shattered as the eggs by now.

I see him appraising me, a sardonic half-smile adorning his handsome face. Gradually, in a flush of horror, the realisation dawns of the exact nature of the vista before him. Me, kneeling submissively at his feet, dabbing his shoes with kitchen roll and asking him to take his trousers off and give them to me. The awful, excruciating black comedy of it sweeps across me and I think I might burst into tears.

As I'm struggling to resist the pricking behind my eyes, a bellowing laugh bursts forth from Dan. My humiliation is complete. I am a laughing stock.

'Susannah, just get up and let Ken do the cleaning,' he splutters. 'I think he'll do a better job than you. And I'll keep my trousers on, if you don't mind. I don't fancy walking home in just my boxers.'

I stagger up from my uncomfortable position, my legs shakier than just the lack of blood flow warrants. I catch his eye and for a second, the tears threaten anew. And then his complicit smile that invites me to share the joke with him draws me in and I see the funny side. I start to laugh, and in moments we are both roaring our heads off, the shopkeeper Ken, also unable to keep a straight face, chuckling wryly in the background.

'Your eggs,' I manage to articulate, when I've regained my breath and before collapsing into another round of helpless mirth, 'I must replace them.'

'It's fine. Don't worry about it.' Dan wipes his hand across his eyes and manages to affect a serious expression for a few moments. 'But please, look where you're going in future – most of my clothes are dry clean only.'

We both burst into another gale of laughter.

'Oh dear,' I say, eventually, 'I hope Charlotte won't be too cross. About the extra washing, I mean.'

Dan emits another laugh, but it's a different kind this time. 'Oh God, she doesn't do the laundry. Agnes, the housekeeper, takes care of all that stuff.' His laughter recedes and he smiles kindly at me. 'All the more reason why you really don't need to worry. And I was always going to change when I got home anyway – we've got a whole host of people coming to lunch and Charlotte will want me wearing something smarter than my old jeans.'

The jeans are extremely exclusive and expensive designer ones, and don't look that old, but obviously I don't say anything. Everything's relative and Charlotte and Dan's idea of a casual wardrobe item is clearly rather different from mine. But I do note that Miriam's concern, made at the party, that Dan doesn't help Charlotte with the chores was obviously somewhat misplaced, given that Dan is asserting that Charlotte doesn't do them either. I thought Agnes was just a cook – but a full-time housekeeper! That must cost more than most people earn. The luxuries that money can buy you – not just things, but services and, ultimately, time! No wonder she can indulge in so many hobbies. No wonder she always looks immaculate.

Dan steps aside to allow Ken to wield his mop efficiently

over the last of the egg. He takes a new box from the shelf and leaves the money on the counter, then pulls the door open and gestures me through. Outside, he gives me a friendly wave goodbye as he heads towards the manor. 'See you tomorrow,' he reminds me, '11am. Don't forget. And don't make me laugh like this again – it'll put me off my serve!'

*Don't worry*, I think, *there's absolutely no chance of me forgetting*. As for the laughing – I can't say right now. But I do know that I can't wait for a game of tennis; it's been far too long and I feel much more relaxed about playing with Dan now we've seen each other again and I know that our first joke-filled encounter wasn't a one-off but that we do really get along.

'Of course,' I call back, 'I'm looking forward to it.'

Whatever difficulties exist between him and Charlotte, there's no doubt that on the surface he appears nothing less than perfect. Sorry to be old-fashioned about it, but he's the kind of man any girl would dream of marrying. The kind of man I thought I had married when I walked down the aisle with Justin. It's not that I was – or am – marriage-obsessed, just that I'd grown up being indoctrinated by certain expectations about the 'right' way to live – get hitched to a suitable male, buy a house, have kids – and the 'wrong' way – don't do any of these things, or do them in the wrong order.

It seems so hopelessly out of date now, so retrograde, despicably anti-feminist, anti-equality, anti-women's lib. But that's the way it was. In many ways, I think it probably still is.

Perhaps remarkably, everything went along swimmingly for a dozen years after Justin and I tied the knot. I had my two amazing children, we bought a succession of ever-larger houses due to the success of Justin's business, and had lovely holidays in Italy and the South of France. Looking back on it now, Justin and Dan have – had – so much in common. That's until it all went belly up, before the lies were exposed and the hollow emptiness that lay beneath everything I had held dear was laid bare. Justin wasn't able to stand strong when the financial world collapsed, whereas Dan seems to have not only weathered the storm but also flourished during it, if appearances are anything to go by: enormous house, designer clothes, disgustingly expensive watch and sunglasses, sports car et al.

As I approach my own house, tawdry, squat, and ugly in comparison to Charlotte and Dan's manor, I see my parents' Ford Mondeo parked outside the front gate, exuding staid and stolid middle-age, just like Marjorie and Dennis themselves, who sometimes come across as pastiches of characters from an Alan Ayckbourn drama. I started calling them by their first names when I was in my teens and my younger brothers were born, wanting to distance myself from this family I no longer felt truly part of. It's a habit that's stuck, though Jamie and Luke think it's weird and always call them Grandma and Grandad.

Pausing for a moment, I take a deep breath before continuing up the path and through the front door. The plan is to have lunch and then go for a long, healthy country walk.

That's all I have to manage.

In the end, the day goes well, considering. The only real flash point comes during dessert, when the cream precipitates the conversation about money and my lack of it that I have been dreading.

'Sometimes we have to make do with what's available in the village,' I explain, seeing Marjorie's raised eyebrows in response to being passed the pot by Luke. 'I can't afford Waitrose anymore and it would be too far to drive there for every little thing even if I could. I do a big shop at the Lidl ten miles away once a week and then incidentals – well, the general store down the road has to fill in the gaps.'

Marjorie visibly balks at the mention of Lidl, as she had at the sight of the words UHT.

'If only you hadn't ... I mean, it's such a shame you—' she falters, and stops abruptly.

I reach across for the cream and pour it, slowly and deliberately, over my crumble.

'Go on, Mum,' I say, mixing the fruit and cream together with my spoon, 'what were you going to say?'

'You know what I mean,' she snaps.

Jamie is looking first at his grandmother and then at me, eyes wide with horrified curiosity.

'I'm not sure that I do,' I reply calmly – or at least as calmly as I can manage. I spoon stewed apple and oats and sugar and cream into my mouth and chew. It is sweet, smooth, calorie-laden, and delicious.

Marjorie sighs. 'If it wasn't for ... what happened.'

My father Dennis coughs and puts down his spoon, letting it clatter noisily into the bowl. 'Marjorie,' he intones, his voice heavy with the bored disapproval that this particular subject always induces in him. 'Is now the best time?'

It seems that he, too, is conscious of Jamie and Luke's pricked ears. Perhaps he's even sympathetic to my plight, unlike Marjorie, who will plough on like the proverbial bull in the china shop if allowed.

'If you've finished, boys, then go off and play.' My words are an instruction, not an offer, and the children understand them as such. With a scraping of chairs and kicking of table legs, the boys depart, seemingly keen to get away from the tense atmosphere of the dining room.

'The point is,' continues Marjorie, as they are in the process of leaving, 'that if Susannah had finished her university course and graduated instead of ... well, instead of dropping out, she wouldn't be in such a dire situation now.' The 'now' comes out as a pronounced whine that grates on my nerves. 'If she— If *you* were qualified, if you'd passed the exams, you'd be able to get a good job.'

I feel myself crumple from the outside in and have to pause to quell the tears before I can speak.

'Sorry,' is all I manage to articulate.

I give in. I'll never be able to exonerate what I did, the trouble I caused, the consequences I brought down upon myself.

'The actual point is, Susannah,' interjects Dennis in the self-satisfied tone that particularly irritates me, 'that whatever happened in the past, if you and Justin had saved a little more during the good times, you would have had something to fall back on when disaster struck.'

I clench my spoon so tightly in my hand I think it might snap in half, and drop my eyes to my empty bowl where creamy swirls pattern the red earthenware. I refrain from mentioning that savings would have helped Dennis, too, when he lost his job and our world turned upside down. If he had had money put aside, I might not have had to change schools, for a start. I keep my reply firmly focused on Justin and on Dennis's accusations.

'He'd probably have had to use it all to pay his debts. Or he'd have hidden it away somewhere. In fact, I don't have any way of knowing that he hasn't done that. Whatever, I'm quite sure there would be none left for me and the boys.'

I get up and begin robustly clearing the table, roughly gathering crockery and cutlery towards me and piling everything in uneven heaps ready to carry into the kitchen. As I leave the room, I feel utterly, miserably alone. Despite all Justin's failings, I miss him.

In my nasty kitchen, I make coffee, taking an age about it so that I have time to compose myself. Biting my lip, I trudge back to the dining room with the tray. I hate all the mean, undersized separate rooms in this house but I know I'm lucky to have a roof over my head at all. I force myself to hold my head up high and determine that I'll make finding a job an imperative. At least that way, I'll be showing the world, as well as myself, that I can look after myself, that I'm neither a quitter nor a basket case.

'Perhaps you could do a secretarial course,' muses my mother as she pours milk into her mug. It's as if she can read my mind. 'Become a PA. It's a steady job, reasonable money.' She stirs her coffee even though she doesn't take sugar. 'Or what about teaching?' She checks herself. 'But no, that wouldn't be possible.'

'Let's leave it for now, shall we,' I request, making it sound like a statement rather than a question.

The stony silence that follows is thankfully, if chaotically, broken by Luke coming back into the room saying that he's kicked his football into next door's garden and asking permission to climb over the fence and retrieve it.

Later, we go for our walk. On the way back, we pass Charlotte and Dan's mansion, the gates wide open, the driveway full of cars, indicating that they are also enjoying company, although perhaps the notion of enjoyment applies more to them than to me. I hope Dan didn't get into trouble for being late back with the eggs and then wistfully imagine the brunch Charlotte will have rustled up, the huge table in that gorgeous kitchen groaning under the weight of delicious breads and salads, tortillas and interesting Mediterranean dips made of avocado and aubergine that I can't afford and anyway, that my parents wouldn't touch.

Marjorie sighs over the beauty of the Queen Anne architecture and the sheer size of the property in her best 'that could have been my daughter' way.

I sigh over the whole sorry mess of it all.

# *Chapter 13*

## *Charlotte*

Dan comes back from the shop, his legs covered in some sort of white stuff, dried up and crusty, that looks like ... well, I won't say what it looks like but leave it to the imagination. I take the eggs as he explains that you bumped into him and caused him to drop a box onto the floor, hence the state of his jeans. You did strike me as someone who might be clumsy. Those carrying a bit of extra weight often are.

Personally, all I seem to do these days is watch the scales and fight the flab. I make all this delicious food, but I don't eat it.

The Kitchen Aid whisks the egg whites with the sugar to perfection. When the mixture stands in stiff, tall peaks, I take out a palette knife from the drawer and spread the meringue, thickly and evenly, over the top of the key lime pie where it sits, like a blanket of the most immaculate snow, waiting to be blow-torched.

We've lived in so many places that sometimes I forget which came in what order, whether Toronto was before or after Tokyo, Seoul a longer or shorter sojourn than Jakarta.

But I know that it was in New York that I learnt to make this dish. Pregnant with the twins and over my morning sickness, I craved it, gorged on it. I put on so much weight – well, one does, with multiples – that oh God, I was enormous by the end.

When the babies came, I swore that would be it. Both for the overeating and the other thing. There would be so much to do, I wouldn't have a chance to get up to anything I shouldn't. And it's true that having twins meant that I barely had time to breathe some days, let alone go to the toilet or clean my teeth. I think about four weeks went by after they were born when I didn't even manage to brush my hair. But it's amazing what time you can find when you really want to. The odd fifteen minutes when both boys were asleep, ten when they were playing on their mat. Oh yes, I found the time for the thing that really mattered. Even if it was the most destructive thing of all.

Whatever else I was getting up to, though, I never neglected the children. But however well you cope with becoming a mother, something has to give and for me, as with a lot of new mums, it was sex. I was going to say that Dan did not take this lying down but sadly that's exactly what he did. Just not with me.

He began an affair – the first of many –with a work colleague. Her name was Anaïs, which is a slap in the face for any wife for a start, with its overt connection to the erotic writings of Anaïs Nin. Perhaps Dan was missing the Far East more than I thought, because Anaïs was of Chinese heritage. She was everything I wasn't: tiny, perfectly formed like an exquisite doll, black-haired and dark eyed. Next to her, especially carrying twins and then the pregnancy weight that took ages to shift, I felt like a galumphing moose, too tall and raw-boned, too washed-out and pale.

Whenever we met at company events – because I started insisting on accompanying Dan, despite the exhaustion and the childcare issues – she would always regard me with that supercilious gaze of hers. It seemed to me that she took a sadistic delight in deliberately standing next to me so that her petite frame would accentuate my over-large one. Sometimes she dropped hints, saying how much she admired financial acumen in a man, and how few men there were in the world who had immaculate dress sense.

I'd turn around and see Dan, master of the hedge fund world, attired in a handmade Savile Row suit that fitted his lean, athletic frame like a glove, and know exactly what she was really saying. Which was, 'I'm fucking your husband and it's going on right under your nose and there's nothing you can or will do about it.' Because somehow, I've no idea how, Anais seemed to understand that something was tying me to Dan, that however badly he behaved, I would cling on like a limpet to a rock. She'd probably seen it before. Most wives don't give up without a fight.

She knew, and I knew, and Dan knew, that I would never, ever let him go. Because without him, I would have nothing, be nothing, own nothing.

In the end though, the battle was won before it had been fought. Anaïs became an irritant to Dan. I'm sure she pestered him to leave me and he had never had any intention of doing that. Like so many men, he just wanted to have his cake and eat it. I confronted him and he promised me that he'd never do it again, never take a 'mistress', never have someone who everyone else knew about and who made me look like a total fool. And I trusted him on that.

I really did.

However, the experience with Anaïs, as I'm sure you would understand, made me wary. So far, though, she's the only one I've ever been really worried about. I understood that all of the others were mere dalliances, nothing serious, never intended to be more than a way for him to pleasurably pass a few hours just because he could. Men who are that good-looking and that rich and that powerful know that they can have who they want, when they want.

I always keep my eyes open though. I'm constantly on the lookout for the next Anaïs, always suspicious. Is it Naomi? In all truth, the jury's still out on that one. But even if she hasn't come along yet, there's one thing I'm certain of.

One day she will.

And just the thought of it makes my blood boil and the urge for revenge swell in my belly. Sometimes I wonder what I would be capable of, if someone were to really come between me and Dan.

# *Chapter 14*

## *Susannah*

Today is the day of the tennis match. I shouldn't think Dan's spent more than a few seconds, if that, anticipating it. I, on the other hand, have been obsessing about it since the time and date were set. My tennis whites are laid out in my bedroom, having been retrieved from the back of the wardrobe, and I pull them on and survey myself in the mirror. Their tightness testifies to the fact that I must be the only woman in the world who puts on weight after a break-up.

Charlotte's comment on my 'sturdy arms' floats across my mind and I push it away. I'm sure she didn't mean to be hurtful and it's not as if it's untrue – though 'powerful' would have been a kinder choice of word, or 'athletic' perhaps. I'd even settle for 'strong'. I scrutinise myself again, standing side-on and flexing my biceps, moving my forearm up and down. Sadly, I concede that 'sturdy' probably is the most apt description. Despondency threatens to descend and I shake it off. I've got the chance to do something I enjoy and, moreover, that I am good at for an hour and I'm going to focus on that, not on all my many and various physical faults.

And not on what's arrived in the post, either. I kick the letters on the mat to the side so I can open the door, not even bothering to pick them up and check them. I don't want or need to know their contents right now.

I take Jamie and Luke to the manor and see them through the gate. They gambol happily towards the house, chatting eagerly about the paper chase they're soon to take part in. I'm grateful they're engaged in a healthy outdoor pastime for a few hours. If the newspapers are to be believed, most pre-teen boys spend more time accessing hardcore porn on the internet than exercising in the fresh air. I don't linger to watch them go inside but instead turn hurriedly away, hoping I don't encounter Dan; I need the solo walk to psych myself up for the game.

I get to the club bang on eleven and hesitate outside the automatic doors for a moment, debating with myself whether to wait or go in. Waiting might make me look feeble, as if I need Dan's permission or accompaniment to enter those hallowed doors. Going in, on the other hand, carries the risk of looking too eager and overly keen, and I don't want to give Dan that impression. I want him to think I'm like Charlotte: confident, self-assured, coolheaded.

'Hi there.' His sonorous voice, so cosmopolitan, rooted somewhere between the UK and the US, cuts short my dithering. 'Sorry to keep you waiting.'

'Oh no,' I blurt out, 'no, I only just got here myself. No waiting.' I laugh, nervously and unnecessarily. Bang goes that idea of being like Charlotte.

Dan is eyeing me up and down and I shift awkwardly from one leg to the other.

'You're changed already,' he says, sounding surprised. He is in his jeans (a different pair, not egg-stained) and I kick myself. I should have realised that the cool people change when they get here.

'Looking good,' he adds, as if to mitigate my obvious discomfort.

'Uh, thanks,' I manage to stutter. He's being so kind and trying to put me at my ease but I wish he didn't feel he had to. At the same time, though, something stirs inside me, a twinge deep down in my belly that I haven't felt for a long time. Since Justin and I split I've become invisible, a woman past her best, cast aside, unwanted. I force myself to relax, to take Dan's compliment and enjoy it – a passing appreciation that's better than being forever ignored.

'After you.' Dan gestures me ahead of him and we turn towards the doors. 'I hope you don't mind but it's just us, I'm afraid, after all – the other couple have had to pull out. Family commitments or something.'

He frowns as he says this, as if family getting in the way of anything is unfathomable, but then turns it into an infectious grin that has me smiling too, though I don't really know why. We are inside the building now and I have a sudden, heart-wrenching assault of memory induced by the smell of rubber trainer soles, of freshly-laundered kit and, drifting in from open windows, of newly cut grass. It takes me back nearly twenty-five years, to when I was my county's top female player for one blissful season. It didn't last. Things that good rarely do.

Puberty made me heavy and sluggish and at the same time I lost interest in the constant training and practice, the gruelling matches and the relentless competitiveness. By the age of twenty I had given up competing and only took part on a recreational basis. I can still play a decent game; I was in the Barnes ladies' team and I'm confident that I'll be able to give Dan a run for his money, although I was looking forward to the cover that doubles provides. Singles is so much more exposing. Dan will be able to see clearly all my flaws and faults; as he doesn't seem to have any himself, this is all the more troubling.

A flurry of activity to our right catches my eye and, like a tornado coming into land, a woman whirls towards Dan and grabs hold of his arm.

'Dan!' The voice is earthy and has what might politely be called a 'local' accent. 'The best player in the club! My favourite member!' There's a pause and then a loud, hooting laugh rings out. 'As the actress said to the bishop!'

I would have laughed myself in any other situation but I've realised, immediately, that this is the infamous Naomi, source of Charlotte's anguish.

'Naomi. Lovely to see you.'

Dan's greeting, cool and collected, confirms my supposition. On hearing his measured tones, Naomi seems to visibly calm down and shrink a little, like a mating bird that halves in size once its boastful, plumped-up and ostentatious feathers are smoothed.

'Susannah,' Dan says, turning to towards me and then back to Naomi, 'meet Naomi. Naomi, Susannah.'

Naomi hoots with laughter again. 'You're always so polite, Mr Hegarty.' She looks at me. 'Isn't he? Such a gent?'

I nod, feebly. Naomi's ebullience is rather enervating.

Dan, not knowing that Charlotte has already imparted more information to me about Naomi than he would probably like, carries on talking.

'Naomi is the incredibly talented head chef and manageress of the cafe here. Before she came along, we slummed it on rock cakes that lived up to their name and curled-up cucumber sandwiches, but now we feast upon quinoa salads and deliciously moist carrot cake.'

Naomi drops her eyes bashfully for a second and then reverts to type and gives Dan a playful thump. 'Are you teasing me? You are awful.'

I grit my teeth as my blood temperature rises, perhaps not quite to a boil but definitely a gentle simmer. I totally understand Charlotte's anxiety and, though she didn't express it as such, her resentment at Dan's open acceptance of Naomi's enthusiastic attentions. She's simpering at some joke Dan has made that I didn't hear with all the adulation of a well-trained dog to its owner.

Poor Charlotte. It must drive her mad – as well as being disconcerting and somewhat worrying. But on the other hand, I ponder, left out of the Dan-Naomi mutual admiration zone – they're discussing some new protein balls she's put on the menu now – if Charlotte spent more time with Dan, involved herself in his hobbies, came to play tennis with him, the Naomi threat would inevitably diminish. Then I remember that it's her bad back that prevents her from being part of it all and I feel sorry for her, and guilty for being critical of her for even a second. She can hardly sit around in the cafe all the time Dan's here just to keep an eye on its manager, after all.

Naomi lets go of Dan's arm, which she's been gripping like a vice, and turns to me.

'New to the village, are you? Well, there's lots for you to find out about this man but just remember that he's mine, OK? I'll not be letting anyone else get their hands on him.'

I gulp, speechless. She's obviously joking but still ... It's all a little surreal, like walking in on an episode of a reality show where some dolly bird is blatantly trying it on with someone else's man on national television.

I'm struggling to think of anything to say in response when Dan steps in.

'Enough already, Naomi,' he says, teasingly. 'We've got a court booked so we'll catch you later.'

'Don't forget to come back for your balls,' Naomi hollers after him, and the raucous guffaw that follows echoes down the corridor, ricocheting off the bare white walls.

'She's ... very lively,' I venture hesitantly, as Dan ushers me towards the courts.

Dan laughs. 'She tends towards the overenthusiastic. All totally harmless, of course.'

'Of course,' I echo, my words sounding unconvincing even to me. I'm not sure how much I should ask about the nature of their relationship, or how deep I should delve. I don't want to find out anything I'd be happier not knowing, or that would leave me with a dilemma as to whether to tell Charlotte or not.

'Charlotte doesn't like it much,' Dan continues, as if reading my mind. 'But as she only comes to watch me play once in a blue moon it doesn't really affect her,' he concludes, bluntly.

'Oh.' I think about this for a moment, feeling that I must defend my new friend. 'I suppose it's a bit boring just spectating, isn't it? I'm sure she's got so many things to do she doesn't really have time for it.'

Dan merely shrugs in response and then the moment is gone as we step outside where the brilliant green grass glimmers in the morning sun.

'Toss for first serve?' I need to keep my mind on the game and not let myself be distracted by the puzzle of Dan and Charlotte's relationship, their somewhat troubled marriage, Naomi's involvement, and what it all might mean.

Dan wins the toss. As the match progresses, we both work up a sweat. I notice how the muscles in his arms become more pronounced as the perspiration gleams upon them, how deceptively youthful is his agile body.

Dan wins, but only just. It wouldn't have taken much more from me to have beaten him fair and square but men's egos don't always respond well to losing. And Charlotte has already warned me about Dan's.

'That was the best game I've had in a long while,' he says, after his winning point. He reaches over the net to shake my hand, which I've hastily wiped on my dress to get rid of the worst of the sweat. A tingle runs through my body at his touch, at the firm hold he has taken of my fingers, his palm pressed against mine.

Since I separated from Justin, I have hardly touched anyone. No one tells you that when you no longer have a partner, you will forget the feel of human warmth, the sensation of skin upon skin, the solidity and comfort that comes from simply holding someone's hand. The only bodies that come close to mine now are those of the boys and it suddenly hits me that once they have outgrown cuddles and hugs, which won't be long, there will be nothing. I will be an island, alone in a sea of indifference and exclusion, just like I was after … Well, suffice to say it won't be for the first time, but I really prefer not to go there, to leave that part of my history as just that – the past.

Dan's handshake has morphed into a hand hold but amidst my bleak thoughts I'm so distracted that I've hardly noticed. Now that I do, I realise that my legs have turned to jelly and that my stomach is fizzing with suppressed excitement.

I snatch my hand away as if I've been burnt. I can't believe what I'm feeling, how for a split second there I forgot that Dan is someone else's husband. My friend's husband.

'Susannah?' Dan's questioning voice brings me to my senses.

'I'm sorry,' I say, trying not to sound too flustered, 'I was miles away then. You were saying?'

'I was just saying that you play very well?'

It's a question not a comment, demanding an explanation. I force myself to focus on my answer.

'Thank you. I played a lot when I was younger.'

Rubbing my towel around my neck, I think about what to say, how much to explain. What to put in and what to leave out. I'd like Dan to know that I once had talent, but I don't want him to think badly of me for not exploiting it, for squandering the one thing I ever had going for me.

'Competed, that is,' I venture, hesitantly. 'But I was never in the highest echelons of the game and ... well, since I've grown older it's become a hobby and a way of keeping fit, no more than that. I've always tried to keep my hand in, but it's been quite hard recently to find the time – and the money, if I'm honest. It's nice to find out I can still hit a ball.'

I can feel the perspiration beading on my upper lip. The day has turned out warmer than expected. I wipe the towel across my face. When I lower it from my eyes, I see that Dan is smiling in his beguiling way.

'You can certainly do that.'

He's so direct, so candid. Despite my earlier, inexplicable thoughts, I can understand that some women – those, unlike me, who are not old enough to know better – might interpret his manner as flirtatious, as leading them on. Some men just have that way about them, and some women – mentioning no names Naomi – fall for it.

'There are a lot of other club members who'd love a game with you – something that would really challenge them.'

'You're too kind.' I do everything I can to suppress the incipient blush I can feel rising on my cheeks. 'I need more practice, though,' I soldier on, filling the silence with my prattle. 'I'd like to play regularly but I can't afford the membership fees. Since my divorce, you know ... money's tight.'

Immediately, I regret the words. I am being too forward, divulging too much about my personal circumstances.

Dan pauses as we're walking. 'I'm sorry, Susannah,' he says, softly. 'I'm being a dolt. I didn't realise how bad things were for you financially.' He casts his eyes around as if looking for the solution then lifts his arms in a gesture of resignation.

'Hopefully the situation will improve,' he continues, 'and in meantime, it's all sorted. I'll sign you in and the two of us will play regularly.'

I smile gratefully. 'That's really kind of you ...'

Dan's eyes are full of concern as he looks at me. 'I can sense a but,' he says.

'I don't want to impose. I'm worried that you're inviting me because you feel sorry for me.'

Dan bursts out laughing. 'Nothing,' he splutters, 'could be further from the truth. I'm full of admiration for you. You're so strong and capable, and you shouldn't have been left penniless like this by your twit of a husband.'

Charlotte must have filled him in on the details of my perilous state, close to homelessness and penury.

'You shouldn't have been left at all, in fact,' he adds, 'but you and I, we'll get to play tennis, don't you worry.'

It's no longer an invitation but a demand. I'm learning that Dan Hegarty simply presumes that no one will say no to him.

And most of the time, I'm willing to bet, they don't.

He offers me a lift home, but wants to have a quick shower first. He says Charlotte doesn't like it if he turns up sweaty and smelly. I'm shallow enough to feel a frisson of excitement at the thought of a ride in his Porsche so I say I'm happy to wait. Luke will die of jealousy – he loves cars and everything to do with them, and the ancient Ford Fiesta that was all I could afford when the hire purchase companies claimed back Justin's Alfa Romeo and my Golf is a constant source of embarrassment to him. He yearns for a Tesla and, in meantime, lives in a permanent state of relief that the primary school is walking distance so there's no need for me to shame him by turning up to collect the boys in the car.

I haven't brought a towel or any shampoo, so I linger in the corridor whilst Dan showers, letting nostalgia wash over me as I imbue the smells and sounds that remind me so intensely of my youth. Eager youngsters in hoodies that hang off one shoulder and super short shorts bustle past me, on their way to the youth training session. Just like I would have been, twenty-five or more years ago. I'd so love my Jamie to be in their midst but there's fat chance of that unless I suddenly unexpectedly inherit a fortune.

Or find a rich man to marry. Well, it happens in books, doesn't it? What about that one where the vulnerable, damaged protagonist not only lives in the flat beneath a stunningly handsome, single, eligible young man – but he also just happens to be a consultant psychiatrist so can heal her mind as well as fulfilling all her romantic desires and paying for her dinner?

I laugh ironically to myself. It's fiction, I say to myself. It's not *true life*, to use one of the boys' favourite phrases from when they were younger.

I stop to read the club noticeboard, idly scanning the postcards selling used kit, offering private lessons or racket restringing services. One particular postcard catches my attention. It's headed with the words 'Position vacant' and goes on to advertise the cafe's need for a waitress-stroke-deputy manager, weekdays from 9am to 3pm, evenings and weekends negotiable. No experience necessary but a professional appearance and knowledge of and interest in tennis desirable.

Instantly, I seize my phone from my bag and type in the contact number. This is a much more realistic answer to my prayers. The money won't be great, that's for sure, but it's exactly what I want in terms of hours and, topped up by Justin's maintenance contributions, however paltry these are at present, it might leave me with an income that the boys and I can just about live on. At least I'd be working and not scrounging; I just can't get my head around applying for benefits. I don't want to give myself time to think myself out of it, so I press call, and hurriedly try to think what they might ask me and what questions, if any, I should pose. I needn't have worried, though, as the call goes straight to answerphone.

I leave a message and end the call. Just as I've done so, my phone rings, loud and strident in the hush of the club corridor. I jump and look at it in astonishment, thinking for one idiotic moment that they're ringing back already.

But it's not the job, it's Charlotte.

'Jamie won again,' she says, as soon as I pick up. 'How about you? Did you put my husband through his paces?'

I laugh and explain to her how the game ended, and then thank her for passing on the news about Jamie. Charlotte never seems in the least bit jealous that Jamie beats Toby hands down every time. She really is so good with children, so fair and supportive of all of them, whether they belong to her or not. Some might say she's over-indulgent but as I've got to know her I've come to see that it's just her way; she's over the top about everything and child-rearing is no different. And the way she looked after Luke when he had his accident was amazing, so kind and caring. I wish I was always so magnanimous about other children doing better than mine; I know that I get a vicarious lift from the boys' successes. I suppose the difference is that there's nothing lacking in Charlotte's life, nothing that she's messed up on, so she is able to be generous. Nevertheless, I should make more effort to take a leaf out of her book.

'When I see you next, you can dish the dirt on Dan's playing and tell me how many points he shamelessly argued with you. And give me the inside information on his secret life at the club,' Charlotte says, before adding a goodbye and ringing off.

Dan emerges from the changing room. He is gleaming from his shower and impossibly handsome, with his etched cheekbones and his still-wet hair standing in adorable boyish peaks on top of his head. He's strapping his watch on his wrist – not the same one he was wearing at the party but another one that looks every bit as expensive.

'My weakness,' he explains, when he sees me looking at it. 'Watches. I know it's an indulgence, but ... well, I've earned every penny I've got through hard work so I reason that it's OK to spend it on things that make me happy.'

I nod. 'Of course.' I think of all Justin's gadgets and gizmos. He would have given the same justification. But I'm not sure they really made him happy. And the thing is that, unlike Dan, he couldn't really afford them; he just wanted everyone, including himself, to believe that he could.

We head for the exit but just before we get there, Dan ducks into the cafe. 'I want to get some of Naomi's new protein balls,' he explains, as I trot along behind him. 'Her cooking is the best, so I'm sure they'll be excellent. And she'll never let me hear the end of it if I don't.'

I look around with interest, trying to get an idea of what it would be like to work here – and also secretly wondering what Charlotte would think to hear Dan use a superlative about the cooking skills of a woman who is not her. Naomi is busy with the lunchtime rush and her reaction to seeing Dan is a lot more restrained than earlier. As he pays, I consider her carefully. Bit of a joke or serious threat? Right now, I'm not sure I know which she is and it seems that Charlotte doesn't, either. As well as all its other advantages, getting the job would be the ideal opportunity to find out.

I resolve to call again if I don't hear back tomorrow.

# *Chapter 15*

## *Charlotte*

I'm worried.

I cover it as best I can, trying to act naturally, using my breathing techniques and mindfulness, and Dan's never said anything. Neither has anyone else. So I can only assume my subterfuge is successful. But that doesn't mean I'm not sick with fear on the inside.

Right now, nothing's happened for a few days. And that's what's bothering me. No drop-down calls. No sign of the black car. Does that mean they've given up on me? Or they're planning something bigger? The fear never leaves me; it buzzes inside my head like a gargantuan bluebottle or a swarm of bees. In quiet moments, I hear the frenzied cries of my children pleading, 'Why did you do it, mummy? How could you let us down like this?' And Dan adding, 'What were you thinking?'

I'm on edge, constantly watching. Waiting. Knowing they'll come back.

I'm walking from my bedroom, along the balconied corridor that curves round to where the stairs begin their majestic descent to the marble-floored hallway, when it catches my eye. My heart stops, my blood freezes, and I gasp involuntarily.

There's no one else in the house. Agnes doesn't work Tuesdays and even the au pair has taken herself off for the day, shopping in Winchester. I'm all alone.

And there's somebody on my doorstep.

Paralysed, I couldn't move even if I dared to. The black shadow passes in front of the decorative glass panes that surround the door. I didn't imagine it. My heart is beating frantically, wildly. I can hardly breathe. There really is someone there, dressed in black – black coat, black hat. Hat? Who wears a hat at this time of year?

A person who doesn't want to be recognised.

I clutch the balcony rail, craving reassurance from its cool solidity, needing something to hold on to. I can't see the figure anymore; he's either standing right in front of the door so he's not visible through the glass or he's gone.

Gripping the rail even tighter, I start to count slowly in my head. One. Two. Three. When I get to thirty, that will be long enough. That will be enough time to know that the man has gone.

Four. Five. Six.

The screech of the doorbell stops my heart, shatters my nerves, and makes me jump sky high. I begin to hyperventilate, and as I do so I sink slowly to my knees, my legs no longer strong enough to hold my weight. Despite my collapse, I'm still poised, my brain on alert, working out what I'll do when he tries the door handle. When he kicks the door down.

What the fuck will I do?

Tears spring into my eyes and I am filled with a sudden self-loathing. I brought all of this on myself. I might have summoned up the willpower to have stopped now, but the years of falling, of succumbing, are catching up with me nevertheless.

*But I couldn't help it*, I can hear my inner self bleating to me, to whoever might listen. *Yes I could*, I retort, furious with myself for my weakness, my lack of self-control. I could have filled the idle hours with baking or crochet or doing charitable works, like normal people do. Like good people do.

But I didn't.

Twenty minutes pass, then thirty, before I manage to haul myself upright. The bell hasn't rung again. I don't know if the man has gone; I daren't look in the direction of the door. I retreat, heart banging against my chest, to the back of the house where its huge antiquity and grand history means there is a second staircase, for the servants of yore. I go down that and into the kitchen where I make myself a strong coffee with a nip of something for my nerves before I realise that I've got to get out of here.

I run the few short steps between the back door and the car and then, just before I jump inside, I remember that it's out of petrol. Completely out. To the point where I only just made it home yesterday. I meant to text Dan to ask him to do something about it, bring some petrol home in a jerry can 70s-style, or get the garage to come round. Whatever is necessary. But I forgot. I stand, frozen, suddenly and terrifyingly incapable of moving. I don't want to go back into the house, where I'll have to check every door and every window one hundred times and even then won't feel safe. But I can't take the car.

Blindly, like a fugitive, I put my head down against an imaginary wind and slink around the corner of the house. I race across the circular gravel driveway where the ornamental cherry stands proudly as if there's nothing at all to worry about. I reach the side gate, wrest it open and head out onto the green. At least there are people here, not just me, all alone. I look around me. Actually, there aren't any people. On the main road through the village on the other side of the grass a few cars pass, but that's it. I walk, as fast as I can, in the direction of your house, seeking sanctuary. Sanity. Self-preservation.

I've just started to breathe more easily when I hear footsteps behind me. It's hardly possible for me to speed up because I'm going so hurriedly already, but I try to, heedless of how obvious it makes my fear to my pursuer. It must be him, the man in the hat. The shadow figure. I'm so frightened that I can't work out if the breathing I can hear is mine or his.

I feel sick.

The hand on my shoulder makes me jump out of my skin. I let out an involuntary scream, high-pitched and animalistic. Why the fuck did I come out when I knew the man in the hat was prowling?

'Charlotte! Goodness me you're jumpy! Whatever's the matter?'

Miriam. Not him. Just dear, sweet, innocent, irritating Miriam.

I'm weak and floppy with relief that quickly turns to anger

at her scaring me like this, and then contrition as I silently acknowledge that it's not her fault.

I shake my head. 'I'm fine,' I say, curtly. 'But as you can see I'm in a bit of a hurry.'

'I'm sorry,' she responds, 'I came to see you about the foraging club. I called round at the house but there was no answer so I assumed you were out and about somewhere.'

'I was,' I reply, curtly. 'I'm out and about here, on the village green.' It dawns on me, now my heart has stopped racing and my brain clicked into gear, that she's dressed all in black, including her deeply unflattering black bobble hat. There was no stranger at the door. It was just Miriam. I take a long, deep breath. I'm becoming paranoid, unhinged. I've got to stop overreacting like this.

'I just wanted to ...' Miriam starts but quickly tails off as I give her a dismissive wave and start walking again. I need to get away from her, from her tattling and prattling.

'I'll ring you about the foraging,' I call back to her over my shoulder. I'm going at such a pace she trails in my wake and I soon leave her far behind, a shadow figure on the green, staring uncomprehendingly after me. I can't worry about her. I've got enough on my plate. She'll get over it; she always does. Her adulation of me never fails. I clench my fists and force myself not to be cross with her for frightening me so badly. She doesn't know that callers to the house give me the heebie-jeebies. Why should she? I should just be grateful it wasn't who I feared it might be.

'No!'

I realise that I have cried out audibly into the quietude of the mid-morning village. The first sign of madness is talking to yourself, or is that the last? In any case, what really matters is that it wasn't who I feared this time. But next?

I arrive at your house, panting and sweating, partly from the rapid walk and partly from the icy fear that trickles through my veins and, these days, never, ever, completely leaves me. I take a moment on the doorstep to calm myself before lifting the knocker and hammering loudly.

Your door opens to a flurry of white that rises up from the uneven wooden floorboards. You let me in and, like Hansel and Gretel with their breadcrumbs, we follow the trail along the hallway to the kitchen. In your sink sits a sheaf of elder-flower, creamy blossoms spreading themselves assiduously across every surface.

Ostensibly, I've come to offer you congratulations; fortu-nately, my brain wasn't so addled on the way here that I failed to muster a reason for dropping in like this. You messaged me a couple of days ago to tell me that you've got the job as deputy manager at the tennis club cafe. This is news that's worth celebrating. Having a bit more cash will make life so much easier for you. Plus you'll be happier with a focus, a job to give meaning and structure to your days.

I wish I could tell you the real reason why I'm here. But of course I can't.

'Been out foraging solo?' I ask you, determinedly focusing on the here and now rather than the perils of the past – and future.

I'm surprised, as even though you've expressed interest in the group, you haven't actually attended a get-together yet. And

I wasn't aware that you knew anything about what to gather or how to make things with it. You seem altogether too citified, too pristine, to have ever gleaned that sort of information.

'Oh no,' you scoff, confirming my surmises. 'I don't know the first thing about it, and there's been so much rain recently. I'll definitely be a fair-weather forager.'

I might have guessed as much. My own interest in the club is all to do with that need to play a part that was so overwhelming when I first arrived in the village, having secured my ideal house, my ideal life. Being some kind of earth mother, tapping nature's bounty for sustenance, was an idea that held so much romance I simply couldn't resist. Plus it would set me up as an innovator, bringing fresh initiatives to the somewhat benighted locals. After all, it's not just Eva Peron's prerogative to want to be adored. And actually, the more I foraged and the more I learnt, the more I got into it and now I love it.

And though I clearly don't need free food, I do need a foil for all the nefariousness of my past, not to mention the excesses of life with Dan.

You fill the kettle, only just managing to get it under the tap as there are so many elderflower stalks in the way.

'Miriam dropped by earlier,' you continue, 'and gave me all this.' You indicate with a flick of your head towards the frothy mass. 'She says she's going to come back later and show me how to make elderflower cordial – she's convinced the boys will love it. I didn't like to tell her that Lucozade Sport is more their thing.'

I raise my eyebrows in sympathy. I've spent what feels like half a lifetime convincing my boys of the benefits of wholesome fruit drinks rather than the mass-produced fizzy products of multi-national corporations. It's not easy.

I wonder if Miriam had been on her way back here when I saw her just now. My behaviour will probably have well and truly put her off. She'll have seen where I was headed and decided to keep a wide berth. For your sake, I hope she makes it at some point or you'll have to get rid of this lot some other way.

'I'm loving the idea of it for the cafe, though,' you continue, oblivious to my distraction. 'I think there'd be huge potential for introducing foraged and homemade items onto the menu. It's so on trend right now. I'm definitely going to talk to Naomi about it.'

The kettle boils and you make coffee. I can't stand instant coffee but I don't refuse. It's funny how these conventions of manners never get left behind, isn't it? I think about all the countries I've lived in, all the cultures I've been part of, and try to find one where it would be acceptable to say, 'No thanks, I don't like your coffee', and I can't think of one. So I guess we humans are more alike than we sometimes think.

'Well done for getting the job,' I say, and take a quick sip before putting the mug back down on the table. I should ask you to be my spy, my secret agent keeping watch on Naomi but I don't want to be too obvious. I decide to wait for you to offer, but you don't.

'Thanks,' you say instead. 'I'm really looking forward to it. Just …'

'Just what?'

You grimace self-deprecatingly. 'I bigged up my experience

in customer service etc from running my gift shop – but I kind of left out the fact that it was well over a decade ago.'

'So?' I don't know what you're worried about. Surely anyone can sling a cup of tea and a slice of cake on a table, or add up the takings at the end of the day, can't they? What qualification or evidence of recent experience would one need for that?

'Well,' you reply, and shrug defeatedly, 'the thing is that Naomi didn't ask for a CV but if she does ... I'm not quite sure what I'll give her.'

I emit a short laugh. 'I really don't think you should worry about Naomi's judgement. I should imagine she's just pleased to have been able to recruit someone as amazing as you.' I take another, very small, sip of coffee. 'You know, Susannah, the thing about most women around here – and sorry to say it, but it is a woman's kind of job – is that they don't need to work. Or rather, if they do need or want to work, they already have a career, and if they don't, it's probably because they've got no intention or need of getting one.'

I don't want a job. But I need one desperately. I've got to pay the debt off somehow. They'll be chasing me every second of every day until I do. Whilst I owe them, I'll never be free of them. Giving them more money seems the best – the only way – to free myself of the continual terror I'm living in. I can't get any more from Dan – he's so generous in the amount he transfers into my account every month as it is. I have to dress exclusively in designer labels to justify what he gives me, so I shop on eBay and have parcels delivered to a PO Box address. Most of my 'hobbies' are fictitious, just an excuse for asking for more cash. I've done it all – yoga, reiki, life drawing ... You name it, I've pretended to have an expensive obsession with it. Dressage was the most ridiculous one but nevertheless, Dan didn't question it, didn't bat an eyelid, just wrote the cheques. Believed me when I said I had to give up because of my knees.

It's deceitful, I know, and wrong, I'm sure. But what options do I have? If Dan knew what I'd done, the lies I've told, the secrets I've kept, the trouble I've got into ... he'd never forgive me. And despite all his flaws – and hell, we've all got flaws, haven't we? – he is my husband; we are committed to each other by our marriage vows. I do love him still, though it's hard to remember that sometimes, through all the guilt and despair and the pretending. The pretending is the worst of it all. It's doing my head in, as the children would say.

They don't mess around, these people. Back in Hong Kong – our second sojourn there – things went rapidly downhill. I got my fix by joining gatherings communicated only by untraceable phone messages and word of mouth. Remember, this is before the internet kicked in and changed everything forever. Back then, you had to take part for real; there was no online option that enables a distance to be kept between participants.

For me, I think it was partly the thrill of the subversive that constantly garnered my enthusiasm and spurred me on, the addiction to breaking the rules, to stepping outside the cloying prison of the expat world into something so much grittier, earthier, more raw. Of rubbing shoulders with gangsters, criminals, the population of an underworld that people like me normally only ever see in the movies. It's amazing the resources you can find within yourself, the things you do that you could never imagine, when you are in the grip of a passion.

But one day I'd no way to pay. I'd maxed out my credit card, spent all my cash. The cigarette burn was only a small one. I managed to cover it up; Dan never noticed it. It was meant to be discreet. A warning. And it worked. I didn't participate without sufficient funds again. Not until right at the end, anyway.

By that time, it was out of control. The leeches can spot when the flesh is weak, when it will be easily punctured and bled dry. And that's what they did. We left just before it all blew up. They only let me out because I said I was pregnant. I begged for more time to pay for the sake of my fictitious unborn child, swore on my existing children's lives that I would.

Sometimes I'm not sure if the worst thing is the deed itself, or the person it makes you become.

So my immediate problem is that I need money and I can't ask Dan for any more. Recently, I've been putting my hopes in my talent for photography. I'm going to write a book about foraging, a glossy, illustrated volume that will grace coffee tables across the land.

How ridiculous is that? How unlikely that I'll ever make a bean?

They say hope springs eternal and that's never been truer than right here, right now. Which is more absurd, the hope that I'll get the money from somewhere or the hope that they won't find me before I have?

Even if the caller today wasn't them but stupid Miriam, they still know where I go and follow me when I leave the house. I'm sure they do. I have a constant feeling of being watched, spied upon, studied. I see the black car everywhere, cruising along the streets, cool as you like. Sometimes it drives me crazy, sometimes to despair. I know they're waiting for me to put a foot wrong, to make a mistake. To miss a payment again.

If I told you, you'd probably say, 'go to the police', or 'tell Dan, it's always best to be honest'. But I can't. If I tell the police, they'll know immediately and that will be the end of me. The UK forces of law and order are hardly going to give me twenty-four-hour protection, are they?

At that thought I instinctively look around me. It's insane. The only window faces onto your enclosed backyard. It's bleak and bare outside, nothing and no one in sight.

I've put into Dan's mind that my low mood is due to worrying about growing old, being past my sell-by-date. Everything in Dan's world can be fixed by throwing money at it, and ageing is no exception. The cash he gives me for Botox and fillers is the only cash I actually spend as I say I do, because it would be impossible to take such large sums and then explain away a face that is still covered in wrinkles.

Maybe that's the solution, it occurs to me now. Plastic surgery, giving myself a new face and a new identity, like they do for people who turn in South American drug barons or Mafia bosses. But I'm not sure even that would put off those who are after me. They're cleverer than that, and a whole lot more determined.

They say someone's past always catches up with them. But I'm sprinting like the wind to outrun mine.

# Chapter 16

## Susannah

The time had to come and now it's here: I'm out on my first forage. There's a fresh breeze in the air that blows away the cobwebs and invigorates the blood, and I have to say that I actually feel really, genuinely, positively enthusiastic about being here, not to mention about my new life in the country in general. I've got a job, a friend, a fascinating hobby to participate in – it's all a bit too good to be true. I stop myself there. This is a theme in my life and I'm not going to jinx my current happiness with thoughts of what's gone wrong in the past.

Instead, I look around me, taking in the bucolic surroundings, the silvery leaves of oaks and sycamores rippling in the wind. Behind them is a bank that drops precipitously down to a babbling brook that could have come straight out of child's picture book. Although, somewhat marring the idyll is the rather incongruous form of Miriam, floundering at the water's edge, clutching at a clump of some kind of plant life.

'Now, let's see what we've got here!'

Her voice wafts up towards me as she pulls and tugs at various strands of greenery. She gave me a lecture on how important plant identification is when we were making the cordial and now is obviously time for the practical.

'This is my secret spot of chickweed!' she calls. 'Quite rare down here in the south, much more common in Scotland.'

She plucks a bunch of the plant that looks, from my perspective, identical to cow parsley.

'Come on, dear, what's the hold-up?' she barks at me as I teeter on the brink of the bank. 'I need you to get really close, so that you can make a positive identification on your own.'

'Right,' I reply, glancing down at my pristine tennis shoes. With a pang of regret, I register that they're not going to stay that way for long. I shouldn't have worn them but I don't really have anything else; I didn't have the kind of footwear in London that easily lends itself to mucking around in waterlogged ditches. I can't for a moment imagine why that is, I think, uttering an internal ironic laugh. And I haven't bought anything new for months, not even a pair of wellies, though I can see now that this is something I definitely need to invest in.

Slithering down to where Miriam is waiting, I catch sight of Charlotte. She's busy selecting tender young dandelion leaves to make a salad. I'm eager to get some of those for myself; consulting the internet, I've discovered that they are far more nutritious than lettuce. No wonder rabbits are so healthy. I remember as a child spending hours collecting for my pet bunny, whom I had named Roberta, and enjoying watching her guzzle through a pile of greenery as big as she was. It had never occurred to me that humans could eat them and if I'd suggested such a thing to Marjorie, she'd probably have fainted in horror.

'So, pay attention now,' Miriam is saying. 'You know it's sweet cicely – or chervil – by the smell of aniseed. That's the first thing. Here ...' Miriam squeezes the bunch of stems and fern-like leaves she has in her hand and thrusts it towards my face, causing me to take a sudden step backwards that results in me crashing down onto my bottom. At the top of the bank, Jamie and Luke burst out into bellows of laughter.

Hauling myself upright, I turn to them and shake my fist in mock threat. As I move, the sharp pain in my ankle causes me to yelp. Jamie's laughter turns immediately to concern.

'Are you all right, Mum?'

I hate to hear the note of panic in his voice. He has been so sensitive to the slightest sign of anything going wrong, to me being ill, to our parlous financial situation worsening, since our lives imploded. His need to take care of me is simultaneously heartwarming and heartbreaking. He's far too young to have such a burden in his life.

I smile to mask the pain and shout up to him that I'm fine. The ankle hurts but I'm sure it's only temporary and I determine to ignore it. Anyway, what with work, tennis with Dan, and my new fitness regime of running and weight-training in the club gym (now I have a free membership, courtesy of the job), I can't possibly allow for an injury – I simply don't have time.

I reach out and take the bunch of leaves that Miriam is proffering towards me. Inhaling deeply, a strong aroma of aniseed fills my nostrils.

'It smells good.' I can't suppress my surprise that a bunch of weeds could have an appetising scent rather than the whiff of damp grass and earth that I had been expecting.

'Of course!' exclaims Miriam, coming right up close to me. 'Now, if you look here,' she explains, intent on educating me, 'you see the white splashes?'

She straightens up and wipes her hand across her brow, leaving a brown streak of mud behind. 'That and the smell are how you identify it.'

'Right.' I peer forward to take a closer look.

'We'll pick a nice handful of this and you can make a lovely salad with it,' she burbles on. 'How much do you pay for a packet of leaves from the supermarket? When this is here, plentiful – and free!' Miriam is on a roll, gathering leaves and uttering exhortations with equal vigour. 'Come on, dear, there's a lovely clump right next to you!'

Only minimally aided by my contribution, her carrier bag is soon stuffed full and she heads back up the bank like an oversized but appropriately shaggy Himalayan goat. I clamber up behind her, and go to find Charlotte where she has disappeared behind a clump of scrubby trees and bushes.

'How's it all going? The job? Naomi?' she asks, casually.

I consider for a moment before replying. The truth is that I've been so busy since I started, learning the ropes and getting used to being on my feet all day, that I haven't taken much notice of her; she spends a lot of time in the office, putting in orders and dealing with paperwork, or cooking in the kitchen, whilst I am out front with the customers.

But it's undeniable that she appears like magic whenever

Dan is around, and fawns and fusses over him like a mother over a newborn. And their interactions do seem to have a familiarity that indicates a certain level of – how should I put it? – intimacy. I'm sure it's nothing more than a particularly demonstrative friendship. Although, on the other hand ...

'Well?' Charlotte prompts, sounding anxious. 'What are you not telling me?'

'Nothing,' I reply hastily. My face must have given me away, indicating my doubt even when I'd determined not to let on. 'She's fine,' I continue eventually, deciding that the best course of action is to play the whole thing down. I don't want Charlotte to get upset, especially when there's probably nothing behind any of it, but I do find it hard to lie.

I breathe in sharply before continuing. 'I mean, she's just one of those people who's naturally over-effusive so her behaviour with Dan isn't out of charac—'

'Still all over him like a rash, then?' Charlotte's question shoots out with bullet-like velocity, cutting over the end of my sentence.

I pause once more before replying, still not sure what to include and what to leave out.

'Well, yes.' I can't help but grimace and unfortunately I think Charlotte sees so I hurriedly try to mitigate her understandable concerns; I can't bear to think of her worrying herself to death about this, especially over someone as annoying yet inconsequential as Naomi. 'But, as I say, it's just how she is. Nothing to worry about.'

Charlotte bends to retie a shoelace. She's wearing a beautiful pair of lightweight, waterproof walking boots that somehow

135

manage to look elegant as well as practical. I laugh inwardly to myself as I think that; this is the first time in my life that I've ever spent time admiring outdoor footwear. I guess it shows just how much things have changed.

'If I question him too much about it,' she mutters, almost as if she's not listening to me, as if she's talking to herself or addressing the ground beneath her feet, 'he'll think I don't trust him.'

She stands upright and looks directly at me, meeting my eye.

'But you don't,' I reply.

A cuckoo calls, the first of spring.

'I mean, you've told me that you know he's been unfaithful in the past ...' I blunder on, trying to make up for my frankness, and merely digging myself a bigger hole in the process. I force myself to stop so I can regain my composure.

'Look,' I resume, eventually, 'you know you can trust me. And you know I'll keep tabs on Naomi Numbskull for you.'

There's a long silence during which Charlotte seems to have retreated to somewhere else entirely. I wonder what she's thinking but I'm not brave enough to ask. Instead, I tilt my head to one side and listen intently for the cuckoo. But it's gone and all I can hear now are some squawks and chirps that I can't identify.

Eventually, the silence becomes unbearable and to break it, I call to Jamie and Luke. There was an awkwardness in that last exchange that I don't like and, though I try to reassure myself that it's no threat to our new but burgeoning friendship, that it's just one of those discordant moments that happen sometimes, I'm worried that I've really put my foot in it.

It's always hard to judge, when someone asks for one's truthful opinion, whether they really do actually want it. Or not.

Charlotte is gathering handfuls of a plant that looks like cow parsley but surely can't be, as I cannot believe this ubiquitous weed is fit for human consumption. But, when I question what she's collecting, it turns out it is.

'Oh yes,' she laughs, 'not only is cow parsley edible but rather tasty, especially at this time of year. Not so much in the height of summer; it tends to be tougher and rather bitter by then. It's also known as wild chervil, and it smells like a mixture of parsley and aniseed.'

Chervil, sweet cicely, chickweed, cow parsley ... with all these 'c' words and scents of aniseed, I'm struggling to remember which is which.

'What would you use it for, though?' I ask. 'I wouldn't know what to do with it.'

'Cow parsley soup is lovely. Or, even more delicious, you can make pesto with it.'

I wander a few steps away from Charlotte so she doesn't feel that I'm invading her patch or crowding her and begin to pluck, somewhat dubiously, at some cow parsley of my own. I remain to be convinced that a roadside weed would be a fitting substitute for basil, one of my personal favourite herbs but, on the other hand, if it really does taste good, it certainly could be another unique avenue to investigate for the cafe. If I could introduce something really on-trend and newsworthy, and increase footfall, that would certainly help to consolidate my position and make me indispensable. Which would do no harm at all, considering how much I need this job and the wages it pays.

We harvest away in silence for a few minutes and then Charlotte stands up, elaborately straightening herself out. I'm filled with sympathy; it must be terrible to suffer the pain and restrictions a bad back gives you. I'm very lucky not to have any such troubles.

She looks over in my direction and suddenly the back is forgotten and she's leaping towards me as if I'm on fire and she needs to put me out.

'No!' she cries, urgently. 'Not that. Don't even think about eating that plant.'

I look down at my armfuls of frothy-headed white-flowered stalks in dismay. I don't know what I've done wrong.

'What's the matter?' I ask.

Charlotte is shaking her head as she examines the contents of my arms and then wrests the whole lot away from me and distributes it to the four winds.

'This is one of the most poisonous plants in the British Isles,' she explains, frowning.

'Oh!' I am dumbfounded, and look down at my malevolent crop, now scattered far and wide. I keep my head lowered until I can feel the flush that's risen over my cheeks subsiding. 'So it's not cow parsley, then?'

'No, it absolutely is not.' Her voice drops to her conspiratorial whisper and she casts a glance over each shoulder as she takes a step closer to me. 'It's hemlock. What the ancient Greeks used to finish off Socrates after he was convicted of corrupting the youth of Athens, poor bastard. And what

Shakespeare refers to as "the insane root" in Macbeth.'

'Gosh.' My heart is thumping and my palms are sweating. 'Well, good thing I didn't try and make it into salsa verde for the cafe then, isn't it?' My voice is high and squeaky with relief. 'Just imagine if I'd done away with half the customers ... It doesn't bear thinking about.'

'No, it doesn't.'

Charlotte bends down and picks up one of the discarded stems and points out the giveaway hollow stalks and purple blotches that enable correct identification.

'This is the one place I know where hemlock grows around here,' Charlotte explains. 'So as long as you avoid it, you should be fine.'

I try to concentrate and focus, but I can't see too clearly in the half-light, definitely not well enough to be sure I could get it right myself – either recognising the patch or the plant. I contemplate making some revision cue cards on everything I've learnt today, like one does in school to learn French irregular verbs or important historical dates.

The fun of the forage diminishes after this discovery, which leaves me feeling distinctly deflated. The rest of the group are starting to get weary so we call it a day. Slowly, we trudge our way back along the crumbling, pot-holed tarmac of the little-used back road, gathering up the boys and the stragglers as we go.

We're chatting in a desultory way amongst ourselves, me, Charlotte, Miriam, and a couple of others, when I hear a car on the road behind us. This is unusual as it's a rough, single-track lane that's been supplanted by a parallel two-lane road that gets any driver to exactly the same destination much faster. There's no reason to come this way unless you're either lost or for some reason wanting to put your car's suspension to the test. It's more common to hear horses' hooves than the swish of tyres.

But nevertheless, it's definitely a car. I glance behind me and see it, gleaming black, approaching far too fast.

'Boys!' I shout. 'Watch out! Get into the side.'

Obediently, my sons flatten themselves into the hawthorn hedgerow. I follow suit, glancing at Charlotte. She doesn't move, seems to be frozen to the spot. And then suddenly she jumps up the grass bank and tries to squeeze herself into a tiny gap in the dense bushes. Her face is deathly white and dandelion leaves spill out of her basket. I see that her hands are trembling. She looks terrified.

She's still trying to dive headlong through the hedge as the car passes us. It's slowed down considerably in deference to so many pedestrians and practically crawls by. It's sleek, dark, and expensive, with enough exhaust pipes to power a tanker and tinted windows that prevent anyone from seeing inside. With no driver visible, in this quiet, isolated country lane, it's like a ghost vehicle or the beginning of a horror movie.

It passes us and curves around a bend. The birds begin singing again, the crickets chirrup and everything is normal once more. No mad axe-murderers. No chainsaw-wielding psychos. No headless horsemen. We are safe.

'At least some people are considerate,' I say. The only other vehicle we've seen whilst we've been here today sped past at about ninety miles an hour.

Charlotte nods weakly. She looks as if she's about to throw up, and is still staring over her shoulder, though the car has long since disappeared from view.

'Are you OK?' I ask, worriedly. I can't think why she's so upset. It might be reasonable if her children were here and had somehow been put in danger by the car, but they're not, and mine are fine. So why so distraught?

Charlotte coughs and takes a few deep breaths. 'Oh yes, of course,' she replies. 'Just came over a bit funny for the moment there. Some weird bug I'm throwing off.'

'Poor you,' I say, pulling a sympathetic face. It seems a bit odd as she was fine earlier but viruses can do that, I suppose. 'I hope it clears up soon,' I add.

At the top of the road that leads into the village centre, the boys and I detach ourselves from the group and head for home. An idea is fomenting in my mind. Charlotte spoke about the book she's writing. Well, perhaps I could take a leaf out of her book – oh, those puns again! – and write one too. Food for thought, I muse, out-punning even myself.

Later, once the boys are fed and in bed, I scrabble around amongst the pile of languishing boxes behind the sofa in my living room. Eventually, I find the one I want. I brush off the light covering of dust that has settled already and pull open the flaps. There are some reference books on top, the kind of book one seems to collect but is never sure where they came from – Greek Myths, a guide to an exhibition at the Royal Academy, a map of Cornwall that I must have kept thinking it would come in handy one day. I put them all to one side. Beneath them lie two or three heavy tomes that I heft out, one by one, and place next to each other on the threadbare carpet.

There they are, my course textbooks, the works that should have helped to furnish me with a degree in Pharmacy and Toxicology. I've never been entirely sure why I've kept them – some kind of nostalgia, I suppose, for what might have been. I've forgotten nearly everything contained within them, but the sad fact is that I should know it all. If I'd completed my degree, I would do. They hold the keys to what I needed to know, before, when I had a career path in mind, a future, prospects. Before everything changed forever.

The course has long been discontinued, the toxicology element discarded. If I had completed it, I would be one of the few people in the country to have such a qualification.

*If.*

# Chapter 17

## *Charlotte*

The photographs are good. I'm pleased with what I've got so far. Once I've put them all through Photoshop and fiddled around with them, they'll be perfect. At least something is going well. The last foraging trip was horrendous, what with the car turning up, passing us on the road, deliberately slowing down to get a good look at me and making sure I got a good look at it – though of course it was impossible to see inside. This was not a figment of my imagination. This was real. Thank God I wasn't alone out there, on that deserted country lane. But assassins don't care, do they? They'd shoot in front of a few women and children, run over, plough through anyone who got in their way. Who or what would stop them?

I'm suddenly struck with the thought that they might have mistaken your two boys for mine, who weren't with us that day. What if they'd ... Oh God, no, it doesn't bear thinking about.

My mind is running away with me and I force it to stop. I haven't been out for days. The only place I feel safe is at home, inside my own four walls, with all the doors and windows

143

locked. It's summertime and hot, and Agnes and the au pair are always trying to fling the windows open and let in the fresh air but I firmly forbid it.

I can't dispel the fear that it's not just the breeze that might enter.

I go back to my pictures. I've captured details precisely as I wanted them. They're exactly the kind of glossy images that I imagined when I first had the idea for the foraging book. It almost feels too easy, using a digital camera and a computer programme, but that's technology for you. Sometimes I think back to the old days of darkrooms and developing fluid. Those shadowy images that had to be so carefully nurtured if they were to come to fruition. It felt like real work, then. Work that needed expertise and dedication and perseverance.

I developed photos with my father. He was an amateur photographer in the old sense of the world, someone who probably knew more about lenses and films and shutter speeds than half the professionals. That's what it used to be like, to be an amateur. When I think of my dad, I try to only think of that, of the quiet of the darkroom and the smell of developing fluid.

Smell is the most evocative of the senses. If I smelt *álcool*, the sugar-cane fuel that all Brazilian cars ran on when Dan and I lived in São Paulo, I would be immediately transported back to the chaos and noise and bustle and traffic jams of that giant megalopolis. I would see the piles of cashew fruits, orange, yellow, and red, looking just like peppers, and recall their bittersweet taste with the acidic burn at the end. I would hear the rhythms of samba and merengue and lambada and remember how we danced, Dan and I, to whirl all our troubles away. And the scent of jasmine will always take me back to Greece, to Athens, where the cloying, honey smell was a blessed relief from the traffic fumes and the insane summer heat.

So that chemical aroma, if I were ever to experience it again, would put me straight at my father's side in the makeshift darkroom he would conjure up in the bathroom. The rest of the family had to make sure they went to the loo before we got started, because once underway, nothing could be allowed to interrupt the process.

Imagine that! Only one toilet in the house. Not like my incontinence mansion, where every bedroom is en suite and there's a separate guest cloakroom and bathroom too. Not to mention the sauna in the basement and the facilities in the pool house. It cost a fortune to do all the plumbing and electrics in a Grade I listed building, but as I said to Dan at the time, it has to be right. If we're going to do it, we might as well put everything into it and do it properly. It makes sense.

But I digress. These days, there's hardly any barrier between the professional photographer and the hobbyist. Anyone can upload their work to iStock or Shutterstock or wherever and sell it and have it used on websites and magazines. But in the old days, by which I mean twenty or thirty years ago, everything was different. You could enter competitions, or send your photography away to magazines and wait months with bated breath to see if they wanted it. The answer would come by post – either the photo returned in an envelope marked 'do not bend' or a cheque for a fiver. Dad didn't submit his work very often, though, despite how passionate he was about photography. Other crap got in the way.

My father was an addict.

The dictionary definition of 'addicted' is to be physically or mentally dependent on a particular substance and unable to stop taking it without incurring adverse effects.

Dad could get addicted to anything. Alcohol. Star Trek. Taking pictures.

If there was an opportunity to do whatever it was to an unhealthy degree and to the exclusion of what he should be doing – i.e. going out to work and earning a living for his family, caring for his children, securing them a roof over their heads and so on – then he would do it.

He indulged in many things to an unhealthy degree but his real downfall was gambling.

Internet research tells me that 'behavioural addiction' is a compulsion to engage in rewarding non-drug related behaviour regardless of any negative consequences to the person's physical, mental, social, or financial wellbeing.

It also tells me that there's a gene that addicts have, and that it's often handed down through the generations.

I could read that and excuse myself my actions, talk myself down from the cliff edge of guilt and anguish and helplessness. But I don't. It just makes me hate my father and everything he did to me and my siblings even more.

His gambling lost us our house. We were homeless, out on the streets. If I tell people that, it's usually the worst thing they can possibly imagine. But he caused us another loss that was even more terrible.

Our mother.

She left, walked out one midsummer morning, and moved in with a man she'd met at the Citizens Advice Bureau, when she was trying to sort out what she was entitled to, what benefits she could claim given that she had no income and no way to support herself and her three children.

He advised her all right.

I'll always believe that if she'd stuck by Dad, if she'd tried to get him help and encouraged him, he could have beaten the addictions. But she didn't want him, and nor, as it turned out, did she want us. Me and my two younger siblings.

We went to live with our grandparents and I hardly spoke to my mother ever again. Or my father, because he passed away shortly after the house was taken, found sleeping rough on the streets, dead from alcohol poisoning.

I picked myself up, turned myself around and determined that I would never find myself in either of my parents' situations. But the best laid plans and all that. I'm completely dependent on Dan. If the worst came to the worst and we did divorce, at least the laws are tougher these days and maintenance payments are rigidly enforced. But still. I wouldn't be able to live the way I do now, nothing like. I'm not sure I'd be able to live at all. Not just in the survival sense, but metaphorically. I'm as reliant on him as I've ever been on any of my ... habits, shall we call them.

And if the truth came out I'd more than likely lose the children, be deemed an unfit mother, a bad influence, or both.

So the worst is not going to come to the worst. It's not going to happen. I want my children to grow up with a mother and father and to have the secure and happy childhood I didn't have. I won't let anything or anyone – not Naomi or any other jumped-up floozy – come between us.

I won't let myself and my sins and misdemeanours come between us, either.

# Chapter 18

## Susannah

I'm starting to notice that Dan really does come to the cafe an awful lot; he's been in every day this week, breezing past me in a sophisticated flurry of expensive aftershave, easy bonhomie, and the self-possession of the affluent. He says he starts work late because he deals with west coast US so he has to wait for them all to wake up.

Today, he's in as usual for breakfast and orders his customary flat white accompanied by homemade granola with summer berries.

'Did you forage for them?' he asks jokingly, gesturing towards his bowl that is brimming with redcurrants, raspberries and blueberries as I fuss with my ordering pad and the arrangement of the salt and pepper pots on the table.

'No,' I confess. 'They don't grow wild around here and I think I might cause a bit of a stir if I raided the village allotments.'

I pause to allow him to smile, which he does, obligingly.

'But the lunchtime soup is a *caldo verde* of cow parsley

149

and wild rocket that I gathered myself,' I tell him, with faux primness. I've got much more confident with my plant identification these days, and I've revisited the patch of verge where Charlotte showed me the difference between the edible plant and the toxic weed several times. We're pretty much at the end of the cow parsley season now, though – much longer and it will be too tough and unpalatable.

'So if I stay for lunch do I get it cheaper, if all the ingredients are free?' Dan retaliates. 'A discount at least, surely?'

At this point, Naomi comes bustling over, all huge breasts made even more prominent by her apron, which sports an image of a naked female body, private parts naively obscured by fruits. I think she finds it amusing.

'My favourite customer,' she gushes, running her hand down Dan's cheek and then pulling him into an embrace that involves his head being engulfed by the aforementioned bosom.

Dan doesn't bat an eyelid. Well, he hardly could, given that his eyes are more or less subsumed by Naomi's chest and arms, submerged in a sea of flesh. But even when released he remains as dignified and unruffled as ever, taking it all in his stride.

'Can I get you anything else, my darling?' she asks, fishing a notepad out of her apron pocket. I hang around, feeling redundant.

Dan waves her away. 'Susannah's got this,' he says firmly. 'All in hand.'

I just about manage to stop myself from giggling; I can only imagine the parts of Dan that Naomi would like to have in her hands. I make him his second coffee and then observe him surreptitiously from across the room as I serve another customer. I get it – Naomi's infatuation, I totally get it. He's gorgeous, muscular and toned, his flawless tennis whites showing off strong, agile legs. It's hardly surprising that a cafe manager in a provincial village with not much going on in her life should find him irresistibly attractive. I wonder what to report back to Charlotte, if anything. There's something on her mind and I wouldn't want to add to her troubles so perhaps it's best to keep quiet, in a *least said, soonest mended* sort of way.

Dan and I meet again the next day for our Saturday match that has become a regular fixture. I've bought a new tennis dress with my earnings from the cafe, and I'm feeling pretty chipper. My money worries have eased, mainly due to finally making a wage but also because I have to say that Naomi is very generous. She allows me to take home food that's still perfectly edible but past its expiry date so the cost of my weekly shop has dropped dramatically. In addition to this, Justin is seeing more of the boys, taking them out every other weekend. We meet halfway at a motorway service station and undertake a kind of hostage handover. I don't like seeing them go but I know they need to spend time with their father – and I can't deny being grateful to have a little more free time, especially now I'm working.

Justin is still living in London, and he's only been able to afford a one-bedroom rental so far so they can't really stay over, but he's confident he'll be able to get somewhere bigger soon. He told me proudly that his priority, over and above his own accommodation, was to increase his maintenance payments so the boys didn't suffer. Clearly, this is only what he's legally obliged to do but I dutifully thanked him nevertheless, and I can't deny that the extra cash is a lifeline.

Everything combined, I've begun to make a dent in my overdraft at last and the satisfaction of seeing that red number diminish, even if only by the tiniest amount, cannot be overstated. I'm so used to my money disappearing like ice cream on a summer's day that to have a little extra is a wonderful novelty – hence the celebratory new sportswear.

So I step onto the court this particular morning with a spring in my step. It's hot already and the grass is no longer immaculate but scuffed at the service lines and browning at the edges. Dan is already ridiculously tanned, and his slanting eyes seem darker than usual, full of the confidence and allure of success. He must have been striking some really good deals recently.

'How are you doing?' he asks me.

I give a dismissive flick of my head. 'What, since we last saw each other all of twenty-four hours ago?' I tease.

'Since whenever,' he counters. 'I'm genuinely interested.'

I can't help but let out a sigh. Though in general things are going well, there are still plenty of flies in the proverbial ointment. For example, the struggle to get the boys to do their homework when all they want is to go out and play football, the sordid state of my house and its desperate need for regeneration – even with more funds coming in, there's still nowhere near enough to undertake a renovation project. But, I remind myself, Dan doesn't want to know all about my niggles.

Except, maybe he does.

'That sigh sounded heartfelt,' he jokes. 'What's bothering you?'

'No, no nothing,' I say. 'Things are really good – better than I have a right to expect them to be. I'm glad I made the move here.'

Dan's eyes crease seductively as he grins. 'I think we're all glad about that.'

A twinge pulls at my chest and I circle my arms to release it. My warm-up routine must be leaving something lacking, I think, and make a mental note to stretch more thoroughly in future.

'But,' he continues, 'I can see you've got something on your mind.'

I shrug and grimace resignedly. 'Oh, you know, it's the stupid little things around the house that I should know how to fix myself but don't, and it makes me feel so useless ... For example, the kitchen tap needs a washer. It drips incessantly into the metal sink like some kind of Chinese water torture,' I explain. I shake my head to show how annoying but at the same time trivial this little matter is. 'And I don't know any plumbers around here and I'm a bit anxious about how much one would charge me, anyway. First world problem, I know,' I apologise in conclusion.

Now it's out, and I feel more helpless and stupid than ever. But Dan takes it completely differently.

'That is a right pain,' he agrees. 'What would you have done in the past? Got your ex-husband to sort it?'

I nod glumly. 'Yes, Justin would have done it. I mean, it's

not difficult, is it? I'm just useless at that sort of thing and I'm worried that if I tried, I'd make it worse, cause a flood or something.'

Dan smiles his lovely crinkly smile. 'I know I don't look like Mr Fix-It,' he says, 'but a washer I can do. And actually, I quite enjoy DIY. I never do any at home because Charlotte won't let me – doesn't trust me, I think. She'd rather get tradesmen in who charge her an arm and a leg and let them mess it up instead.'

'Oh,' I splutter, somewhat surprised. Dan's right. I didn't have him down as someone who's handy around the house, as well as all his other talents.

'I'll come round and do it for you,' he suggests, not sounding in the least as if he feels he has to offer. 'One day this week ... I'll let you know when I'm free.'

'Thank you,' I reply simply. I don't know what else to say. It's so unexpected but so delightful that I'm nonplussed. A multi-millionaire who's not too self-important to mend a tap. That is someone truly special.

The match is a tough one. Dan has muscle and height, but as well as being more fleet of foot, I have precision on my side. And I've built strength and fitness over the past few months so I'm feeling better than I have since my youth. You could say that, as tennis opponents, Dan and I are perfectly paired.

The first set goes to him, and I have to muster all the resilience I have to up my game in set two. I win it, six-four. Set three goes to a tie-break, which I take by a hair's breadth.

Dan is surprisingly magnanimous in defeat; perhaps

Charlotte has painted an exaggeratedly bad picture of him to me. As he shakes my hand, his eyes meet mine.

'Nicely done, Ms Carr,' he congratulates me. 'There was a fluidity and determination in your game – or should I say in yourself – today that I had no chance against.'

I incline my head graciously and accept the compliment. I even do it without blushing.

'Quick coffee?' Dan asks. 'Charlotte doesn't like anyone around and interfering when she's cooking.'

She's invited me and the boys to lunch – it's not one of Justin's weekends – and I'm looking forward to a feast. I'm also keen to see more of the inside of that beautiful manor house. I've only really been in the kitchen to date. We head for the cafe and I wonder how Naomi will behave when she sees Dan – will it be her normal embarrassingly over the top reaction? – but she's busy in the kitchen and it's one of the local schoolgirls doing her weekend shift who makes and brings our drinks.

'You're playing better and better,' Dan says, leaning forward as if to show how serious he is. His right knee brushes against mine as he shifts position.

'Thanks,' I say. I should add something witty and clever but as always, I can't think of anything right now. It'll come to me hours too late, when I'm in the shower or cleaning the loo as is usually the way.

'We should enter the league,' he muses, furrowing his brow in concentration. 'I think the playoffs start really soon, with the final at the end of September.'

He sips his steaming coffee. 'Not a patch on the flat white

you make,' he comments, smiling. But then his expression changes, eyes narrowed in concern.

'Have you noticed anything odd about Charlotte lately?' he asks. There is an insistent, intent tone to his voice, as if he is determined to get to the bottom of it, whatever 'it' is. 'Anything about her behaviour or her mood?'

I squirm and sit back in my chair to hide it. I hate talking about people when they're not there. It always makes me feel as if I'm being disloyal – even if it's good things that are being said. And discussing Charlotte, the person who's held out the hand of friendship so generously since I've been here, makes me particularly awkward. I shift uncomfortably in my chair, clumsily crossing and uncrossing my legs. My knee inadvertently ends up in a position wedged against Dan's. It feels a bit awkward and overly intimate, but I leave it there, feeling that to snatch it away will only draw more attention.

'She does seem worried about something,' I venture cautiously, considering how she's been acting strangely for weeks now, all jumpy and nervous, her face pale and drawn despite all the 'work' she's had. I don't think it's disloyal of me to let Dan know I have concerns, but on the other hand, if Charlotte wanted him to know about something that's bothering her, I'm sure she'd tell him. Sharing and confiding is what husbands and wives do, one of the many reasons why partnership is so valuable and sought-after.

The only reason not to let on would be if one had something to hide – and I can't believe that of her. Although on the other hand, one never knows ... And then of course there's the state of their relationship to consider. It just doesn't seem,

156

to the casual observer, to be very healthy, if truth be told. Charlotte *says* she loves Dan, but there's no evidence of this in the way she acts with him or how she speaks to him. In fact, there's plenty to the contrary.

Dan is looking at me intently, his eyes narrowed in concentration. 'Worried in what way? About what?' he questions. And then, without waiting for my answer, he blurts out, 'I knew it. I absolutely knew it. She won't come anywhere near me, won't let me touch her, doesn't want to—' He breaks off mid-flow, as if aware he's about to say something revealing. 'Well, let's just say she's very distant,' he resumes, returning to his usual measured tones, 'and I can't seem to put a foot right.'

I bite my lip, something I always do when I'm unsettled. 'Perhaps it's that she's missing the twins now they've gone back to school,' I venture, 'and even the younger two aren't around much, are they? It makes her feel old, to see her babies growing up. That's what it's like for women. It's natural. She'll get over it.'

A tentative smile breaks across his face, and the rather charming, anxious furrows on his forehead gradually smooth out. 'Yes, of course, you're right. That's what it is, all it is.'

He seems to be thinking hard about something, then his next words come out in a rush. 'I'll find something to treat her with. Perhaps a piece of jewellery from that place she likes in Marylebone ...'

I listen to Dan going on about whether Charlotte would prefer rubies or diamonds, gold or silver, a necklace or earrings or both.

'Right now,' I interject, suddenly realising the time, 'I think she'd just prefer us to get there in time for the lunch she's making. Drink up!'

Dan nods and finishes his coffee in one gulp. 'Sure. Let's go.'

The Porsche is parked outside on the street. 'The car park was full when I arrived,' he explains. 'And people are so careless. The spaces are really tight, everyone's in a hurry, and I've had a couple of scratches and scrapes. All those mums dropping their kids off here, there, and everywhere, rushing and not even noticing that they've bumped someone. Sometimes I think it's safer to stay out here.'

He gestures to the road, which is wide and spacious, and fairly sparsely occupied. As he does so, we both see Miriam approaching, scurrying along in her characteristic head-down, determined way, like Mrs Tiggy-Winkle.

'Look at you two!' she cries as she spots us. 'Don't you look the vision of health and vitality! You should be the pictures on vitamin supplement boxes!'

Dan and I catch each other's eyes and I suppress a giggle. She's truly batty.

'The ones for the more mature age-groups, I presume you mean,' I laugh. And then, realising what I've insinuated, add, 'Only speaking personally, of course.'

Dan grins and Miriam beams.

'I must get a snap for the foraging newsletter,' she goes on, in what seems to be a non-sequitur.

'Why?' I enquire, mildly.

'To show the benefits of eating wild food – you are the living proof!'

Before we can comment further, she's whipped out an

ancient iPhone and started snapping away. I know I'll look dreadful, my hair, only just released from its ponytail, still staying resolutely behind my ears rather than framing my face the way I want it to, my cheeks still flushed from the strenuous exercise of the match.

'Fantastic!' exclaims Miriam, appearing happy with her work. 'You could be a couple, you two; you *match* each other somehow.'

I'm overcome with mortification – poor Dan, being associated with insignificant lil' ol' me when he's used to the glamour queen that is Charlotte. Miriam's peering at her phone, bending over, and I make a *what–is-she-on?* face at Dan above her head. He grins, unphased as ever.

'Look!' cries Miriam, wielding the phone at us. 'Just look at you!'

Nervously, I take a peek. We stand there, the crown of my head fitting neatly underneath Dan's chin, perspiring gently in the sunshine. Or at least I am. Dan looks immaculate, a George Clooney-esque aura of perfection about him.

I shrug. 'I honestly think you're mad,' I say to Miriam, 'but if you must use it, I suppose it's my only chance of ever being a cover girl!'

Dan also gives his blessing.

Escaping Miriam's clutches, we get into the car. The Porsche does the journey in nanoseconds. Fast cars, expensive jewels, a beautiful house and a gorgeous husband; there's plenty to envy in Charlotte's lifestyle.

It's a good thing I'm not the covetous type.

# Chapter 19

## *Charlotte*

My phone pings to signify a message. It's from Miriam and I don't open it immediately as the potatoes need basting – yes, potatoes are on the menu, due to public demand. When everything is back under control a few minutes later, I pick up my phone to see what Miriam wants – something about next week's foraging schedule or the exact quantities required for sorrel pesto probably.

I punch in the passcode and see, instead of what I'm expecting, a photo. It's of you and Dan, standing outside the tennis club. Dan's gaze is directed straight at the camera. Typical. He never loses an opportunity to pose. But you. You look as though you've been caught unawares; your eyes are averted and you're glancing down as if hurriedly smoothing your skirt or checking the buttons of your shirt are done up correctly.

Or as if you don't really want the photo to be taken.

Using my thumb and forefinger, I zoom in on your face. Our country air and locally-foraged produce seem to suit you. Your gently tanned skin glows with health – though you should watch that. Too much sun is *so* ageing. But you look lovely and I wish, not for the first time, that I could think of someone who would be suitable for you, someone I could introduce you to. I know you're lonely, I know that more than anything else you desperately want a man, but unfortunately, though Biglow has many positive attributes, a healthy supply of single, eligible gentlemen is not one of them.

Perhaps you should sign up to one of these online dating sites. I don't think they're just for young people anymore; apparently there are ones that specialise in the over-forties. Or maybe Guardian Soulmates would be best – you are a bit of leftie, and Guardian readers are mostly bleeding-heart liberals, just like you. Or eHarmony, maybe. It worked for a friend of a friend of mine; unlikely though it sounds, she found eternal love with a man from Minehead who breeds miniature schnauzers. Perhaps I'll suggest it, when the time is right. The dating agency, that is, not the breeding of irritating yappy pooches!

I take another look at the photo. Something catches my eye and I hesitate, zooming in again, even further than before. The earrings you're wearing are very pretty. And they look expensive. They must date from your former life, when you had a husband and he had money to spend on you. If I remember, I'll ask you where you – or rather, he – got them. Finding a new jewellery emporium is always fun.

I'm absorbed in contemplation of your accessories when the sudden blaring of the front door bell makes me jump out of my skin. My heart skips a beat and a shock of fear runs through me. I let the phone drop from my hand and focus on steadying my breathing. I'm just regaining control when a deafening ring, combined with a low thumping, disturbs the silence anew. My mobile. I glance towards it, then irritatedly snatch it up, fear replaced by annoyance. It's Dan.

'Charl,' his voice booms down the airwaves, using the name he knows I hate, 'can you let us in? I told you I didn't take keys but you're not answering the door.'

'Coming,' I reply, curtly. I stride towards the door, spending the time it takes to get there composing my face into an expression of welcoming bonhomie.

The meal I've laboured over is greatly appreciated and, though I say it myself, delicious – rack of lamb with rosemary potatoes (which you and I both giggle about as I serve them), broccoli puree and caramelised carrots, followed by a pear tarte tatin that melts in the mouth.

After we've eaten and the boys, who I managed to get to play outside whilst you and Dan were at the club, have disappeared to the fustiness of the indoor games room, and Dan to his study, you and I retreat to the drawing room. The French windows are open, revealing the flawless green lawn that the gardener spends so long perfecting. In the beds that surround it, the roses are flowering profusely. At the end is the ha-ha, its visual trickery extending the manicured garden into the lush, tree-studded meadow that stretches into the distance beyond. This separation, it suddenly occurs to me, seems to reflect my life at the moment, divided into the part I understand, which is being a mother and carer and wife, and the part that I don't, which is ... well, so many things, but mainly, of course, my tormentors. And Naomi.

Nevertheless, despite everything I feel quite relaxed as we settle ourselves on adjoining sofas. I opened wine in your honour and somehow between us we've managed to polish off two bottles. I'm concerned about your drinking. I will mention it sometime, when the time is right. It might not be a problem. It might just be that really good wine is a treat for you these days.

I'm about to ask you how school is going for the boys when the phone rings.

My heart stops.

I break out into a cold sweat that instantly makes my palms and my armpits feel clammy. My heart thumps so loudly I'm sure you can hear it. It's the landline and I race for the handset before anyone else can get it. Neither Dan nor the boys ever answer but still, every time I panic that this will be the time that one of them will. And that, instead of a drop down, in place of silence, there'll be someone there who'll talk.

Breathless from my sprint, I snatch up the receiver.

'Charlotte! So glad to have got you! I thought you might be out enjoying the weather. So pleasant, isn't it? Though perhaps almost too hot ...'

It's Miriam. As her voice prattles on, going on about the photo she took of you and Dan and how it would be perfect for the newsletter, my chin sinks to my chest and I'm suffused in a hot flush of relief. I concentrate on four-four breathing to calm myself: breathe in for four, hold for four, out for four, hold for four ... By the time I've recovered, I realise that Miriam is asking me something and I haven't heard a word.

'Charlotte, are you all right? You sound rather peculiar – a bit like a heavy breather, actually!'

She guffaws loudly at her own joke and I manage a little titter.

'I don't know what you mean,' I counter, feebly. 'Must be a poor line.'

'So I can put you down to contribute some seasonal blooms for the church flowers next week, Friday, for the Joyce wedding on Saturday?'

'Yes, yes, of course,' I splutter. I'd agree to anything right now, I'm so thankful that it's harmless Miriam on the other end of my phone and not who I always fear it might be.

I walk very slowly back to the drawing room, regaining my composure with every step. I'm OK for now.

Another stay of execution, but for how long?

# Chapter 20

## Susannah

'Just Miriam,' Charlotte announces, as she returns and sits back down on the sofa opposite me. She is her normal, self-assured self once more; on the surface, there's no sign of the frightened rabbit who leapt off her chair as if a bomb had gone off as soon as the phone rang.

Whatever's on her mind has not gone away. I wonder what Dan will do about it and whether he'll ask me again. I wonder what *I* should do about it.

'She wanted to know about flowers for the church,' Charlotte continues.

'You are wonderful,' I say. 'Is there anything you don't take part in?' I know I should be more involved in village life but I just don't have the time, with work and the boys and I'm still sorting out the house. That's a task that feels like it will go on forever.

'I think it's so important to contribute where you can,' replies Charlotte, somewhat obliquely. I'm not sure if she's implying something about me or not. 'And when it comes to flowers – well, I've got plenty at this time of the year.'

She waves her hand towards the overflowing beds in the immaculate garden beyond the doorway as if I've asked for evidence. I nod in acknowledgement as I pick up one of the many photos from the side table next to me.

'So when are you off to Corsica?' I ask, appraising the image. In it, an infinity pool drops away to a sweeping cerulean bay, at the tip of which lies a jumbled fishing village, picturesquely located at the foot of steep cliffs. I think that, if I owned something so idyllic, I'd be there every possible moment. But I suppose if you have such luxury permanently at your fingertips, it's difficult not to take it for granted.

'This is the place?' I add, checking my assumption is correct as I continue to gaze at the vision of paradise in the picture.

'Yes, that's right,' Charlotte confirms. 'And before you say anything, I know how lucky I am. We are,' she corrects, presumably thinking of her children as well as herself.

Ruefully, I ponder what my summer will be this year – namely, me working my socks off and the boys lucky to get a day out at Camber Sands. Although Justin has vaguely alluded to taking them camping in the Lake District, so you never know. They, at least, might get a change of scene. I wonder how long Charlotte will be away for and I'm suddenly aware of how I've come to rely on her friendship and how lonely I'll be if she's gone for two months; there's no one else I'm remotely as close to. Certainly not Miriam. Or Naomi. Of course there's always Dan and the tennis, as I understand that his work commitments mean that he never joins his family for the entire duration of their stay abroad, but it's not the same with a man. I can't confide in Dan, tell him my secrets, unburden myself to him in the same way I can to a girlfriend such as Charlotte.

'When are you going?' I ask, inwardly chastising myself for thoughts that, if spoken, might come across as me resenting Charlotte and her boys their summer break.

'Oh, I don't know yet,' she replies, airily.

I interpret this as the last-minute approach of the well-off – no need to plan half a year ahead to be sure of getting the best price with the low-cost airlines.

'The thing is,' she continues, falteringly, 'that I … well, I don't think I'll spend all summer in Corsica this year.'

Spoken in such an uncharacteristically hesitant manner, her words take me totally by surprise.

'What?' I ask, involuntarily.

'Corsica,' Charlotte repeats, somewhat sadly. 'I don't think I'll go to the house for the whole of July and August.'

'Whyever not?'

'I'm not sure I should leave Dan alone for so long. You know what they say: while the cat's away, the mice will play.' Charlotte's face has visibly fallen, her eyes downcast and her lips almost trembling.

I'm taken aback, so much so that I don't answer immediately, needing to choose my words carefully.

'Don't be silly,' I say eventually, trying to sound as encouraging as I can without coming across as pushy or overbearing. 'You can't let the Naomi thing get to you to such an extent that it interferes with your summer – or the boys' summer, for that matter.'

I brush a speck of dust off the photo and put it back down

on the table. 'And anyway,' I add, thoughtfully, 'they say that absence makes the heart grow fonder so you'd probably find that some time away from Dan would put everything into perspective and do your relationship a lot of good.'

Our respective sofas suddenly seem a million miles away so I get up and go and sit next to her. Her hands are tightly clenched together in her lap and I give them a gentle squeeze. They feel hard and bony, resentful somehow, as if they are gripping the weight of her uncertainty, the extent of her troubles, whatever those might be, and finding it hard to let go.

'You absolutely must go. I insist on it,' I conclude, and then utter a short laugh of mitigation. It's not like me to be giving instructions to Charlotte; our relationship tends towards the opposite. 'Come on,' I urge, 'you can't let a silly girl like Naomi rule your life.'

Charlotte shakes her head at the same time as attempting a wan smile.

'How about this,' I continue, hating to see her so sad and forlorn and grasping for anything that might make a difference. 'I'm going to be here all summer and I promise you that I'll keep an eye on her, make sure she keeps her claws out of him.'

At this, Charlotte finally seems to relax somewhat, running her fingers through her immaculate brunette hair in her habitual gesture. It feels good to know that this is how much she trusts me, that knowing Naomi will be under my eagle-eyed surveillance is the key to her peace of mind.

'You'd be crazy not to go to Corsica,' I add, warming to my theme now. 'You love it so much and you deserve a break. It might be a good idea to have another word with Dan about Naomi, put your mind at rest about it all. I mean, clearly, there's ...' I hesitate, not quite knowing how to put what I'm thinking into words, not wanting to make anything worse or increase Charlotte's worries, 'I mean, there probably is something there. But it might not be as bad as you think. It's always best to get things out into the open,' I conclude.

Whilst she is pondering this, I contemplate the long weeks of July and August that stretch ahead. Even if I don't have a whole bunch of friends to miss yet, there's something about the annual emptying out of the country, when everyone who possibly can heads off somewhere that's not home, whether it be Cornwall, Croatia or Corfu, that I've always found difficult. Of course it's fine if I'm one of the ones who's on the move, too – but so often in my life I've been the one left at home, going nowhere and doing nothing. This year will be exactly the same, and suffice to say I'm not relishing the thought.

I wonder about what the village will be like when everyone is on vacation and then think that the thing that will really affect me, when Justin has the boys, will be my own loneliness. So often I long to be free of the work and responsibilities that children entail, but when they're not there I miss them like one of my own limbs.

'But are you really not going anywhere?' Charlotte asks, interrupting my chain of thought, changing the subject from herself.

I shrug. 'No holiday for me,' I say, with fake cheeriness. 'I mean, I've only just moved here so I'll enjoy the good weather and play some tennis. I can't take time off from the cafe so soon after starting the job, plus the summer is the busiest time and Naomi has said it's all hands on deck,' I continue. 'And anyway, where would I go and who with? I've no money and no partner. Justin will have the boys for a few weeks – there's talk of camping – so I won't even have them to keep me company.'

I raise my eyebrows and, as I do so, catch your eye. We both laugh.

'I know,' I say, 'rather them than me sleeping in a tent. But it's all he can afford and he is their father. I don't want them to grow apart from him or lose touch – and I don't want to be someone who lives in bitterness and resentment, however much Justin hurt me with his secrets and lies.'

Secrets and lies.

Charlotte seems to have quite a few of those. Whilst she pretends to be so open and forthcoming, in reality she's a clam that I haven't even got near to breaking open yet. She opens her mouth to speak and I feel my whole body tense, wondering if this is the moment she's going to reveal all. But before she's got started, the door bursts open and Jamie and Toby come running in.

'Can we go down to the river to swim?' they shout in unison.

The moment of disclosure is gone.

I hesitate, looking to Charlotte to see how she will respond to the request. I'm not sure how I feel about unsupervised activity around water but there are four of them and Jamie and Toby are tall and fit and strong so I'm sure they'll be fine and are more than capable of looking after the younger two. But Charlotte can be quite a fusspot of a mum, and I wonder which side of her will dominate this decision – her need to protect her children against the outside world balanced against her inability to ever deny them anything.

'Please, Mum,' yells Luke, who's jumping up and down behind his brother. Then Sam turns up, trailing a beach towel behind him, already prepared for a 'yes' answer.

Charlotte looks at me and waves her hands in a gesture of despairing acceptance. 'I don't think we're going to be able to stop them, are we?' she says. A good old-fashioned 'no' would have done it, in my opinion, but when it comes to her children, I don't think Charlotte knows how to use that word.

In any case, the boys have already taken her response as permission granted and they melt silently away.

'You were saying something,' I say, leaning towards Charlotte in a way I hope inspires the sharing of confidences.

She shakes her head.

'Was I? I can't even remember. Whatever it was, it was nothing important.'

A silence descends, in which we are both lost in our own thoughts. I visualise the letter that arrived this morning, the all too familiar franking stamp. Not a debt collector, nor an accounts department. Instead, something that I've been dreading all my life; the researcher from the production company is tenacious if nothing else. It's the third one I've received, forwarded courtesy of the Royal Mail from my old address in Barnes. I press my fingers to my temples where a sudden tension headache is pounding, then look back up and give Charlotte a bright smile.

I've no idea what she's hiding but whatever it is, can it really be worse than what I am?

# PART 2

*Stars, hide your fires; let not light see my black and deep desires.*

— *Macbeth*, William Shakespeare

# Chapter 21

## *Susannah*

Charlotte's gone to Corsica after all, despite all the vacil-lating and hand wringing about whether she should leave Dan alone. I know that she was about to say something, to reveal something, when the boys exploded into the room with the force of a hurricane, begging permission to go swimming in the river. Once they'd disappeared she denied it. But I'd spotted the signs of a confession coming on. The lowered eyes, the husky voice, the contrite expression. I'd seen them all in Justin, after all, when he finally came clean about the extent of his debts and the trouble he was in.

And not just in him.

Because the thing is that, long before Justin, I'd been there before. My husband isn't the first man who has abandoned me, nor the first who deceived and dissembled. Oh no, not at all. Even after all these years, I still think about him all the time … My first love. Mourning him, cursing him, missing him.

His name was Charlie.

I met him at university. He was sitting at the bar in the

Malet Street student union building, incongruously drinking a pint of milk. Everything he did was unconventional, unusual, unique. I fell completely and utterly head-over-heels in love with him. He was my protest boyfriend, my beautiful, clever, funny, intelligent bad-boy from the rough end of Bristol, brought up in a tower block on the wrong side of the tracks by a drug-addicted and depressed single mother.

The first date we went on, he took me to Pollo Bar in Old Compton Street, famous for being the cheapest eaterie in town. Even now, I clearly recall the crowded space, rammed with booths in oxblood leatherette, all occupied by people talking at the tops of their voices. My eyes swivelled from side to side as I tried to take in the assault on my senses, the mural-covered walls and the dusty 1960s light fittings, everything shrouded in a haze of cigarette smoke. There didn't seem to be any possibility of sitting down anywhere and it was hot as an inferno. Charlie ploughed on nevertheless and eventually, after much sliding sideways and avoiding legs and arms, we arrived at a narrow, twisting staircase that led down to a basement almost as packed as the level above. Formica tables and chairs jostled for position in the cramped, low-ceilinged space, all so close together there was scarcely space to move between them.

Somehow Charlie found somewhere for us to park ourselves. He ordered and the dish arrived within minutes, a huge, overflowing plate of spaghetti puttanesca, the sauce staining the yellow pasta strands red, forming the combined colours of a sunrise.

Or a massacre.

The waitress plonked it down between us, handing us both a spoon and fork wrapped in a translucently thin paper napkin.

'The servings are big enough for two here,' Charlie grinned. 'No point in paying for one each.'

He picked up his fork, swirling it around and around in the dish until it was wrapped in a huge tomato-blood-spattered spaghetti bandage with multiple trailing strands, at which point he plunged it into his mouth. I watched, mesmerised, stabbing ineffectually at a few strands of pasta when he asked me why I wasn't eating.

Despite how fast Charlie was ploughing through the food, it seemed to take forever for it to be finished. We forced our way out of the restaurant and onto the brightly lit, buzzing street. I'd been feeling choked by the heat and cigarette smoke and steam in the basement and I remember how relieved I was to take a deep breath of fresh air.

'I should be going,' I said.

'Don't you want to come back to mine,' he replied, and it wasn't a question.

Having sex with Charlie at his digs was awkward to say the least. He shared a bedroom with a pot-smoking philosophy student named Ptolemy who never seemed to go out but rather spent the majority of his time lying flat on his back on his bed, eyes closed, puffing on a joint. To any casual observer he looked like a complete no-hoper, a student who would – literally – burn through his grant and leave uni with no more qualifications than he started with. But of the two essays he'd handed in so far, he had achieved firsts in both, Charlie said, despite the fact that he never attended lectures. He was just naturally brilliant and the dope appeared to magnify his genius. In the end, he graduated with a first.

'Like Coleridge and Shelley on laudanum,' I suggested, hoping that the comparison with such literary heavyweights might help me convince myself that a more or less permanent bedroom companion was something other than inconvenient.

'I guess,' replied Charlie. 'Although I think he takes his inspiration more from Bob Dylan.'

That night, the first occasion of love making, we had to throw Ptolemy out and make him go and sit in the kitchen. The flat's sitting room had been turned into a bedroom for another two students, so there were four people living in a space designed for one or two at the most. Ptolemy thought it unnecessary that he should leave; he wasn't interested in sex – it was too elemental and messy, too real. His interests were purely esoteric and never involved the intermingling of body fluids. We could do what we liked, he would take no notice. If we didn't mind him being there then he didn't mind us.

I most emphatically did mind. Ptolemy was duly banished.

'The ice queen melteth,' whispered Charlie in my ear after I had climaxed. I nodded, replete, a goal achieved, a triumph recorded. It was my first time.

After a few months, I moved out of my student accommodation on the Camden Road, a four-lane highway permanently choked with traffic, and Charlie and I moved into an apartment high above the Finchley Road, a six-lane highway permanently choked with traffic. We shared with the pot-smoking Ptolemy and a couple of other lads, cramming everyone in to save money. It was cramped and noisy and messy, and Marjorie, on her one visit, was horrified. Her righteous disapproval only made me more sure I'd made the right choice.

Charlie was my rebellion and as such no one, apart from me, was surprised when it didn't work out.

He cheated on me and then left me for a petite and immaculate French girl he met on his year abroad. Clichéd, right? But true. All too true.

The betrayal was complete, the cruelty absolute. To be treated like that by the man I loved through and through broke my heart.

It took a long, long time to get over Charlie.

Eventually, nearly a decade later, I met Justin and began what was my second, and as it stands right now, last relationship. I'm sure my parents, brothers, aunts, uncles, grandparents and every member of my extended family breathed a sigh of relief that I'd finally come to my senses, found someone suitable and sensible, and hopefully put the past behind me. My mother and father were on tenterhooks until Justin finally proposed; when he did so, they could hardly believe it was true. I don't think I could, either.

After Charlie, it was hard to trust anyone.

So in Charlotte (a name, I note, that is often shortened to Charlie) I recognise all the signs of what suspicion does to you; I've been there myself. Now that she's out of the way for a while I can do some digging, see if I can shed any light on what's wrong, what it is that's eating away at her. Sometimes she has a look about her, as if she's petrified about what's behind her. Every now and again she'll glance over her shoulder and I know, at those times, that she's not listening to me anymore.

It's as if she's being hunted.

And I too, because of Charlie, am being pursued.

Perhaps Charlotte and I are more similar than either of us realises. I look down at the letter in my hands, pulled out of the bunch of bank statements and circulars that have just been deposited on the doormat. The tell-tale franking stamp of the production company leaps out at me and, as always, it's addressed to my maiden name. I don't need to open it to know it'll be from that researcher again.

I rip up the letter and bury it in the bin, pulling a banana skin and piece of cellophane over the top of it as if that will somehow diminish its power and weaken it, like garlic to a vampire. He's obviously read about me, this researcher, in the newspaper reports from the time, of which there were many, some so lurid I could hardly recognise myself, and has mercilessly tracked me down. He doesn't seem to know my married name or my current address.

But if he found me the first time, it's surely only a matter of time before he finds me again.

# Chapter 22

## Susannah

Unlike the ne'er-do-wells of my past, Dan is as good as his word.

Three days after our weekend match and lunch at his house, he sends me a text asking if today is convenient for fixing the leaky tap. As it's my morning off, I tell him not only am I in but I'm free to go to the hardware store with him, too. The boys are out on playdates and I had been planning to spend the time pulling together some chapters of my book, the idea for which has crystallised recently. It will be a compendium of British flora, along with each plant's chemical constituents and the ways in which it can be used for herbal or medicinal purposes. I'll include any instances where the plants have been used in fiction or real life for beneficial or malevolent purposes. I'm hoping it will be the sort of coffee table work that will really intrigue people, a casual read but also informative and interesting. I want to make inroads on my project when the boys are away on the oft-mooted Boys' Own camping trip to the Lakes. But the tap badly needs some TLC and Dan's offer is too good to turn down so …

He picks me up in the Porsche and there's something pretty cool about pulling up next to the shabby white vans and battered Ford estates in the car park and sauntering across the hot tarmac to the shop's open doors, all eyes upon us. I have to hide my delight in the novelty of it all, obviously. I'd like Dan to think such a lifestyle comes as naturally to me as it does to him.

Back at my house, he pulls out our £2 mixed packet of washers and some assorted tools he's brought with him and gets to work. I offer him coffee but he declines. He doesn't say so but I can tell he's already clocked the lack of an expensive Italian coffee machine and realised it's going to be instant. I pour him a glass of elderflower cordial mixed with sparkling water instead.

The job takes him no time at all.

'There you are,' he says, turning the tap on and off in a demonstration of how beautifully it now works. 'No drips and you won't have to use so much power on it now!'

Laughingly, I brandish my biceps to demonstrate that I'm strong enough. Then immediately regret it as I remember Charlotte's 'sturdy arms' comment.

'You won't be needing those muscles anymore,' jokes Dan. 'It's smooth as butter. Anyway, your sleek, toned physique has far better uses than forcing dodgy spigots open and closed.'

He turns away to tidy up the tools and the spare washers, his comment hanging in the air between us, images of what those better uses might be flitting through my mind.

'I actually really enjoyed that,' he continues as he pours various rubber circles back into the plastic packet, oblivious to the effect he's had on me. 'Using my hands, doing something practical – and useful. I wish I had the opportunity more often.'

I pull myself together, banishing the disturbing, delightful thoughts I'm having. He didn't mean anything by his comment. But still ...

'From now on,' he continues, wheeling around in my cramped, grotty kitchen and smiling broadly, 'you can keep your strength and power for tennis. That's where it can really come into its own.'

I laugh, slightly hysterically. I'm all at sixes and sevens, feeling a little overwhelmed. Dan's been so kind to give up all this time to me, and his unexpected handiness is yet another string to his already impressive bow of talents. Plus, he's kind and full of compliments and I really can't fault him in any way. To have his attention and friendship is like being bestowed with some precious, rare gift and I can't help but enjoy it.

He gestures towards the glass of cordial. 'Is this for me?' he asks, immediately assuming it is and reaching out his arm to pick it up. He drains it and licks his lips appreciatively. 'Wow, that's good,' he says. 'Homemade, I'm sure?'

I nod my assent.

'Multitalented, as I say,' he laughs.

'Likewise,' I jest, indicating his handiwork with the tap.

And then we're both laughing and it feels so natural for him to be here, doing things Justin would have done (albeit with a great deal more nagging beforehand) and I stop feeling ashamed of my minuscule house and tatty decor. I am what I am – and Dan's not judging me anyway. This is probably the most relaxed I've ever been with a man and the novelty value of that is a long way from wearing out.

The interlude with the tap fixing turns out to be one of the best moments of the next week or so and one my mind frequently returns to when I'm feeling down. The boys go off to the Lakes with Justin as promised and I'm left to my own devices. I have ample time to stress about the TV researcher, imagining him closing in on me, narrowing his search until, one fine day, he arrives at my door. Dan spends a couple of nights in London for work so I don't even have him and his visits to the cafe to break the monotony, leaving me nothing to do but dwell on the past – and my fears for the future. Without my boys being around, I don't even have the mundanity of endless meals and shopping and washing to take my mind off things.

For the first time, I truly envy Charlotte being able to escape to Corsica on holiday, to get away from it all. Of course, the reality is that I know this is not what happens. Wherever you go, you take yourself with you.

On top of everything else, memories of Charlie continue to assail me, beckoned by Naomi bringing to the cafe fragrant bundles of herbs reminiscent of the fateful trip I took to visit him during his year abroad, the first time I ever encountered fresh coriander, basil, and thyme. The pungent smells of those plants will forever evoke recollections of the Mediterranean and Marseille, of meals cooked by Charlie in the apartment he shared with four ultra-glamorous French girls who took it upon themselves to teach him as much about French cooking as they could. Any man's dream, right? But I was so naïve and trusting that it never crossed my mind that Charlie would stray.

Even when I went over to visit him, I didn't realise straight away. It was only when I saw that those vixens rarely left his side, that they constantly surrounded him with their *Ah, oui's* and their *Je ne sais pas's* that it dawned on me. One, in particular, was leech-like in her dependency on Charlie, always needing him to help her to translate something for her English degree or to show her how to make tea '*ze Engleesh way*'.

Her name was Josephine.

Charlie's increasingly complex experimentation with haute cuisine needed a sous chef and I, evidently, was not up to the job. Josephine, of course, was. She was his ever-present acolyte, delivering his elaborate, herb-adorned dishes to the table with all the devotion of a religious ceremony. He pretended not to notice her adoration and when I brought it to his attention, he dismissed out of hand the very notion that she was making a play for him.

I abhorred her sexy accent, sexy pout, and sexy apparel. In the rising warmth of late April, she wore boob tubes and micro-mini skirts and ostentatiously washed her tiny, translucent underwear by hand in the kitchen sink, draping it alluringly over the Juliet balcony to dry where it was on full view to anyone in the sitting room. At a time when the only smalls England had to offer were of the sensible and practical Marks & Sparks variety, or polyester fripperies from a sex shop, the expensive but flimsy fabrics of her barely-there knickers and plunging bras were something truly exotic. And threatening. Those frith-froths of embroidery and lace were like bunting proudly proclaiming a celebration.

Or a victory.

I wanted to get away, to get out of the huge but claustrophobic apartment, far from all the fawning minions. I'd checked out a small hotel on the waterfront in Cassis; in the photos it looked charming, a whitewashed bedroom with muslin curtains that fluttered in the breeze, the window overlooking the picturesque cluster of pastel-hued buildings nestled around the harbour. A small beach nestled at the foot of high cliffs and, though the water would be too cold for swimming, sunbathing under a milky spring sun would be perfect for my English skin that hadn't seen a ray since the previous August.

But Charlie vetoed the expedition on the grounds of expense, our lack of any mode of independent transport, and the fact that the weather forecast was bad.

'What's the point of spending all that money just to sit in the hotel room and watch the rain pour down?' he asked plaintively, like a small child wondering why he has to go to school.

The three weeks of my stay seemed to pass so slowly. Charlie was out of sorts throughout, as if his displacement to another part of Europe made him mildly allergic to the presence of anything British. Namely, me.

But as soon as I left, I easily persuaded myself that it had all been nothing, just Charlie's stress at having to integrate someone from one part of his life with people from another. He found transitions difficult, was always grumpy when going to sleep or waking up, just like babies often are. I clung to the fact that, once he came home, everything would be OK, everything would return to normal.

The Finchley Road flat was no more; I'd moved back into halls, not wanting to be there unless Charlie was and anyway, without us as a couple living in one room, I couldn't really afford the rent. My heart was set on getting a flat together for our final year, just the two of us, where we could do what we liked when we liked. Walk around naked. Make love on the sofa or the kitchen table. Have a coffee table strewn with important and erudite books that we would actually read rather than just watch Ptolemy roll joints on. Hope for the future kept me going through that lonely year.

Those hopes were dashed in the cruellest, most heartless way.

I watch Naomi now, as she chops and dices and tastes, and wonder whether she really has designs on Dan. It's more and more apparent to me that, even if she does, Naomi is not Charlotte's main problem and neither, I don't think, is Dan. She wants to hang onto him, of course she does. Women generally do, from habit if nothing else – though in Charlotte's case, I imagine that it's the lifestyle he offers her that plays the biggest part in her tenacity. What can she possibly see in handsome, charming, multi-millionaire Dan, I ask myself ironically.

That being said, the truth is that if Dan is going to walk off into the sunset with a trollop from his sports club, Charlotte might learn the hard way that there's not much she's going to be able to do to stop it. You can't make someone love you; you can't make them stay if they are determined to go. That's just the way it is sometimes.

I picture Charlotte in Corsica now, imagine those long,

dreamy, sun-filled days, the photos from her drawing room coming to life before my eyes. The stunning view from the terrace, the blue sea dotted with white-sailed yachts, the cloud-less sky, the town basking dreamily in the midday sun, its ancient houses clinging to the hillside that plunges down towards the harbour. And all around, the sensuous scent of lavender, basil, and mint suffusing the air. She's lucky. At least she has that place, that beauty.

And then the picture mutates and it's not Charlotte in my mind's eye anymore, but me, climbing the steep steps from the beach, laughing, a flowing white kaftan billowing out around my tanned legs. Dan heaves into view, leaping the treads two at a time, revealing how fit he is. Entering the house, we make our way to the bedroom – to what must be our bedroom, because we proceed there quite naturally together – and as soon as the door is shut Dan pins me to the wall and is kissing me whilst deftly pulling at my clothes, releasing my breasts from my bikini, lifting my dress—

Shock brings me to my senses. The vision fades and recedes and I'm back in the cafe, clearing tables of soiled cutlery and ringing up prices on the till. I can feel myself blushing like a love-struck teenager and have no idea what on earth I'm doing thinking such things.

'Morning!'

I jump out of my skin at the greeting and my heart hammers against my chest.

It's Dan.

I'm sure he can read my mind and see what I've been dreaming about. My flush deepens.

'How are you? Enjoying summer?'

'Oh, sure,' I reply, fighting hard to regain my composure, forcing the heightened colour to drain from my cheeks. 'All good and the boys are with their dad so I'm young, free, and single for a while!' I laugh to show I mean it ironically. 'Sort of, anyway,' I add, just in case there's any doubt.

Dan nods distractedly. 'I'm jealous,' he says.

I raise my eyebrows questioningly. 'Of me?' I can't keep the surprise and bewilderment out of my voice. I can't imagine what about me Dan could possibly be jealous of.

'Oh no, not you,' he replies, hastily.

I am suitably crushed, my stupidity revealed.

'I meant your husband,' Dan continues. This is equally mystifying. Justin is divorced and single, not to mention being bankrupt – not a condition that usually inspires envy.

'Oh,' I gulp, inadequately.

'Yes,' Dan muses, seemingly lost in thought. 'I sometimes wish I'd made more time for my sons, gone off on adventures with them, you know, with nothing but a torch, a bit of tarpaulin and our own wits to guard against the elements, wild camping, sharpening sticks with a penknife, hunting and shooting and fishing ...' His voice trails off as the fantasy grows.

'Well,' I stutter, not sure how to respond. 'I mean, I guess it sounds nice ... daring and testing and all that man stuff – but personally I'd say that a luxury villa in Corsica would be a much more preferable option.'

Dan smiles and looks suddenly more relaxed. 'Yes, you're right,' he agrees, 'I've provided them with everything money can buy. They want for nothing. I shouldn't feel guilty. It's just that ... well, Charlotte monopolises them so much, she excludes me all the time – she always has – until I feel that I'm not necessary to their happiness, that all I need to do is provide the money and that's my job done.'

He looks so sad and woebegone that I can hardly bear it, and I'm also taken aback by these revelations and the confidences they contain. It's more than he's ever divulged to me before. Really, Charlotte has no business making him feel bad when he does so much. Earns so much.

'I think you're being far too hard on yourself,' I say. 'After all, we all have our faults.' I desperately want to lighten the mood, to make Dan feel better. 'Me more than most, I'm sure,' I add, in a feeble attempt to do just this.

Dan smiles, humouring me. 'I doubt it,' he laughs. And then, with a voice that exudes finality, 'enough already with the soul-searching! Charlotte's ensconced for the duration with the boys in that luxury Corsican villa you mentioned and yours are out of your hair.' His grin widens. 'You should enjoy a bit of downtime, cut loose. Do the sort of things two children in the house prevent you from doing.'

I'm silent for a moment, my earlier daydream flashing through my mind again before I manage to banish it once more. Obviously he doesn't mean to be suggestive, any more than he did when he made the comment about my athleticism when he was mending the tap. Men are like that; they don't load everything with dual meanings like women do.

But then he obviously does realise that his comment is open to misinterpretation because he hastily adds, 'As in, play lots of tennis without worrying about getting back to cook the dinner.'

He plops himself into a chair and scans the menu purposefully, for what reason I cannot imagine because he must know if off by heart and always orders the same thing according to what time of day it is. I'm relieved, in any case, for a break from the intensity. But as I wait for him to make his order, my mind wanders again, to his strong and dextrous hands, to his athleticism that belies his age, to that gorgeous crinkly smile that he seems to be bestowing on me more and more frequently these days.

'Sit down, why don't you?' he says, gesturing to the chair opposite his and then around the almost empty cafe. He's right; it's really quiet just now but it will fill up soon. Everything is happening a little later during the summer holidays – morning visitors at nine-thirty or ten instead of eight, lunch at two or three instead of one.

I sit.

'How's Charlotte getting on over there, anyway?' I ask.

'She's fine,' Dan replies, shortly. 'I think they've been keeping themselves fairly quiet, not too much of a social whirl. It always takes Charlotte a while to recuperate once she's there, catch up on sleep and rest, et cetera, et cetera.'

I smile and nod understandingly. There's a lot to do, running a house the size of hers, organising the daily housekeeper. And of course families are full on, even when half the children are away at boarding school and there's an au pair to take care of the remainder. I'm so glad she's getting the chance to recharge her batteries.

I leave a short pause before responding.

'She still seems very anxious about something,' I say calmly, smoothing down the pages of my order pad. 'You mentioned it to me before, and I hadn't really noticed it myself at that stage. But since then, well, I've started to get the same feeling as you. I don't want to pry or interfere but something's definitely getting to her and, um ...' I hesitate and glance around the cafe, checking Naomi is out of sight before meeting Dan's gaze head on and continuing, 'I'm wondering if she's in some kind of trouble.'

Dan's face loses its habitual charming openness as his expression turns quickly to one of surprise and then hastily masked annoyance.

'I don't know what that could be,' he states firmly, shaking his head in denial. 'I can't for the life of me think of anything. What kind of trouble could she be in?'

I shake my head as I reply. 'Maybe it's just the suspicious mind that living with Justin gave me,' I muse sagely, 'the knowledge I gained from that of how people you think you know so well can be so good at covering things up, but how, afterwards, you always realise that there were signs.'

Now Dan looks alarmed.

'Do you think she's betraying me?'

The speed and frankness with which he says the words stuns me into a momentary silence. It seems the lack of trust between these two is mutual.

'Oh no, no!' I reply with a smile. 'Of course not, nothing like that. What I mean is, she just seems to have something on her mind that's really bothering her. But having said that, I don't have any evidence ...' I pause for a moment then continue, emphatically, 'I shouldn't have said anything.'

'She has ample opportunity though, doesn't she,' ponders Dan aloud, as if he hasn't heard what I've just said. 'All the hours I'm working late, all my trips abroad.'

It crosses my mind that this says more about the accuser than the accused. On the other hand, there's such a lack of nurture in the way Charlotte so often talks about Dan that maybe he is just jumping to a logical conclusion.

I place my hands firmly on the table and take a deep breath. 'She's away now for another six weeks or so and presumably out of the way of temptation – although I suppose the French do have a reputation ... but no. Let's not even go there. And as for anything back here, I'm sure that there's nothing going on, no one you should know about. Absolutely sure of it.' I pause. 'There's definitely something, though. Something's not right.'

My mind's turning it all over again, probing anything and everything that could be at the bottom of Charlotte's distress. She drinks a lot – I've noticed that on frequent occasions. She's even alluded to the fact that *I* can put it away; the accuser and the accused, again. I wonder if she could have got into trouble because of alcohol, or clandestinely joined AA or something. But it doesn't really make sense; being an alcoholic is hard to conceal from people you live with, especially over a prolonged period of time.

And I'm not convinced that that's shameful enough to hide; these days, it's practically mainstream, as well as being so much better understood. If her problem were drink, I can't see why she wouldn't be able to share it with her husband at least, even if no one else. And Dan is clearly as clueless as to what is going on as I am. Another possibility is drugs but again, surely there would be times when she was out of it, when it was obvious that she'd been taking something. And she looks so fit and healthy that I can't believe it's that either.

I consider what other addictions Charlotte could be suffering from. Maybe she's a compulsive shopper, racking up thousands on credit cards. She does have a never-ending supply of new clothes, all designer brands. I've never seen her wear the same thing twice. Her jewellery collection could fill the front window of Asprey's. And the house is full of the latest gadgets and gizmos – matching Smeg toasters and juicers and what have you, two different Kitchen Aids, three coffee makers. All her back-to-the-earth foraging could just be a cover for what she's got herself into: consumerism on steroids.

Dan's face is still creased in concentration. 'I think it's me,' he blurts out. 'It's not that she's seeing anyone else, just that she doesn't love me anymore.'

His tone is so woeful, his face so crunched up with anxiety, that my heart goes out to him. Being unwanted is the worst feeling of all. What's most hurtful is when it's cumulative. When there have been numerous opportunities to see that one is surplus to requirements, but one hasn't picked up on them – and the guilty party hasn't had the guts or, probably even worse, cared enough to come clean.

When Charlie returned from Marseille, we got that dream flat together, just the two of us. Of course the reality was far more prosaic: a basement in West Hampstead with the usual problems of damp on the walls and mould on the bathroom tiles, but to me it was perfect. I found it, I decorated it with love and care, arranging the furniture, hanging the curtains, revelling in the joy of creating a little nest for him and me. And then, just before his finals and my third-year exams of my four-year course, she came to stay.

Josephine.

Uninvited – by me, at least – but she was never the kind of girl who would let manners get in the way of anything she did. She didn't know the meaning of the word. She invaded my home and immediately I knew it was the beginning of the end. When I came back from uni early one day to find them having sex in my bed, between my treasured antique linen sheets that I'd purchased in the flea market on that ill-fated visit to Marseille, I both couldn't believe it and knew I'd been expecting it. I felt violated, as if I'd been physically assaulted. Even thinking about it now, after all these years, makes my stomach turn over in fear and pain.

It induced a kind of madness in me, a madness that haunts me to this day. As my plan for revenge fomented in my mind, it grew and burgeoned until I no longer controlled it and it burst forth, taking everyone by surprise – including myself.

If only it hadn't led to me taking the catastrophic actions that had robbed me of getting my degree, of forging my own career, then maybe things would be different now. But I was young, and foolish, and as the judge said, I suffered for it. It doesn't seem fair that I should have to bear the consequences for the rest of my life.

Everything I did was the result of betrayal.

'I know what it's like to be unsure of someone,' I mutter

quietly. *Don't mention Charlie*, my rational self is hissing at me. Nobody knows, and it needs to stay where it is – consigned to history. Stick to Justin. He is much safer territory.

'When Justin's business was going down the pan and everything was falling apart, if I'm honest with myself I knew things weren't right. But I pushed those doubts away because I didn't want to deal with them, to find they were true. In retrospect, that was such a stupid thing to do because if I'd known, if I'd faced up to it and confronted Justin, I – we – might have been able to mitigate it, prevent the worst of the fallout. And then it wouldn't have been such a terrible jolt when it all came crashing down.'

Dan shakes his head again, at my catastrophe rather than a potential one of his own this time. 'I'm sorry you had to go through so much.'

He reaches his hand across the table and clasps mine in a grip that is strong and cool and reassuring. I feel immediately self-conscious. I look around me; a sudden influx of customers has filled the room and they're all glancing across at me, waiting for me to arrive by their sides and take their orders like a little elf wielding magic. God, it would be nice not to have to do this job. For a brief moment, I'm filled with real envy of Charlotte: of her lifestyle, of long holidays in sunny places and a bank balance that never has numbers in red.

But I need to get back to work.

I turn to go but Dan is still holding my hand. His fingers tease along mine as I release my hand.

'Susannah,' he says.

I halt and turn back toward him.

'That match we've booked Friday evening, are you free for dinner after? I'd like to thank you for being such a good listener. And ... perhaps we can have a bit more of a think about Charlotte, about what might be wrong.'

I'm completely taken aback, but at the same time honoured to be asked, to be confided in, and I beam back at him like an awkward teenager. An evening out! An evening of not eating a lonely slice of cheese on toast in a cold, empty house.

'The Thai place along the high street is really not bad at all, if you like that sort of thing,' he suggests.

'I love it!' I reply. 'That would be fantastic, thank you.'

# *Chapter 23*

## *Susannah*

I'm on my way out to meet Dan for our match when my laptop starts buzzing on the kitchen table. It's a Skype call from Charlotte so of course I put down my racket and my bag and connect; I'm desperate to hear all her news, how she's getting on, and what she and the boys have been up to. As soon as her image comes onto the screen I see the difference in her. The fact that she looks fantastic is nothing new – she always does – but there's something more to her radiance today. Her tan sets off her brown eyes and her brunette hair is even more glossy and glistening than usual. But more than both those things is that she looks relaxed in a way I've never seen in her before, as if a weight has been lifted off her shoulders. I've heard it said that Corsica is a magical place and now I see its sorcery for myself.

I don't have time to ponder this further, however, as straightaway Charlotte is asking me about Naomi. I reassure her that her nemesis is no better or worse than usual.

'She's been keeping Dan fed, that's all I'm aware of,' I report.

'The other day it was some noodle dish she insisted on giving him in a plastic container to take home so that "he doesn't waste away", in her words.'

'Oh!' A cloud of worry passes across Charlotte's hitherto untroubled countenance. 'Dan loves his food, especially anything Far Eastern. Or curry, as long as it's super-hot. I don't ever make him that sort of stuff. I'm more classic French or Italian.' She pauses, grimacing thoughtfully. 'Perhaps I should?'

'Maybe,' I shrug. 'I wouldn't get too worked up about it. I mean, he said it was delicious but whatever they say about the way to a man's heart being through his stomach, I'm not sure that Tupperware meals are that romantic. Although if curry is his favourite …'

I see how her face drops, alarm flickering across her eyes.

'Only joking,' I interject hastily, trying to dispel her fears with a conspiratorial laugh. 'Vindaloo isn't known as an aphrodisiac, as far as I'm aware, nor soy sauce.'

The fact is though that Naomi slaves over the dishes she makes for Dan, and openly revels in the praise she receives. The other day she had a massive smile plastered on her overly made-up face for hours afterwards. It must have driven him mad the way she pestered him about it for the next two days, asking him every time he came in if he'd finished the portion he'd taken home. If he put it straight in the bin, he had far too much tact to tell her so.

I'm actually never quite sure what he does with all the goodies she plies him with – usually, when it's homemade protein energy balls or flapjacks, they disappear into his bag and are never seen again. He always says, next time he's in the cafe, that whatever it was tasted delicious, in the same way that he always tells her how lovely she's looking. Which I guess would be true if peroxide-blonde locks, alarmingly thick and prominent eyebrows, orange-tinged foundation and false eyelashes were really his idea of beauty, which somehow I doubt. So the conclusion that I draw is that he's adept at those little white lies that oil the wheels of social convention and that's probably another reason why he's such a successful businessman.

Few of us are immune to flattery and charm, after all.

'I've been doing a lot of thinking,' Charlotte suddenly announces.

'Oh?' I ask, conscious that I'm short of time but realising there's something she needs to get off her chest. Perhaps she's finally going to reveal all and tell me what's bugging her.

'I've left Dan out too much, monopolised the children, not allowed him in. All of that has to change.'

'Right,' I say. So no revelation, after all – or at least not the one I want her to make. This admission about the way she presides over all aspects of childcare, shutting Dan out, is only what he identified and told me himself so recently. 'OK. That sounds like a good decision to make.'

'And sex,' she adds, out of the blue. 'I need to have sex with him. More often than we have been – which, if I'm honest, is hardly ever recently. Men need that, don't they?'

I'm blown off course by this disclosure. I mean, Dan has hinted at their lack of physical intimacy. But men generally have a distorted view of sex and how regularly they should be getting it. It's a rare long-term relationship when both partners have exactly the same needs in terms of frequency of intercourse. I wonder if Dan puts pressure on her, if that could have anything to do with her despondency. Perhaps this is all it is, all that's causing her diffidence, her perturbation. That bizarre mix of concern and guilt that women feel when they're not doing something someone else wants them to.

'You should never feel forced into sex, Charlotte,' I say, keeping it gentle, trying not to sound prim. 'It's not an obligation.'

'It's just that I've been putting him off so much lately,' she pauses. 'Well, always, actually,' she concludes, sadly. 'I'm just not in the mood, and I hate how it messes up my hair. But really it's because I've got too much on my mind. You see ...'

I cast a surreptitious glance at the clock. I'm going to have to go.

'I don't think you should be worrying about it right now,' I cut in firmly. 'You should be concentrating on relaxing. That's what you're in Corsica for, after all.'

Charlotte's face hovers closer to the screen. 'I was just going to say that ...'

I need to go. A blur in the background behind Charlotte morphs into Toby. He stops at the threshold of the door and starts yelling something about Sam.

'I'll leave you to it,' I laugh, as Charlotte turns to wave a threatening fist at her son. 'Speak soon. Bye!'

I press the button that, with the familiar robotic beep, sees Charlotte disappear from my screen. It's only when I get to the club that it dawns on me that she had been about to make a revelation. That maybe she had finally been going to share something with me, something more than she already had when she told me about her and Dan's sex life. Damn! Foiled by the children interrupting again.

Brushing the mystery to one side, I stow my bag in a locker. I can't do anything about it now and I'm looking forward to this match with Dan. I take a quick look at my reflection, loosening my ponytail slightly; I never think it's flattering to have it pulled back too tightly, pram-face style. I stroll outside to wait for Dan, who arrives only minutes later. I notice the grey in his hair tonight, but far from ageing him, it makes him look distinguished and wise, like the kind of man who can be depended on. This is not a man who would let his entire world collapse around him, who would leave his wife and children with neither a penny to their name nor a roof over their heads, like Justin did.

He kisses me on each cheek, and with the kisses comes an enticing waft of subtle aftershave and warm skin. Then he pulls a coin from his pocket and throws it flamboyantly upwards, catching it with a slap of one hand over the other. I win the toss to serve first and a tingle of anticipation ripples through me as I propel the ball into the air and then smash it over the net. Playing with Dan releases something in me: an animal instinct to get one over on him, to second guess his every move so that I can counter it; an urge to win because I can tell – I know – that much as he hates losing, he admires a winner above all else.

And, after a gruelling three sets, I am declared the victor by a whisker. We've played often enough now for me to know that he's definitely not letting me win because I'm female or Charlotte's poor, abandoned friend or even his friend. I triumph on the occasions that I am the better player.

He looks me in the eye as he congratulates me.

'I've never been put through my paces like you do,' he says.

I smile and feel my cheeks redden – again. 'Flatterer,' I murmur in reply. I still haven't quite got my breath back after the last, decisive rally.

'No, seriously,' he continues, an urgency in his voice that I haven't heard before. 'I play because it keeps me fit and I enjoy it so much more than a solitary sojourn in the gym. But you play like a professional, like you could go places.'

I pull my mouth into a lop-sided grimace. 'Could have gone places, once upon a time.' It's a struggle to keep the bitterness out of my voice. 'If I'd pursued it when I really had the chance. But it's too late for regrets now.' I look at him and try to smile. 'Anyhow, at least I'm beating you fair and square.'

He laughs, his eyes crinkling in their sexy way, his expression all kindness and admiration.

'You are so right. Your athleticism is too much for me. However, in another context ...'

He lets the sentence hang, unfinished.

These statements that have a *double entendre* seem to be happening more and more often. Perhaps it isn't just my overactive imagination.

Hurriedly, I snatch up my towel and racket and head off to the changing rooms. Out of the corner of my eye, I see him watching me depart and I'm conscious of his eyes upon me until I'm out of sight. Under the pounding water, I soap myself thoroughly, eradicating all traces of the sweat induced by the game, emerging cleansed and fragrant. Though, unlike Charlotte, I'm not a big drinker, I'm looking forward to one tonight. It's been so long since I've been without ties or responsibilities, the children elsewhere, nothing to hold me down. Even before any alcohol, I feel light-headed and dizzy with the unfamiliarity of it all.

It's the first time I've been to the Thai restaurant that stands proudly on the village high street, drawing foodies from all around to sample its authentic dishes. In all truth, I haven't eaten out since I left London, and before that not for at least six months or so. I'm not sure what to order, surreptitiously scrutinising the prices and veering towards the cheaper options until Dan, without looking up from his own perusal of what's on offer, says, 'This is on me, by the way.'

I pause and bite my lip. I should refuse, insist on going Dutch, but if I do, I'll be eating nothing but porridge and dandelion leaves until the end of the month. Dan is not just rich but stinking rich; if he wants to pay, I should let him.

As if to reinforce my thoughts, he continues, 'It would give me the greatest pleasure.' He waits until I'm looking at him and then forces me to hold his gaze. 'I enjoy spending my money on things that I like. My watches, remember?' He pauses, his smile so assured but at the same time so genuine that it melts my heart. 'And taking a beautiful woman out to dinner is about the most enjoyable thing I can think of. Even better than a Rolex.'

The waiter arrives with glasses of champagne I didn't even notice Dan ordering. He picks his up and holds it towards me and I do the same. He clinks my glass and leans forward to me.

'Thank you for coming with me and entertaining me whilst I've been abandoned by my entire family.'

He gives a short laugh and then drinks a large glug of champagne.

A sudden sharp flash of understanding sears through me. He hates to be alone. He hates it when Charlotte takes the boys away from him for extended periods. He hates being left to his own devices, the house echoing, the bed cold and empty.

I sip my drink and, emulating his body language, lean forward.

'I understand where you're coming from. I'm, well, I'm an expert in abandonment,' I confide in him. 'It seems to be my forte.'

A memory is ringing in my ears as if I can hear her voice right now.

'Tout est juste dans l'amour et la guerre.'

Those were Josephine's last words to me as she shut my own front door in my face. The worst thing is that I had to look them up to find out what they meant.

All's fair in love and war.

'I'm so sorry, Susannah,' Dan says, his voice low with sympathy and regret, unaware that Justin is far from the only disaster in my past. 'You don't deserve to have been treated like that.' He clinks his glass against mine. 'Here's to a better future.'

We drink and put our glasses down on the table simultaneously.

'You deserve someone who'll give you everything and think himself lucky,' continues Dan.

I swirl my champagne around in my glass and contemplate the popping bubbles. '*Deserve* doesn't have anything to do with it, does it? Life doesn't work like that.'

I don't want to sound angry, cynical, but I'm afraid that I do. It's hard not to. Involuntarily, I sigh deeply, and he takes my hand, just like he did so recently in the cafe. The waiter is hovering and Dan sends him away with a flick of the wrist.

'If it's worth anything – I'd like you to know that I would never have left a woman like you. I don't know what your husband was thinking.'

Or what Charlie was thinking? I shrug helplessly and struggle to stop the tears that are pricking behind my eyes from pouring forth.

'I'm sure it was me as well as him,' I mutter, unable to meet his gaze as I speak. 'We were probably both—'

'No,' Dan interrupts, forcefully. 'Don't excuse him or find reasons to justify what he did. There are none, and that's final.'

I manage a weak smile and nod resignedly. 'You're right.' Then I laugh and, with a wave of my hand, dismiss the conversation. 'But let's not talk about miserable things anymore.'

I pick up the menu and Dan mirrors my action.

'We should order – that poor guy's about to come back over again and anyway, I'm starving. All that vigorous exercise ...'

Dan grins and then glances over at the waiter, who is by our side and bowing respectfully in seconds. Dan is clearly well-known here and holds a lot of clout. I guess all restaurants love their rich clients, the big spenders. No reason not to.

'OK, let's choose,' Dan says, as the waiter hovers silently with his pad. 'I really recommend the green papaya salad, and we must definitely have a pad Thai, but then I also love chilli ...'

His voice floats over me as I sink back and relax, loving the feeling of being taken care of. Dan is so capable, so competent with everything from building a multi-million-pound fortune to ordering the best dishes on a Thai menu. Justin had nothing like his style and Charlie never had two beans to rub together.

The food arrives and I tuck in with alacrity. I wasn't lying when I said I was hungry and I haven't had anything this good since the Sunday lunch Charlotte cooked a few weeks ago. Which, incidentally, I noticed that she barely touched, pushing her helping around her plate and only picking at the vegetables and a little of the meat. Of course she didn't have so much as a single potato on her plate, though they were sublime, flaky and crispy and delicious, just as roasties should be.

Dan notices my enjoyment of his choices from the menu.

'It's so good to be with someone who actually eats!' he exclaims.

I know I should be embarrassed about my healthy appetite but at the same time I can tell he's genuine in his appreciation – and unlike such a comment coming from a woman, there's no side to it, no buried agenda or insinuations contained with it that perhaps I should exercise more restraint. He just really likes the fact that the meal he's paying for is being enjoyed.

His phone rings a couple of times whilst we are eating and he checks it, briefly glancing at the screen, but doesn't answer.

'Someone wants to get hold of you!' I say, the third time it happens.

He shrugs. 'The office. Some of the Americans I deal with don't have any concept of work-life balance. They're workaholics.'

I nod. Ironically, Charlotte has made this very accusation against Dan many times. I can see that making money becomes addictive and hard to restrict to the hours of nine to five on weekdays – but maybe it's not as simple as that. The next thing Dan says confirms my thinking.

'But then again,' he muses, suddenly dejected, 'I can hardly talk. I'd be at home more myself if I felt wanted there. But sometimes, well, sometimes Charlotte seems as if she can manage quite well without me.'

I frown sympathetically. 'That sucks,' I say.

He doesn't reply, just gives a resigned grimace and goes back to the papaya salad. I've had to give up on that – far too much chilli for me to handle.

When the meal is over, Dan leans back in his chair and gives a satisfied sigh. 'That was great,' he states, conclusively and I'm in full agreement. 'But now I feel like going home and relaxing. Want to join me for a coffee and a nightcap?'

I hesitate for a moment. I don't really fancy going to the manor and then walking to my house alone late at night across the green and down the dark road to the unfashionable enclave where I reside. Though there's little danger of encountering hooded thugs lingering on street corners, sometimes it's the dead silence and emptiness of the countryside that I find scarier than urban noise and bustle – especially at night. Like so many other things, I'm just not used to it.

'Um, I'm not sure ...' I begin, wanting to tell Dan the

reason for my reluctance but not wanting to come across as a total wimp.

'Oh!' he utters, as if reading my mind. 'Of course, you're worried about how you'll get home. But I'll give you a lift back or, even better, you could always stay over.'

My face flushes red hot and I shake my head. I'm feeling flustered, not wanting to seem rude by turning down his invitation. It's kind of him to ask and even kinder of him to be concerned about what might be holding me back. But I'm just not sure I should, if it would be appropriate to go back to his house with him.

Dan is studying me intently. 'I mean,' he continues, 'it's not as if we're short of bedrooms. Charlotte always has the guest room made up and ready in case of a chance visitor. You could have a swim and sauna in the morning before you go. It costs a fortune to heat that pool; I'd like to see it being used.'

'Well,' I say, still hesitant. 'That does sound very tempting, I must say. I suppose I could borrow something of Charlotte's to swim in. What luxury! Your very own wellness spa.'

'It's nice,' agreed Dan, 'but terribly underused. The family take it for granted.'

'I guess that's always what tends to happen,' I muse, 'when it's there all the time; it's easy not to be appreciative.'

'So come!' says Dan, gently. 'Be appreciative. I'll be eternally grateful.

I can't help but laugh. He really is such a sweet, kind, generous man. 'I'd love to,' I reply, all reason to resist swept away.

The Porsche has us home in moments.

In Charlotte's elegant drawing room, I accept the tumbler

Dan proffers. I can't stand whisky – or at least I thought I couldn't until tonight – but I don't want to be troublesome by asking for something else. And when I try it, I find that I quite like the peaty, boggy taste that seems to contain the essence of the Highlands. I express my surprise, inadvertently giving away the fact that I've agreed to have a drink I know I don't like.

'You've just been having the wrong whisky,' Dan assures me, in the way he has that makes him impossible to argue with. 'In other words, cheap stuff. You're enjoying this because it's nearly £150 a bottle.'

I almost choke when he says the price. It's more than my budget allows for my monthly food shop. But then I remember how Justin didn't think twice about spending £40 or £50 on wine, which doesn't last nearly as long, and I get off my high horse tout suite. As Dan has said before, if you've got it, why not spend it and I have to agree. After all, there are no pockets in a shroud.

We chat and drink and I start to feel a little tipsy, but in the most pleasant, agreeable way. At one point I suggest to Dan that I really should be off but he begs me to stay.

'Please don't go yet,' he pleads plaintively. 'Let's watch a movie or, well, just talk. It's so nice – Charlotte and I hardly ever do this anymore, just sit here and chat. And anyway, I don't want to spend another evening alone.'

I smile. 'I know how you feel. It's weird when every room is deserted, every door you open leads to another empty space. I'm not used to it at all.'

'It's awful. I hate it.' Dan takes another slug of whisky. 'But it's not just that. It's not just because they're all away. Even if they're here, I'm left out. They're a unit, the boys and Charlotte, and I haven't been part of it for years and the worst thing is that I'm not sure if I've created that situation or they have. I really don't know.'

My heart breaks for him anew. The elite businessman, the go-getter, the walking success story, is as messed up and unsure and insecure as all the rest of us underneath. We're all blustering most of the time, putting on an act, hoping we don't get found out – even Dan, the archetypal alpha male. It seems so wrong that he's been ousted from the family bosom, left to provide the money and not much else. Though Charlotte might feel it's only what he deserves, that he's reaping what he's sown – he simply doesn't understand it. I feel sorry for him, and sorry for her. For a moment, I feel sorry for myself, too.

'It sounds very difficult,' I reply quietly. 'But if it's that bad, perhaps it's time to call it a day? Not all marriages last forever – I can vouch for that. Perhaps you'd both be better off out of it. Happier. Saner.'

We're sitting at either end of a capacious sofa. Dan listens to what I'm saying and then slides himself nearer to me. He stretches his arm across the back of the sofa, behind my shoulders.

'You're so wise, Susannah,' he says softly. 'And so under-standing. I can talk to you in a way I've never been able to with Charlotte. Thank you.'

It all happens so quickly, his arms encircling me, his mouth on mine, that I hardly have time to process it, let alone to resist. Before I can react he's kissing me passionately, long and hard, a kiss that lasts and lasts, and I find myself kissing him back just as urgently, and at first I'm thinking of my friend Charlotte and what the hell is going on, and I can't believe that I'm betraying her like this but then I stop thinking of her and concentrate on the kiss and there is nothing else in the world but me and Dan. The fleeting thought that, as Charlotte so clearly can't really be bothered with him then it's all right for me to have him, crosses my mind before that, too, is forgotten and I sink further into his embrace.

After a while, I've no idea how long, he stands, pulling me up after him, and still kissing me he leads me up the stairs and into the bedroom where he lays me on the bed, rips off my clothes and makes love to me in a way I've never experienced before, not with Justin nor even with Charlie.

By the time it's over, I've lost all sense of who, what, or where I am. He puts an arm around me and nestles into my back and soon I hear his breathing settle into the regular pattern of sleep.

I lie in bed – in Charlotte's bed – wondering what on earth I've done. Until it suddenly occurs to me that it's the innate attraction that Dan and I have for each other that's been fuelling all our encounters, almost since that very first day when he arrived late to the party with a bunch of helium balloons.

That this had always been bound to happen. That however much I tried to be the friend Charlotte wanted me to be, the desire Dan and I have for one another was always going to win out. I have a sudden feeling of panic about whether

Charlotte is definitely in Corsica and all of her boys, too. But I know she is and once I've reminded myself that it's all fine and she's not about to walk in the door and find us here, I fall asleep too.

But not before wondering how on earth I'm going to tell her.

# Chapter 24

## *Susannah*

It's surreal to wake up in Dan's arms, in Dan's house, in Dan's bed.

Charlotte's house. Charlotte's bed.

Racked with guilt, I put my arms over my face, shielding my eyes from the daylight that's streaming in from behind the curtains. I don't know what happened. I don't know why it happened. But I do know it was wonderful.

Dan must have sensed me stirring because I feel him turn over and roll towards me, and then his hands are on my body, caressing me, arousing me. I feel eighteen again, reborn into a time before Justin, before Charlie, before I knew how terribly, badly wrong love can go. How terribly, badly wrong a life can go.

It's as if I've wiped the slate clean and been given the gift of starting over.

Dan's love-making is slower this morning, not the desperate, fervent act of the night before but studied and considered. It's just as good, if not better. I can't believe that

I'm over forty and I've never made love like this before, had no idea how incredible it can be. Charlotte admitted that she and Dan don't have sex anymore – and when I only had Justin, and memories of Charlie to pin my own experience on, I could understand that. But now, now I've been with Dan, I don't get it at all, don't know how someone could voluntarily turn their back on this, could find it not to their liking.

It reveals to me the emptiness of Charlotte and Dan's relationship, the extent to which all fires have been well and truly extinguished. Charlotte may be using her solitude in Corsica to rethink what's gone wrong but she's going to find it's too little, too late. Dan and Charlotte's marriage, it seems to me, is based on keeping up appearances and clinging onto life's comforts, not on any real affection. And this convinces me, as Dan brings me to orgasm, that what he and I are doing is not so very bad. That we could be, that in fact we are, very, very good.

Dan suggests breakfast but in the kitchen he gazes helplessly at the six-burner hob, so I step in and make scrambled eggs on toast. Surrounded by all Charlotte's things, her choices of crockery and cutlery, her children's pictures on her walls, her collection of magnets on the fridge door, I can't stop thinking about her. Only continually reminding myself that there's no love in their union anymore, that their partnership is a hollow shell, enables me to sit at Charlotte's table as if I am mistress of the house. I doubt she'll enjoy getting divorced any more than the next person, but for her it won't be like it was for me. Dan is rich and generous;

she'll get a fabulous settlement and she'll be free of the man who irritates her so much. She'll be able to find someone she does want to have sex with.

Dan asks if I'd like that swim.

'The pool is well up to temperature,' he says, flicking his eyes towards an electronic gadget on the wall that displays a reading of 28 degrees.

'Charlotte likes the water really warm,' he explains, adding, 'costs a bloody fortune, as I alluded to last night.'

Then he breaks off as a dark shroud of doubt descends upon his face. Being confronted by all the wasted years, by the fact that now he has the chance to be with someone who truly loves him, must be challenging. I can understand that.

At this precise moment, his phone rings. 'Charlotte' flashes onto the screen as the noise gets louder and louder, more and more persistent. We both sit and stare at it until, eventually, it rings out.

Slowly, very slowly, Dan reaches out, picks up his phone and puts it in his pocket. He looks stricken, panicked.

'I can't talk to her right now.'

'No.' I try to exude sympathy through my tone and body language.

There's silence for a moment. I imagine what he might say. 'I can't tell her over the phone, but I'll do it as soon as she's back,' or, 'I'll need to prepare the boys for what's coming; I can't let them suffer.'

'When you've finished your drink, I'll drop you home,' Dan continues, not looking at me, making sure not to meet my gaze.

He drains his glass and thrums his fingers on the table

before continuing. 'And then we must never mention this again, Susannah. Do you understand?'

Now, he looks at me. Stares straight into my eyes. 'Charlotte must never, ever find out about this.'

I'm too stunned to reply.

# Chapter 25

## Susannah

Dan has gone to Corsica.

I stare at the message on my phone, dumbfounded. It's not from him; he's made no contact with me at all. Instead, it's from Charlotte, telling me how pleased and excited she is that he's on his way, how she's going to make new efforts to put the past behind them, to make everything right. Absence has made the heart grow fonder and she sees everywhere she's gone wrong, how everything was confused and muddled but now is crystal clear.

She loves Dan. He loves her. Naomi is nothing. She thanks me for looking after him. She appreciates it.

I let the phone drop from my hand. Despite what he said on Saturday, I had still held out hope that, once he'd had time to think about it, and get over the idea of telling her, once he'd spoken to her and been reminded of all that's wrong with their relationship, he'd rethink his decision. Would call me, contrite and apologetic, invite me round, pull me into bed, confess that he can't live without me.

But no.

After all his leading comments, his generous, loving gestures, the outpourings of his heart and his come-ons that I fell for, hook, line, and sinker, the fact is that I've been spurned, used, and tossed aside in the worst possible way. And his reaction to the whole thing is to fly off for a lovely holiday reunion with her.

I phone in sick to work. Naomi will just have to manage without me for a few days. Lying on my bed, I go over and over in my head the evening we spent together, and the wonderful night and morning that followed. Before Charlotte started calling and calling and spooking Dan so much that he felt compelled to get shot of me.

Justin Facetimes but I reject the call. I can't bear for anyone to see me. He makes a voice call instead which I answer in case there's something wrong. But there isn't. He proceeds to regale me with tales of everything he and the boys have been up to in the Lake District – some triathlon challenge or other seems to feature large in the activities list. He's become a fitness fanatic since the bankruptcy and break-up, one of those Mamils we hear so much about in the media, sad middle-aged men in Lycra, using their bicycles as relationship substitutes, and he and the boys have been cycling and swimming and running like maniacs for the past two weeks.

When he first got a bike, my initial thought was about where on earth he had got the money, but now I don't even have the energy to care. Jamie and Luke are fine, which is all that really matters. Though right now, despite how much I love them, I can hardly bear to think of them coming home, of having to function again, cooking regular meals and helping with homework and sounding interested when they tell me about their day.

It occurs to me once Justin has hung up that, with or without the boys, my whole position here in the village is in jeopardy. Just as I've begun to rebuild my life, it has all come crashing down around me. Working at the tennis club will be a constant reminder of Dan, but I can't afford to let go of my job. I valued my friendship with Charlotte but I was so beguiled by Dan that I fell into the trap he laid for me, thinking that he was offering me something real, the solid relationship I craved, a two-parent family for my boys.

I hate myself for being so naïve. But somehow, however hard it will be, I have to pretend nothing's happened; I have to carry on as normal.

Normal. This is about as far as I've ever been from that state since the horror of Charlie and Josephine and its aftermath ...

I wander around the house, unable to settle to anything. I make cups of tea that I don't drink and plates of toast that I don't eat. In the living room, my old course books, together with some newer ones I've borrowed from the library or bought cheaply on Amazon, litter the floor and the coffee table. When time has allowed, I've been beavering away at my book idea; I thought I'd done quite a lot, had made good progress. But now I understand that it's never going to happen, I'm not going to see it through. I never was. All those hours of research and note-making, wasted.

My life, wasted.

I kick miserably at the corner of one of the biggest tomes

that's lying open to the frontispiece. My name, written by me over twenty years ago, my writing large and childish, looks quite different from how it is now. And it's not even my actual name but 'Sue', the shortening of Susannah I adopted for Charlie, who found my real moniker offensive, reeking as he felt it did of elaborate middle-class self-satisfaction. He wanted me to join him in being a working-class hero, which of course I never could be, however much I tried. I went to private school for years, for God's sake.

I sit on the sofa and think of Dan. The extent of my foolishness, the error of my judgement, hits me with full force. Not for the first time, I've been shown up as a credulous idiot who fell for the oldest trick in the book: 'my wife doesn't understand me and I'm lonely'. And now I risk losing everything not for the first, nor the second, but the third time.

When the doorbell rings, I jump out of my skin. A deep sense of foreboding weighs me down like a lump of lead in my stomach. It would feel right, somehow, if it were that researcher, if he'd tracked me down at last after plaguing me by mail for so many months. His latest letters have changed tack somewhat, now containing veiled threats along the lines of '*If you agree to take part, you get to tell your story in your words, your way. If you don't, then we tell it anyway, but in our words, our way.*' However many times I ignore his missives, or put them back in the post box labelled 'Return to Sender', he keeps on trying. I don't know what it will take to make him understand that I'm not going to bite, that I'm not interested. I push from my mind the offer of payment that was mentioned in the very first letter, repeated in every one since. It is quite a lot of money. But despite being perpetually skint, I'm not tempted. I'm not that desperate and my past is not for sale.

*I am not for sale.*

I've slumped onto the floor whilst I wait and hope that the post woman will give up and leave. But instead, the rings on the bell are followed first by knocks on the door and then loud, insistent raps at the window. I crane my neck to see out without being seen. But immediately, my eyes meet those of the person outside, the person who is peering in, hunting the room for signs of life.

I don't know whether to laugh or cry. Instead of the pestilential researcher or a representative of the Royal Mail, it's Miriam, her moon face looming at me through the glass. Relief floods through me that my fears are unfounded, but even though she's not who I dread, I still want to wave her away, to tell her to get lost. But I can't do that. Being rude is not the answer, especially not to Miriam, who has always tried to be friendly and bears no blame for the mess I've got myself into. Cursing under my breath, I go to the door.

'Hi Miriam,' I say, trying to stop my voice from breaking, fighting back the tears that suddenly prick behind my eyelids. 'What can I do for you?'

Miriam looks at me, her head cocked to one side. She's wearing the same black bobble hat she was sporting at the first paper chase back in April, despite the fact that it's now twenty-five degrees outside. She resembles a particularly idiotic garden gnome. She looks ludicrous. 'We had an arrangement, for a get together. Don't you remember?'

'Sorry, Miriam,' I splutter, gesturing for her to come in. I pull a ragged piece of toilet paper off the roll – I've run out of tissues – and dab at my eyes. 'Summer cold. It's really laid me low.'

'Poor thing. Turmeric could be the answer! Do you have any? The Indians have long sworn by its anti-inflammatory properties.'

'Right,' I concur, 'I have heard something like that. But I'm fine,' I lie. 'Nothing a good dose of Nightnurse won't sort.'

Miriam frowns doubtfully. I'm sure she's about to warn me of the dangers of such over-the-counter remedies. If it hasn't come from a herb or a root or been found buried in a hedgerow, it's at best useless and at worse potentially harmful in her eyes.

'Anyway, we had put this afternoon aside to go through your first draft – for me to check your facts and so on and so forth.' Miriam flaps to and fro the cover of the text book she's pulled onto her lap. 'But I don't think now's the right time, is it?'

'No,' I murmur. 'No, it's not. I'm sorry, Miriam, but I'm really not feeling too good. I'm going to go back to bed for a bit.'

'Right you are, dear.' Miriam stands up and puts her hands on her hips in that hearty, fearless way of hers. 'I'll find some-thing that'll do you good, don't you worry. I'm thinking lemon balm and sage, with a spot of echinacea root and perhaps some ...'

She's still rambling on as I shut the door behind her and collapse against it, the tears streaming down my face, this time with no attempt to stem them.

Desolation is always worse when someone is kind.

# Chapter 26

## Susannah

The days pass.

I imagine Dan and Charlotte lying lovingly next to each other on matching sun loungers, sipping cocktails around the infinity pool, the scent of herbs wafting gorgeously around them, Charlotte oblivious to what Dan's done. I wonder if his mind is also constantly replaying our night together like mine is, turning it over and over and examining and re-examining it. In my fevered and addled state, Dan sometimes morphs into Charlie and back again.

My torment didn't stop with me finding him and Josephine in bed together, with having to move out of my home – oh no, it didn't stop there. Hurt piled on hurt like the continuous dumping of rubbish in a landfill site, one truckload of trash upon another.

I managed to find lodgings with a couple of girls from my course, Debs and Simone, who were sweet and kind and full of fascinated, prurient disgust about the way I had been treated. I couldn't face ever setting foot in the basement again so I wrote a letter to Charlie asking him to pack everything up and they went to collect it for me. Which was nice of them.

When they returned in a taxi (that I paid for; Charlie offered no help of any kind, neither emotional nor financial) loaded down with bags of stuff, so familiar and yet now utterly alien, I wanted to burn the lot of it. Its association with Charlie caused it to be shorn of any pleasure I might once have felt in it. Everything felt tainted, even my clothes, which I'm sure in reality she wouldn't touch with a bargepole. But just the thought of my things being in the same space as her sickened me.

Simone and Debs helped me to unpack. They were so kind. So thoughtful. They persuaded me that I couldn't afford to purchase a whole new wardrobe so I needed to keep all the clothes and accessories they had rescued for me, however much I hated the thought. As they talked in soothing, encouraging tones they pulled things out of the bags one by one: jeans, skirts, jumpers, belts. Seeing my apparel like this made me realise how mundane it was, how staid and boring.

Josephine clad herself – minimally – in tiny white leather miniskirts with fishnet stockings and sky-high stilettos, accessorised by exquisite handbags big enough only to hold a mascara and credit card. I wore paisley-print midi-skirts with wool tights and Doc Martens and carried a satchel. It was hardly surprising it was her who Charlie preferred. It was as the truth of this fact was dawning on me like the proverbial penny dropping from a great height that I noticed that Debs and Simone had fallen suddenly silent.

Lifting my eyes from the pile they'd built on my bed, I

saw them both staring dumbfounded at the item Simone was holding, her arm outstretched as if trying to keep it as far away from herself as possible in case it bit her.

My eyes slowly tracked the length of her arm. From her splayed fingers dangled a pair of impossibly delectable French knickers, made of shiny and opulent black silk and trimmed with lace.

'Ooh la la, Susie, what have we 'ere?' laughed Simone, speaking with an exaggerated French accent. 'Where on earth did you get zese beauties? They must have cost a fortune.'

As she spoke, Debs reached out to fondle the fabric, so lustrous and delicate it demanded to be felt.

'Wow!' Her voice was a stage whisper, as if the knickers might be offended by too loud a noise. 'These are so gorgeous. Who would have thought you were hiding such garments under those prim A-line skirts and blouses?'

They both fell about laughing. This was the 1990s. As already noted during my sojourn in France, in the UK sexy underwear was polyester Ann Summers; everyone else wore sensible and practical cotton briefs from M&S. I looked on, stunned. Eventually, my lack of reaction of any kind caused them to abruptly shut up.

'What's the mat—' began Simone, before petering out in a red flush of embarrassment. 'Oh, oh, I see, I get it ... sorry. Really sorry.'

The knickers had dropped from her hand during the fit of hysterics and now lay on the floor in a crumpled heap. Neither of them seemed to want to touch them.

I picked them up and screwed them into a tight ball in

my fist. They scrunched up to nothing. It was what I wanted to do to her, to that bitch Josephine, and to Charlie, too, despite how much my heart still ached for him. One of them – perhaps both, conspiring together, determined to inflict maximum hurt on me – had planted them amongst my stuff. They couldn't have known that Debs and Simone would be assisting me and would see them, too.

No, this pain was intended all for me.

I felt myself collapse then, from the inside out, slowly falling like the Jenga tower when the crucial brick is removed, sinking down and down to end up in a jumbled, chaotic heap, in my hand still clenched the interloper's knickers.

Unlike Josephine, I have the capacity to feel guilt, remorse, regret. And for Charlotte, I do. The justification for my actions is that I thought Dan was serious. I thought he meant it. I thought he and Charlotte were over and there was nothing more to it than waiting for her to overcome the denials and accept the inevitable. Now, with a distance of over twenty years and my experience of being the other woman, I suddenly understand that this is probably exactly how Josephine saw things.

Oh, the irony. The terrible, truthful, irony of that.

The boys return from their holiday, brimming with health, tanned and fit after their wholesome, outdoors-in-all-weathers holiday, both an inch or so taller and more tousle-haired than ever. I try to focus on them, my children, keeping at the forefront of my mind how much they love me and depend on me, how much they need me. Their presence is a balm that almost – but not quite – makes up for the hurt and loneliness.

I can't completely let go, can't lose my mind the way I did after Charlie's betrayal. The repercussions for Jamie and Luke if I trod that path again are too terrible to contemplate. Not just the legal and judicial consequences but the ramifications of all the publicity, too. A blonde in a scandal always attracts attention like crows to carrion; perhaps less when she's forty than when she's twenty, but attention nevertheless. The gutter press is no different now to what it was then, when the tabloids went wild for my story.

The story of how I poisoned Charlie and Josephine.

# *Chapter 27*

## *Susannah*

A flu virus seized hold of me, all those years ago, in my weakened state of not eating, not exercising, not working; heartbreak is a physical as much as an emotional ailment. The saintly Simone took my temperature and it was as she held the thermometer up to the light to read the mercury that the idea occurred to me. Perhaps it was the fever causing me to hallucinate. But whatever it was, the notion took root and, as I gradually recovered, began to shape up as an actual plan, a mission that, once accomplished, would cause Charlie and Josephine to suffer in the same way as they had inflicted such suffering on me.

There were any number of pharmacies dotted around the streets of London, more than one could ever imagine and I visited many of them and in each one, purchased a thermometer. Over time, I accumulated lots of them. They were inexpensive, just a few pounds each for the basic model. Whilst on my shopping spree, going from store to store to avoid suspicion, it was impossible to avoid the Valentine's displays, the serried ranks of chocolate boxes, of hearts and flowers and teddy bears. Each one made my eyes brim with tears; no celebrations for me this year, no declarations of undying love, no partner at all. Equal measures of hatred, despair and hopelessness engulfed me.

At Deb and Simone's flat, which I still could not think of as home, though I'd been there for over a month by then, I spread the carefully collected thermometers out on my bed and counted them. There were enough. Next to them, I placed the expensive box of designer chocolates I'd also purchased. It was closed with a cardboard sleeve and tied with a silky red ribbon, adding to the luxury it exuded. I sat and looked at my goodies for a long time, only clearing them away when I heard one of the girls' keys in the front door.

Next day, my headache and my tiredness laid me low once more. It was Sunday; no need to get up so I didn't. As I lay in bed, feeling the chill dankness of a February day emanate through the glass windowpane, I found it hard to think of any reason to get up ever again.

Opening the drawer of my bedside table to retrieve paracet-amol, I heard the chink and clink of the thermometers as they moved around within the plastic bag in which I'd concealed them. Also in the drawer were the French knickers. They were no longer the tight ball I had stashed there; it had gradually unfurled as I imagined Charlie and Josephine's liaison – I couldn't bring myself to call it love, or even a relationship – had done during those sultry days in the Marseille apart-ment, and ever since they threw me out. Somehow, though I despised the knickers' slutty beauty, I couldn't bring myself to throw them away.

Perhaps having them there was the reminder I needed that I had revenge to exact for a wound inflicted. This mission was the boost that gave me the impetus to get me through the day, the plan that galvanised me into action.

The plan that would bring retribution.

It had to be perfectly executed if it was going to achieve what I needed it to. The first part of it demanded that I was alone in the flat to make the phone call and of course it had to be a weekday. Finally, on a Wednesday afternoon, I had my opportunity.

My hands shook as I lifted the receiver and dialled the number. The nervous sweat on my fingers left damp patches on the plastic and caused them to slip. As the ringing tone began, I swallowed hard and took a deep breath; I was really going to do this.

When the call connected, there was a small delay before I heard the voice of the call handler. Pretending to be our course director, a Professor of Pharmacology, one of the few females in such a prestigious role in the whole country, was easy. Nobody whose job it was just to answer the phone in a poison-control unit would know what she really sounded like. It only took a few minutes to get the information I needed, which I noted down carefully on the notepad in front of me. I thought I had recovered my composure after the initial terror, but as I tried to write, the pen slid in my fingers, making my writing erratic and untidy – though still perfectly legible.

I asked the call handler to repeat back her words, to make double sure I had recorded them correctly. She did so, speaking slowly and clearly as she had presumably been trained to do.

Satisfied, I coolly thanked her and rang off. I checked back what she had told me; it was entirely consistent with what I had understood from my toxicology books and the lectures that had formed part of my course. The satisfying snap of the elastic band as it fastened the notebook closed was the perfect end to the day.

The 14th of February, Saint Valentine's Day, dawned bright and clear, the day for lovers everywhere, the time to declare your feelings and, if you're a man, buy two dozen red supermarket carnations for your partner. One dozen if you're a cheapskate.

It was the day that I'd been dreading because of all the reminders of what Charlie and I had had together and what I'd lost. What he now shared with that strumpet Josephine. But now it was here, there was a fizz of excitement deep within my bowels, a steeliness to my nerves and a steadiness to my intent. It was time for me to get my own back.

It was harder than I imagined to break the first thermometer. I tried firmly rapping it as you would an egg on the side of the metal bowl but nothing happened. Smashing it against the rim didn't work either and nor did trying to snap it. In the end, I put some newspaper on the floor to protect the carpet – I needed to be mindful of my deposit – and stepped on the slim glass tube. A splintering sound told me I'd succeeded.

Hastily snatching the thermometer up, I poured the liquid mercury into the bowl where it slid and rolled in a small, perfectly formed silver-white sphere. The syringe hoovered it up but it barely filled the receptacle – only 0.5g. I broke another, and then another.

My mouth and nose felt sweaty under the mask that I'd taken the trouble to bring from my placement in the hospital pharmacy. As a vapour, broken down into individual atoms, mercury absorbs into the lungs where its poisonous effects are quickly felt. I needed to be careful that I didn't contaminate myself in the process of what I wanted to achieve.

Obviously, I didn't tell anyone what I was planning, or afterwards what I had done. I was naive enough to think that I'd covered all my tracks, that no one would ever be able to point the finger at me.

I truly believed I'd committed the perfect crime.

# Chapter 28

## Susannah

The questioning didn't take long.

I thought I'd be at the police station for ages but I think the officers felt sorry for me; I was so obviously a fish out of water in a cell or an interview room. They weren't in any case in any doubt as to the culprit. I didn't even really care by that point. I just wanted the whole business over with.

Already, I could hardly remember injecting the chocolates, those perfect, shiny brown spheres that resembled the carapaces of cockroaches, with the mercury from the thermometers, wrapping them back up and delivering them to the flat, addressed to that French floozy Josephine. It was as if it were something I'd seen in a movie, not something I'd done myself, lived in my own real life.

Josephine had come home and found the chocolates on the doorstep. Thinking they were a gift from Charlie, she'd immediately opened them and taken one. She might have been skinny but she was bloody greedy. But in the end she'd eaten just the one, only one measly little chocolate. And not even eaten it really as, not liking the taste, she'd spat it out. I'd thought that the strong cherry brandy flavour I'd chosen would have masked the contamination, but it seemed not.

When Charlie came home he'd examined the box and found the mercury oozing out of the holes made by the syringe; he'd called the police and immediately implicated me.

Attempted murder.

That's what Charlie wanted me to be charged with. But of course it wasn't that. The mercury, even if they'd eaten all the chocolates, every last one, would at worst have given them stomach pains and vomiting; in solid form it passes through the intestines so nicely that, in Victorian times, it was used to treat constipation. And anyway, I had proof that I'd checked that they wouldn't die – my call to the poison unit had been recorded. Later, this last simple action was to prove vital in court.

But the truth is that I never wanted to kill Charlie and his French tart. I just wanted them to feel the pain that I had felt, experience the agony they had put me through. To teach them a lesson. That's what I told the police, and they believed me.

I was charged with attempting to harm and released on police bail. The trial would not take place for a few months. In theory, I was free to continue with my life, innocent until proven guilty. But no one would want their medicines dispensed by a pharmacist who'd tampered with toxins, and the university made it clear that I wasn't welcome on their course anymore. Rather than suffer the ignominy of being unceremoniously thrown out, I left. All that work, all those hours of study, all the money I'd spent on books and materials and living in London.

All gone.

My parents were incandescent with rage. They chastised me endlessly, over the phone and in person when they drove up to accompany me to my first bail appointment at the police station. It was a nightmare and, to make matters worse, my own brothers regarded me with barely disguised contempt, and treated me as if I were a stranger, a cuckoo in the nest, unrecognisable as their own sibling.

I couldn't get work whilst I was waiting for the case to go to court; I had no one to ask for a reference and anyway, I would have had to explain to any potential employer that at some point I'd need a period of time off to go to the Old Bailey and defend myself against a poisoning charge, which is clearly not a request on which most employers would look favourably. So, when the end of the month came and the next rent was due, I moved out of the flat for good. Simone and Debs were glad to see me go, of course – too kind to actually insist on it but nevertheless relieved and grateful that my lack of money meant that they didn't have to actively chuck me out. Simone was an evangelical Christian; I wondered what all her God-bothering friends would make of me. Not a lot, it was fairly safe to assume.

Like most people, I'd never been in trouble with the law before. I hadn't even indulged in the shoplifting from The Body Shop in which all the other girls in my class at school had participated. Too scared of getting caught, too intimidated by the prospect of my parents' wrath if I were found out. But now I understood just how awful it is to have the prospect of a custodial sentence and a criminal record hanging over you. It sapped all my energy, removing all desire to achieve anything. There seemed no point when, at some unspecified time in the near future, I might be heading for prison, might be locked up and deprived of my freedom.

The next few months were the worst of my life and there were times when I wasn't sure that I could cope, that I felt myself begin to go under. To cap it all off, an acquaintance, on a visit home to her folks, came to see me and informed me that Charlie and Josephine had got married. A shotgun wedding because she was pregnant.

There were so many reasons why this news flattened me. Not least because, when it came out in court – as it inevitably would – that the only person who had put one of the chocolates in her mouth was expecting a child, was that very moment forming and creating a new life – well, that was surely going to be the kiss of death to my defence.

That's when I gave up.

I can't give up now though. I've got the boys to think of.

Charlotte and Dan are due back at the end of the week. I lie in bed at night, wondering what will happen when Charlotte finds out. Because she will find out. Wives always do. The truth will out, one way or another.

Dan seems to think he's infallible, that he can breeze through life doing exactly what he wants and escaping the consequences and after all, as Charlotte has told me, he's got away with it before. But this is so close to home, his wife's best friend.

That surely changes everything.

# *Chapter 29*

## *Charlotte*

The two weeks Dan spends with me and the boys in Corsica are blissful, like a second honeymoon. I don't know what's happened but I can't remember the last time he was so loving, so attentive. Perhaps it's true that absence makes the heart grow fonder – though I'm not sure that's ever been the case before! Or maybe he's sensed how I've changed, how determined I am to be different, to include him more. From now on, we'll be one big, happy family, everyone mucking in together, sharing our joys and our disappointments like proper families do.

The fantasy lasts right until the moment we get home and I climb into bed, pleasantly tired from the journey. I altered our flights so that we would all return together. It cut a week or so off the time we'd intended to stay in Corsica but I couldn't bear to say goodbye to Dan. I want our newfound bliss to last forever. Now, as I lie in bed enjoying the natural, rather than air-conditioned, cool, Dan is downstairs quickly writing an urgent work email. I suppose some things will never change. But I don't mind; he'll be here soon.

The housekeeper has put fresh sheets on the bed and I luxuriate in the crisp white linen. It's been line-dried outside so that it smells of an English summer day. I remember that I left an unfinished detective novel on the bedside table and reach out a hand to pick it up. It can't have been very compelling if I'm not desperate to find out whodunit. But I feel a duty to the author to at least read the last few pages and see if I'm surprised by the outcome. The book isn't on the table so I lean over and scrabble around under the bed in case it has fallen. Agnes is great in many ways, reliable and trustworthy, but she is very much of the 'out of sight, out of mind' school of cleaning. If the book has been knocked to the floor by a frenzy of the vigorous hovering at which she is particularly adept, she won't have noticed it.

My hand makes contact with a block of paper and cardboard. But not just that. Next to it, I feel the cold solidity of metal, the slinky ridges of a chain. Ignoring the book, I pull what must be a piece of jewellery out from its hiding place and examine it closely. It is a silver chain with a collection of charms hanging from it: a die, an arrowhead, and a heart. I notice that the chain has not been undone but is broken. Easy enough to replace. I lay it carefully down on the bedside table, turn onto my back and lie completely still, staring at the ceiling.

The necklace is not mine.

But somehow it's got into my house, into my room. Into my bed.

When Dan enters the room, I'm sitting up, the pillows propped behind me, my eyes fixed on him as he opens the door, smiling in anticipation. He's wearing just a towel, his erection pushing it proudly forward. He must have showered in another bathroom so that, when he came to me, he'd be ready for action. He moves forward to stand beside the bed and lets the towel drop.

I say nothing, but just hold the necklace out towards him, the chain dangling from my fingers, the charms swaying to and fro. If I weren't so upset, I'd think it was funny the way his erection disappears, dwindling away in a matter of seconds, leaving his penis flaccid and dropping. If I had a pair of scissors or a knife I'd cut it off.

And from his reaction, from the dismay that's swept across his face like a thundercloud in the Corsican mountains, it's obvious that he's guilty. He must know this too, as he doesn't even try to explain. Doesn't give any feeble excuses and platitudes, no 'I don't know how it got there', or 'It must belong to the cleaner'. He just looks at the piece of jewellery as if he could murder it. And then bends down to pick up the towel and wrap it back around his waist.

'Go,' I say to him. 'I don't want to be near you anymore. I want you to leave.'

Dan sits on the bed beside me and instinctively I jerk my legs away. Even though I've got the duvet between me and him, the thought of touching any part of him nauseates me.

'We should talk about this, Charlotte,' he says, his voice hushed but insistent. 'I can explain.'

That's when I scream. I throw my head back and let the sound come out, as loud and terrible as I can manage, until my throat is sore and I have to stop.

The silence that follows is the most profound I've ever heard. I can't believe I haven't disturbed the boys but they're probably in the basement still, or with earphones rammed so deep in their ears they're incapable of hearing anything except whatever mind-destroying rubbish is emanating from their devices.

'Just go, Dan,' I say. 'Just get out of my sight.'

He stands up, holding the towel to make sure it's secure, as if he's read my mind and knows what I'd like to do to him.

'There's only one thing I want to hear from you right now,' I blurt out, unable to stop myself, much as I don't want to engage in any dialogue with him. I take a deep breath and steel myself for the answer.

'Is it hers?'

I force myself to meet Dan's eyes.

'Well, is it?'

Dan blanches visibly, a pallor I've never seen before engulfing his face. It's the first time I've seen him utterly floored, so completely disquieted. He opens his mouth as if to reply and then closes it again and swallows so hard I see his Adam's apple moving.

Impatient now, I ask for a third time.

'Are you shagging Naomi?'

Even as I say it, I realise I don't really believe that Naomi is the guilty party. But if it's not her, who could it be? Dan wouldn't bother bringing someone he works with in London all the way down here to the sticks, he'd just go to a hotel in town. And another reason against it being Naomi is that the necklace is far too tasteful, too understated and chic, to belong to her. She's the type who wears enormous nickel hoops in her ears and fussy trinkets that are more Claire's Accessories than Pandora. Plus I'm absolutely sure I recognise it, that I've seen someone wearing it or something similar, and though I can't quite put my finger on who it is, I'm certain that it's not Naomi.

'Just tell me, Dan. Don't prolong the agony.'

His expression completely transforms, his eyes that had been narrowed widening in astonishment, the anxiety in his tight lips melting away.

'No, no absolutely not. Naomi?' He starts to laugh and then, presumably realising the insensitivity of doing so, stops abruptly. 'Not her, good God no,' he concludes.

For some reason, though he's clearly an even more untrustworthy bastard than I ever knew, I believe him.

'OK.' I pick up the book that had been the start of this episode, deliberately open its pages and hold it right in front of my face. 'Now please do what I asked you to earlier and leave. Not just this room, this house. Immediately. And don't come back.'

I listen for the sound of his car tyres on the gravel drive, for the engine softly purring into the night. I need to be sure he's gone because I don't know what I might do if he tries to come back in here and sweet talk me.

Only when I'm sure he's left do I turn out the light. I don't sleep. Who would, in this situation?

I feel utterly crushed, all the stuffing knocked out of me so I'm limp and flimsy as a ripped rag doll. There's so much emotion in my head that there's none, because I simply cannot even begin to process what is happening to me, to us, to my marriage, and to my family. Everything I've worked for, sacrificed myself for, has been blown away in a single puff. I don't who I am or where I am anymore.

It's not a good feeling.

I'd cry if I thought it would help but I'm not sure it would make any difference. I've played it all wrong, done everything wrong – and now I'm here in this echoing house with no idea what the future holds.

My agony continues well into the small hours. I cannot get the thought out of mind: if not Naomi, then who? In despair, I text you. I just need to vent my feelings, to let out what's going through my head right at this moment. Despite the fact that it's 2am, you reply only seconds later.

*This is horrific*, your message says, *but be strong and don't do anything stupid.*

A well-judged response. Because when I'm as angry as I am now, I don't know how far I could take things.

# *Chapter 30*

## *Charlotte*

A couple of weeks have passed. I still feel at sixes and sevens, unable to settle to anything, my misery unabated. I've spent a lot of time with you – when you're not working, of course. It's September already and the twins are back at school, now joined by Toby. I let Dan say goodbye to him but I drove the children there alone. I couldn't share a car with Dan, no way.

I thought I'd miss Toby like I'd lost a limb but I've been so distraught that I've hardly had the emotional space to notice his absence. The boys think Dan's on an unexpected and extended business trip. The trouble is that Sam is still at home and his continual plaintive questioning, 'When will Dad be back?', 'Where's he actually gone though?', his trembling lip, the incipient tears that continually threaten, all tear me apart. The fact that he's here and not at school many miles away also means that, at some point, he's bound to hear the rumours, the gossip I'm sure is already flying around this bloody village. My fury at whoever caused this hurt to my family quadruples by the day.

After not being able to cry that first night, I've made up for it since. I've sobbed and wept and howled and demolished boxes of tissues, leaving my nose permanently sore and red and chapped. Some days I just want to stay in bed with the duvet over my head and block the whole world out. As well as anger, I vacillate between sorrow and fear and self-pity and cannot settle on any of them.

It's as if I must experience every horror, one by one, in excruciating detail, before I can move on to the next one and be wrung out with pain again. Despite all Dan's previous betrayals, he's never brought someone to the house before. To our home. Our bed. My nest sullied by some trollop, my bed sheets covered with someone else's bodily fluids. Yes, I know I'm being crude, but anyone would be in these circumstances, wouldn't they? I haven't felt agony like this since my mother left us when we were children, and my dad died, a homeless, stinking hobo. I had forgotten that such utter anguish is possible, how much it hurts, how impossible it is to escape it, even for a moment.

And yet, despite all this, the understanding that I had come to in Corsica, that I love Dan and always will, that we have something together that's too good to throw away, is always with me. However much I rage and roar, however injured I feel, however my feelings sway like the treetops in a hurricane, I am clinging on to the knowledge of my love for Dan. The trouble is that I'm simply not sure that I can ever forgive him.

In my hour of need, I've leant on you as a true and good friend.

We're sitting in my drawing room now, the Japanese

anemones, those flowers that signify the last days of summer, tapping at the window glass. It's dark outside, rain clouds gathered overhead, waiting to unleash another downpour. The phone is right beside me but I don't worry about it ringing anymore. At the end of the day, as far as my tormentors are concerned, it's only money they want from me. *They* don't want to steal my husband or end my marriage. So I don't bolt for it when it rings these days, I just answer calmly and of course it's always nothing – a friend ringing for a chat, one of the boys phoning to ask for money or permission for a weekend exeat to a mate's house.

It makes me wonder if all my previous fears were for nothing, just products of my febrile imagination, like Miriam's visit that day. That perhaps there never was a black car following me or members of the cartel tracking me down, that these were just ordinary people going about their ordinary business and I built them into evil persecutors. Even the phone calls could just have been automated ones from call centres where they dial hundreds of numbers at a time and only a small percentage of those who answer will actually be greeted by a real person on the other end.

Perhaps I've been worrying myself sick for years for no reason. It's a sobering thought, another thing to give me cause to re-evaluate my life, where I am now, and what I want for the future. Though I don't usually drink in the day, such soul-searching calls for strong liquor so I pour us both a gin and tonic, garnished with lemon slices from the crop I brought back from the garden of the Corsican villa.

You are full of sympathy for my predicament, and

presumably to demonstrate how deep your empathy is, you tell me about your first boyfriend, how you were betrayed and brutally ousted from your flat by him and his new woman. You had to return to your hometown with all its miserable pretensions, to your unspeakably dull family and their lower middle-class preoccupation with what other people will think. It led you to do something that should be unimaginable, which you now tell me all about.

As you talk, I study you intently.

# Chapter 31

## Susannah

Charlotte listens avidly as I tell her the story of Charlie's treachery, keeping her eyes fixed on my face, bent a little forward so she doesn't miss a single word. It's hard to articulate all the details; though the memory is fresh as a summer's day, the words needed to express it have rusted and corroded so that I must wrench them out of myself with the force of will.

'It was awful,' I say, slowly and tentatively, feeling my way. 'It's hard to believe that another human being could deliver such a devastating blow that it would make someone doubt their own life, their own worth. But that's ...' I stutter, falter, manage to continue, 'that's what Charlie made me feel.'

'It sounds dreadful,' Charlotte says, sipping her G&T, the ice cubes clinking against the glass as she does so. 'Absolutely terrible.' She finishes her drink. 'So what happened next?'

'I tried to commit suicide.'

The words are out. I've never said them before, never told anyone. Not Justin, not any other of my friends. Charlotte's gasp of astonishment makes her cough and splutter. Her drink must have gone down the wrong way with the shock and surprise of my confession.

It's almost gratifying that she cares so much, is taking it so seriously, not immediately dismissing it as a young girl's folly but even so, I don't know why I'm telling her. I don't even know why I'm here, sitting in the elegant drawing room of the woman who has what I want ... wanted. Whatever. I've lost all track of my feelings towards either Dan or Charlotte. But somehow I can't let go, can't turn my back on Charlotte, on our relationship. I can't help it. She's my best friend. I've got no one else, now that Dan is gone.

'I waited until Marjorie and Dennis were out at some Rotary Club do,' I continue, my eyes fixed on the garden beyond the window, my voice monotone like it's on automatic playback. 'I took pills, lots of them. One after the other, swallowing them down with water though they still stuck in my throat. It wasn't hard though. I enjoyed it.'

Charlotte is dumbstruck, saying nothing, just listening open-mouthed. She's finished her drink, I notice. That was quick – but at least she won't choke again.

'I couldn't cope,' I admit. It's so hard to do this, to admit to her – to anyone – that I didn't have the resources, mental, emotional, or physical, to deal with what Charlie and Josephine did to me. Perhaps I'm sharing the story with her to make her feel sorry for me, which will in turn serve to mitigate her anger when she finds out it was me who ... Or to provide myself with some kind of pre-excuse, a pre-emptive strike before ...

I don't know. I really don't know why I'm doing what I'm doing. But I can't seem to stop.

'How did you survive?' she asks, a hint of vicarious pleasure lurking beneath her sympathetic tone.

'My parents came back unexpectedly early – Dennis wasn't feeling well – and Marjorie found me,' I respond, briefly.

We both sit in silence for a moment, absorbing this information, the fact that my mother's chance appearance is all that prevented my life from being over.

'How dreadful!' she exclaims, eventually. 'What an awful shock. She must have been terrified for you.'

I shrug again. It's funny how the memory makes me regress right back to being that confused, mixed-up, desperately sad and lonely twenty-something.

'I suppose so,' I agree. I recall the ambulance arriving whilst I was in a state of semi-consciousness, being rushed to hospital, having my stomach pumped. The concern tinged with reproach shown by the paramedics, the A&E doctors, and worst of all by my parents.

*Why did you do it, Susannah? Surely a broken relationship isn't worth this?* But it wasn't just Charlie and Josephine by then. It was my criminal act as well and they knew it, though they didn't say so.

'Did you suffer any lasting damage?' asks Charlotte, her voice interrupting my reverie. 'I've heard that paracetamol can destroy your liver.'

'I was fine,' I reply, without hesitation. 'No lasting effects. All good.'

There's another pause, during which we are both

presumably contemplating the fragile line that lies between life and death.

I'm glad I've told her, I suddenly decide. I wanted to share the worst time of my life with her. But it's her husband who's hurting me now, I think with sudden rancour, and she has no idea about any of it. I've been clutching onto her friendship from sheer force of habit. And, if I'm honest, to avoid any possibility of anyone in the village pointing the finger of blame at me. The rumour mill is like a river in full spate, flowing out of control, questions being asked about where Dan is, why his car is never in its usual place in the gravel driveway anymore. If Charlotte and I were suddenly no longer friends, it would be all around the place in nanoseconds.

Sitting here now, I have a sudden urge to chuck the rest of my drink in her self-satisfied face, to drench her prurient interest in my tarnished past with the juice of her own bitter lemons. But it's best, I know, to play the long game. To be the considerate, loving friend I've always been, standing by my mate in her hour of need. That way Dan will see my true mettle, will recognise me for what I am: the bigger person, moral and upright.

All I have to do is to hold out until something changes, which surely it will. And when it does, I'll be there, ready and waiting in the wings, and he'll already know that I am far, far superior to his superficial, preening wife. The problem is that I really don't know how long I'm going to be able to keep this up, to maintain the pretence.

And after all, if it came out into the open, if Charlotte knew the full extent of what Dan has done, I'm sure she'd never want to speak to him again. Nor me, obviously. But by then it wouldn't matter because, once Dan knew he and Charlotte were finished, he'd come back to me.

Wouldn't he?

# Chapter 32

## *Charlotte*

It's hard, hearing your story of how you reached rock bottom before you began the slow crawl back up. But it seems incomplete somehow. Call it female intuition but I've got a hunch you're leaving something out.

'Did anything else happen?' I ask. 'I mean, you told me before that you lived with some friends from your course before you chucked it all in and went home. So the ... the attempt on your own life, you didn't do it right away, immediately after you split with Charlie, but some time later?'

I can see that my question has taken you by surprise and before you've had time to think better of it, you're answering.

'I was in trouble with the law,' you say.

I tilt my head to one side questioningly. 'How so?'

'I did something stupid,' you blurt out.

Drawing a deep breath I wait, on tenterhooks, for more. But you disappoint me.

'I'm not going to talk about it,' you say. 'I can't.'

You say the words with such finality I can tell that nothing

259

will persuade you to spill the beans. My mind goes into over-drive as to what it could have been. GBH? Stalking? You come across as so timid and self-effacing but maybe that's not the real you. Still waters and all that, I guess. I'm pondering this when distraction arrives, as it always seems to, in the shape of the children, Luke and Sam happily together, Jamie morose with his pal Toby absent. Luke has cut his hand and you fuss over him like his whole arm has fallen off.

Whilst this is going on, I think of where you've ended up now. Your job in the cafe – long hours, hard work, on your feet all day, and low pay. Not to mention having to work with Naomi. She's not who Dan's been sleeping with, I'm sure of him on that. And the truth is, though she's an acquired taste that I personally am never going to acquire, she's probably not that bad really. I have an urge to bury the hatchet with everyone I've ever had an argument or differ-ence of opinion with. In the face of what I'm going through, everything else seems trivial and unimportant. It's made me reconsider everything.

'I'm so sorry, Susannah,' I mutter once the children have left again, forcing my thoughts back to you and your sad history, wishing I had something more substantial to offer than my sympathy. Of course, the Charlie situation was not one where alimony applied but you don't seem to have got a good deal in your divorce with Justin. At least if Dan and I were to split now, I would be sure of a more than generous settlement. He's not in a position to argue and in any case, I know he wouldn't. But far from hiring a solicitor and commencing divorce proceedings, in all his communications with me, he's been begging me to forgive him, to let him come back, to allow him to try to make things up to me.

You get up and wander over to the French doors. Last time you were here, they were thrown open to the sunshine. Now they are firmly closed in anticipation of the impending rain.

'Has he told you who it is yet?' you ask, as if reading my mind. Your back is turned to me so I can't see your expression. But there's a faltering note to your words that makes me wonder ... do you know? Have you seen or heard something?

'No,' I answer. 'And I'm not going to stoop so low as to ask, not again, not after the first time when he denied it was Naomi.'

'Oh.' There's something about your tone, and your stance, that I can't quite interpret. Is it surprise? Disappointment? I'm about to question you further when you strike up again.

'It's just that ... are you really sure you believe him about Naomi? She was very chirpy all the time you were away and now ... well, now she's been off work for nearly a week.'

You come back from the window and sit down again, perched on the edge of one of the plump sofa cushions like a bird about to take flight. Your hair has grown and no longer frames your face but hangs messily down your back, past your shoulders. I suppose you can't afford the regular cuts and blow-dries that a shorter style would demand, let alone the highlights that would do so much to enliven your rather dingy shade of blonde. I feel sorry for you again. It's hard to be poor. I should know. I always was, before I met Dan.

'He insists it's not her and I believe him,' I reply. 'He seemed to find the whole notion preposterous. All his texts protest that, whoever it was, it was nothing, just a stupid fling, a moment of madness. That old chestnut.' I feel tears pricking behind my eyelids and I squeeze them back. No matter how much I steel myself, how much iron I try to gird my heart with, it gets to me every time I think about it, corrosive jealousy gnawing at my stomach. 'And I can tell that he's still expecting me to invite him back home sooner rather than later,' I conclude, giving an ironic snort of disbelief.

It seems like an age passes before you answer. When you do there's something odd about your face, as if you don't feel too good.

'Look, Charlotte,' you say, a hint of irritation in your tone. 'You're going to need to think really hard about Dan and your next move. I mean, if you did take him back, could you ever trust him again? Hasn't he pushed you over the edge once too often now?'

I'm barely listening, but you plough on.

'I'm not sure,' you persist, 'that if it were me, I could see my way back from this latest dalliance.' There's scorn in your voice, but whether for Dan or for me in my weakness I'm not sure. I'm concentrating too hard on something else to take much notice.

'I haven't decided yet,' I reply tersely. The decision is for me, and me alone, to make.

You sigh and grimace sympathetically and say you need to be off. A dental appointment for one of the boys or something. In the hall, you put on your trademark red coat, liberally distributing bits of dried up and crumpled greenery from the pockets all over my pristine floor tiles.

'Don't worry,' I say tightly, 'I'm always finding weird things in my pockets.'

Once you've left, I give in to the rage that I've been harbouring since I realised. Since I understood why the necklace I found under the bed was familiar, where I'd seen it before.

On you. Around your neck. Matching the earrings that caught my eye in the picture Miriam took of you and Dan outside the tennis club, and which you are wearing today.

'Fucking bastard!' The words explode out of me and ricochet around the echoing hallway like lethal bullets. I've always been a measured person, not prone to violent outbursts of any kind. Fury like this I have never known before.

My rage rises up to almost uncontrollable levels. I pace up and down the length of the drawing room, metaphorically gnashing my teeth and tearing at my hair. The house is too big, too ornate and elaborate, for a single woman, even one with four children sporadically inhabiting it. I don't want to be alone. I had a shit childhood and I deserve a better adulthood. I have never been unfaithful, and I never would be.

After the shock comes the realisation, like the clearing of the sky after the rain. I want Dan. I want my husband, here with me, where he should be, being mine.

If there had ever been any doubt as to whether I would give Dan up for someone else to have, it's gone now. The fact that it's you who wants him makes that all the more certain. How dare you come here with your sob stories about rejection and suicide? Are you for real? Perhaps the idea behind telling me is so that I'll follow your lead, top myself, and leave the way clear for you, the scarlet harlot of Biglow village.

There is no way that is going to happen, no way you will ever get your dirty thieving hands on Dan. So much for you being a shrinking violet. How could I have been so deceived?

I'll make you suffer for your betrayal, be in no doubt about it. No doubt at all.

# Chapter 33

## *Charlotte*

I've called Dan.

He's been phoning and texting twenty times a day and I've refused to respond to anything. But today I give in. It's actually me who picks up the phone to him. I tell him we need to talk and the relief in his voice is overwhelming. I have to make the arrangements quickly and then ring off because I can feel tears welling in my eyes and I don't want him to know. I'm sure there'll be a time for more weeping but it's not now. Not yet.

He's coming for dinner on Saturday night. I want it to be at the weekend so that there'll be less chance of anything getting in the way like a conference call at 10pm or 6am, the usual ridiculous times that are Dan's normal working hours. Plus, I'm nervous and I need a couple of days to prepare. To work out what to say, how much to concede. It's not that I want to prolong anyone's suffering, but if we're going to make this marriage work, we both need to commit to it. And I'm not sure that Dan's quite there yet.

I tell you that he's coming round. I want to know what you'll do. You continue to act like the innocent, as expected, to portray yourself as someone who's only concern is for me and my welfare. Lying bitch. It's good, in a way, to know. Because finally some of my desolation can be replaced by pure anger.

'Is it what you really want, Charlotte?' you ask down the phone line, all faux sincerity and sickly simpering.

'I think so,' I reply hesitantly, playing along. 'I'm not sure at all but if I don't see him, if we don't talk, I'll never know how I truly feel, will I?'

There's a long silence during which I silently wish the rivers of hell to descend upon you.

'I can't say I'd be welcoming him back with open arms if it were me,' you say, your voice tart now like a sour sweet.

For a split second, I am incandescent. 'It's hardly "open arms",' I retort, biting back a much stronger response. 'It's a conversation. That's all.'

'What about food?' you ask, apropos of nothing, completely knocking me off kilter.

'Food?' Do you think I need to challenge my husband not for shagging my best friend but for his nutritional choices? Is the problem not Dan's unfaithfulness but his diet?

Then it dawns on me. 'Oh, you mean what am I going to feed him?'

I force myself to engage in your ridiculous preoccupation. 'I don't know,' I say, bluntly.

I am a feeder, the woman whose culinary repertoire is never found wanting. Who endlessly dishes up delicious and nutritious meals for her family and friends without batting an eyelid. But suddenly, I can't think of anything that would suit and I'm not sure I care. Plus, the very thought of opening a recipe book, going out and doing the shopping, collecting ingredients, drains me.

'Perhaps a takeaway,' I conclude lamely, still not sure why I'm telling you anything.

'No, that won't do at all,' you say, almost before my words are out. 'Look, it's national rice week – I know, who knew? – and in the cafe we're featuring 'curry of the day' for the whole seven days. Saturday will be our finale and I'm cooking lamb massaman. Why don't I make extra and bring some round for the two of you?'

'Thank you,' I manage to mumble as crocodile tears of relief course down my cheeks. I'm good at this, I realise, this dissembling. I'm even starting to enjoy it. It provides some relief from my anguish. And if you want to do the leg work, why should I stop you? It's quite funny to think of you, the scarlet temptress, running around like mad woman cooking for my reconciliation supper. The meal that will finally cement the end of your dream of stealing my husband. I sniff, loudly.

'If just the offer of a curry is making you cry,' you say, in voice that is designed to cheer me up, 'God knows what will happen when you taste it! It's going to be very spicy – and I might add a bit more chilli in the one I make for you because I know how Dan likes it hot.'

Am I supposed to notice this double entendre? It's a low blow, if so.

'Charlotte, one last thing I think you should consider,' you urge, by way of finishing the conversation, 'don't give too much away. Don't make it too easy for him.'

Your sheer bare-faced cheek is utterly astounding I think, as I put the phone down. Straight away it rings again. Instinctively, I reach out to answer it. It's so soon after you rang off that I assume it's you again, that there's something you forgot to tell me. I'm riled up but forcing myself to appear calm. I'm not prepared for the silence. The deafening absence of noise that's so familiar. That makes me certain that there's someone there who wants to frighten me, to intimidate me. That it's them.

Just when I thought it had gone away, when I had begun to believe that none of it had ever been real anyway, when I had started to breathe easily again – in that respect, at least, if not about events with Dan ... I can't bear it, I really can't. Not now, not again.

'Go away,' I shout, knowing there'll be no reaction but doing it anyway, 'just fucking go away and leave me alone. I'm paying the money, what more do you want from me?'

I sink to the nearest chair and run my hand over my forehead, where fear has caused beads of perspiration to gather. When Dan came out to Corsica I had intended on fessing up, laying everything on the table. But we were having such a blissful time that I couldn't bear to spoil it. So I put it off to do when we got home, but I never got the chance. Finding the necklace blew out of the water my carefully conceived idea of telling all.

Now I have to confront the fact that the whole hideous mess of it is still hanging over my head like the sword of Damocles.

A voice sounds at the other end of the line and my heart

stops. There's never been any response before and, though I invited one, I understand now that it's the last thing I wanted or expected. A hot flush of dread runs through my veins.

'Charlotte, it's me.'

Dan.

Oh, fuck. Fuck, fuck, fuck.

'What on earth was the matter just then? Why were you yelling? Who on earth did you think it was? What's all that about paying money?'

I feel sick.

'Dan, I can't talk now. The, um, I've got an appointment. The physio's here – you know, she always comes on a Friday. So I've got to go. We can go through everything tomorrow. See you at 7.30.'

I hang up before he can ask any more questions. He'll know I'm lying – or maybe he won't. Maybe he'll believe me that I'm seeing Maya the physiotherapist now. He doesn't know anything about my routines. He even believed the dressage story. Fell for the idea that once a week I went off and rode a dancing horse, for God's sake. Looking back now, in the cold light of day, it stands as a stark reminder of how far apart we have grown. Had grown. We truly lost sight of each other to such an extent that it became too easy to lie, to know that either our lies would be believed or that the other partner was too indifferent to care whether what we say is true or not. We were living separate lives, preoccupied with different things, forgetting that spouses are a team. That marriage is a collective effort.

I stand up and look in the mirror. Horror at what I am

confronted with momentarily overtakes all other concerns. A pale, drawn face stares back at me, my Corsica tan is all but gone, my hair awry and my mascara smudged. The wrinkles around my tired eyes are minimal, thanks to my recent 'treatments', but the 'scaffolding' in my cheeks seems to have sunk so that they are not firm and rounded but sallow and droopy.

Women really do get dealt the bum hand, don't they, I think sadly to myself. The menopause, with its dry skin and hot flushes and diminishing oestrogen, robs one of the useful function of child-bearing whilst it simultaneously steals one's looks. The thickening waist and protruding belly taunt one, however hard one exercises and diets. A life of toil trying to keep body and soul together is followed by a slap in the face for bothering. For men, grey hair and a lined face can be so distinguished – look no further than Dan for proof of that – whilst the same things on a woman diminish and demean her. But I've not given in to the ravages of time and I'm not going to give in to being usurped.

It's time to fight back on all fronts.

# Chapter 34

## *Susannah*

I'm struggling with the shock of what arrived in the post today.

Not another dreaded missive from the production company. No, this was a small padded envelope, the address typewritten, no note inside. Just my necklace, with the three silver charms, the arrowhead, the die, and the heart. The chain is broken which explains why I have not been able to find it over the past few weeks – it must have fallen off when I was with Dan and he has now returned it. It must be him, because if anyone else had found it, how would they know it was mine? It can't be Charlotte; I saw her this morning and she was perfectly pleasant, though a bit distant, obviously still hurting. It's the absence of any message in the package that seems most significant. No 'Thinking of you' or 'Would have preferred to give this to you in person but you know the situation'.

Nothing at all.

I bury my breaking heart in a flurry of activity. Dan's action – or lack of it – is inexplicable. I don't know how he

271

can love Charlotte more than me. I mean, any man would get bored of a trophy wife like her at some point, I'm sure. She's immaculately turned out but there's nothing behind the facade, no depth, nothing real. I mean, as a friend she can be entertaining, a laugh. But as a wife? A long-term relationship needs more to it than that. In contrast, Dan knows how good we are together, playing tennis, talking, in bed. It seems wilful, self-flagellating, for him to throw that away.

He hasn't come into the cafe, or visited the club at all, since it happened. But I find a new chain and defiantly restring my charms anyway, fastening the necklace around my throat before heading to the cafe. If he does turn up, this will show him that I am unbowed, even though I hate going to work now and can't stand the smell of rubber soles and air freshener and freshly laundered tennis kit that assails me as soon as I walk in the door. It makes my heart jump into my throat and cramps clutch at my gut.

The club is Dan and Dan is the club and I can hardly bear that I still have to come here every day, that the future for me and the boys rests on keeping my job here, that I can't just simply run away. I can't drop out, the way I did after Charlie left me, because I have Jamie and Luke to think about now, responsibilities I didn't have then. I can't so much as contemplate the idea of finding another job or even of moving again. It's far too soon for that.

So I chop and dice and season and taste, and as I do so, some tiny part of my mind that believes in fairy tales and not in real life allows me to fantasise about Dan, to imagine that, despite everything, eventually it will all come right. I think about his and Charlotte's imminent meeting and picture the scene, the looks on their faces when both of them realise that their differences are irreconcilable, that there has been an 'irretrievable breakdown' in their marriage, that citing 'unreasonable behaviour' and adultery will be the best way out of it. How, when that moment comes, Dan will turn to me to pick up the pieces and put him back together again. And how, because we'll be discreet and subtle and take things slowly, Charlotte will never need to know that it was me, always me, for whom Dan was prepared to risk everything.

In the meantime, offering to provide the food was a way for me to make sure that I am present at that meeting, that both of them are reminded of me. Plus, cooking Dan's favourite food – super-spicy curry – something that Charlotte has said she won't do, will make Dan realise that I am so much better – more considerate, nicer – than her.

At this thought, I take my phone out and look, again and again, at the text Charlotte sent me the night she discovered Dan's infidelity, venting her rage, telling me in detail what she felt like doing to her husband.

It's one of those texts that no one should ever send.

# Chapter 35

## *Charlotte*

You call me to make sure I'm in and can take delivery of your gourmet offering. You've finished work for the day; the batch you're giving me is a pepped-up version of the one you've been serving to your customers and you tell me it's gone down a treat. You'll pop over right away with it.

This is my cue to get my act together. I've been up and down all day, my mood vacillating from one of willing conciliation, of desiring to clear things up with Dan, brush all his misdemeanours under the carpet, pretend that none of it ever happened and that nothing has to disturb our comfortable life, to one where I rage and scream at him for what he's done. Why should he get away with the humiliation and ignominy he's dealt out to me, seemingly without giving a second thought to my feelings? I'm going to keep him – but I'm not going to make it easy. My resolve strengthens when I think of the boys, his sons, his flesh and blood. Sam's confused little face haunts me. I don't know if he believes the work trip story. All he wants is for his dad to come home.

By the time you arrive, bearing a large casserole dish and your usual duplicitous sympathetic-but-encouraging smile, I'm all over the place, my hair wrapped in a towel because I decided I needed to lay the table before drying it, clothes strewn across the ironing board because I can't make up my mind what to wear. I want to look smart, resolute, and purposeful, clearly not someone who can be pushed around or suppressed. The Charlotte that I always was, and will be again. But I also want to look seductively vulnerable so that Dan sees what he's done to me and feels deep remorse for it. That's a tall order for anyone's wardrobe and make-up bag and whether I can achieve it or not, I'm not sure yet.

I take your red coat, hang it neatly in the cupboard, then make tea for us. It sticks in my craw to be offering you hospitality but I don't want you to know that I know. Not yet.

Plonking down the mugs of tea, I sweep aside the mess I've created on the breakfast island, which is littered with napkins and napkin rings, silver cutlery, recipe cards for desserts, and a huge packet of plastic straws that Sam got out for some reason and, as always, left lying around. It looks like I'm expecting twenty people for dinner, not just one, and that one my husband of twenty-five years.

You have clearly come to the same conclusion.

'Gosh,' you say, rolling your eyes. 'I'm worried you might be over-thinking this!'

I break a weak smile and nod. 'I know. I'm going to clear it all up. I'll make it look like I threw everything together at the last minute because I've been so busy going out and having fun.'

You take a deep breath and then pause, biting your lip, that habitual tic I've noticed you fall into when you're thinking or are worrying about something.

'It's not my place to tell you what to do, but ...' you say, enunciating each word carefully and slowly as if you're having to work really hard to get them out.

I bite back the retort, 'No, it isn't, you two-faced bitch'. Your statement is instantly recognisable as one of those 'everything before the but is bullshit' moments. And so it turns out to be, when you proceed seamlessly to tell me precisely what I should do.

'Honestly, I've held back from saying this; I've been tactful and tried to understand where you're coming from. But the truth is that I can't believe you're even thinking of giving him a second chance. He's treated you so badly. If I were you, I'd let him run off to whoever it is who's caught his eye this time and be done with him. If you try to force him to choose you, to love you, surely you'll always have that nagging doubt about whether it's genuine. And after all, only a few months ago you weren't sure you even wanted to be with him anymore anyway.'

'Right,' I say, because it's all I can manage. I'm trying to work it all out. To understand Dan. To understand you. I could confront you here and now, lay down in front of you everything that I know.

But I am sure that revenge, unlike curry, is a dish best served cold.

I turn to where I've placed the dish on the worktop and lift the lid. A dense, mouth-watering aroma of thick spices engulfs me – cumin, coriander, and turmeric. I'm not that big on curry but this smells delicious. I take a teaspoon from the drawer, dip it in, and taste a mouthful of the sauce. It's an explosion of flavours that starts off tasty and then, when it hits the back of my throat, has me coughing and choking with the chilli hit.

'Fuck,' I splutter, when I regain the power of speech. 'That is one hot curry!' It's funny how the one thing that a sense of smell can't detect is the heat of the spice.

'I did perk it up a bit from the cafe version,' you apologise meekly. 'But I said I would, remember?'

'Yes, absolutely, you did. It's … well, it's fine. Lovely. Thank you.'

You look at your watch. 'No bother at all,' you reply, sounding relieved. 'I need to be off now though, to take Jamie to a cinema party. He and Luke are waiting in the car. Do you think Sam's ready?'

You're taking him for a sleepover so that Dan and I have the place to ourselves. Agnes doesn't work weekends and we no longer have an au pair. Hana left in the summer and I haven't got round to replacing her. With only Sam at home, maybe I won't. So the house is empty. *No one to hear the screams*, I think to myself, with a hollow, inward laugh, as I fetch my youngest son from the games room. He leaps and bounds down the hallway, distracted from the worry over Dan's absence by the prospect of a fun night with his friend. He shows you a flint arrowhead he found on a school nature walk last week that he's bringing with him to impress Luke with. When I was a child, we found them all the time but they're rarer now. I guess so many have been collected over the years. I take a picture of you and him examining it. His enthusiasm and pride is cute and heart-warming.

Despite this happy moment, a twinge of fear plucks at my heart as I hand you back your red coat and see you off. It's not ideal for my son to be in your care but I need him out of the way and it's vital that Dan doesn't get wind of the fact that I know who he seduced in my absence. Or who he was seduced by. Not before the time is right, anyway.

But as you exit through the back door, an angry, chill wind blows up and I am overcome by a sudden, inexplicable feeling of dread.

Two hours later, in an attempt to bolster my spirits before Dan arrives, and to remind myself of your perfidy, I look at the photo I took. I've opened the wine and had one glass already, and together with the gin and tonic I drank earlier, I'm feeling a little woozy. Normally, I'm just a social drinker and, unlike you, I never have more than a glass or two so of course it's going to go straight to my head. This is a night when I might have to break my no-carbs rule and absorb some of the alcohol with rice and naan bread.

Impatiently, I zoom into the details of the picture, teasing the edges outwards until the part I want to see is centre-screen, blown up to almost life-sized. It's further proof, more evidence, the absolute confirmation of your betrayal.

I take a gulp of wine.

Are you deliberately taunting me by wearing the very necklace I returned to you in the post or is it just that you are stupid? What is the curry all about? Some crazy, half-baked

# Alex Day

(pardon the pun) way to get back at me for trying to reconcile with my husband? A way to get into Dan's trousers?

And, most chillingly of all, how far are you prepared to go to get what you want?

# Chapter 36

## Susannah

I turn in my seat to check that Luke and Sam have fastened their belts. They are chattering and giggling about something, a shared joke, a hidden secret. Jamie is silent, intent on his phone. He's been so quiet since they got back from their time with Justin; I'm sure he knows there's something troubling me, however hard I try to behave as if everything is absolutely normal. Before starting the engine, I rub my hands over my tired eyes, hoping to dispel the anguish that's suddenly engulfed me. An intense pain sears through me. *Shit!* I've got chilli on my fingers from making the curry and I've managed to get it into my eyes. They smart and water and I squeeze them shut in an attempt to dispel the pain.

Suddenly, it all feels too much. I want to cry and sob and roar at the sky about everything that's gone wrong. I want a cuddle and a hug and someone to tell me it'll be all right. But there is no one to do that and instead I am the one who must be strong and indomitable, making sure my boys don't find out that the world is dissolving around us. Again.

At this moment, the boys notice that we haven't actually moved yet, that we're sitting with an idling engine going nowhere.

'Mum!' says Jamie. 'Let's go. We'll be late for the party.'

I nod. 'Yes, sorry, just had something in my eye.'

He's in the passenger seat next to me and I see him looking closely at me, appraising my response, calculating whether it's anything extra he should be worried about. Charlotte regarded me in the same way, just now, in her kitchen. In fact, her whole manner was a bit off, her gaze uncanny.

Remembering that Charlotte's bedroom window looks out on the circular gravel driveway, I release the clutch and move off. She might be watching me, wondering why I'm not leaving. Suddenly, I want to be away from here, out of sight of the house within which Dan held me close. The stones scrunch beneath the tyres as I pull away.

The gates open as I approach, silent and smooth; in the mirror I see them closing behind me, monumental and black, separating the house from the real world outside, preserving Charlotte in well-heeled luxury.

And suddenly I understand. I know, fully and unequivocally, how much it all means to her and how far she will go to maintain her hold over it all – including Dan.

Where that leaves me, I don't even want to contemplate.

# *Chapter 37*

## *Charlotte*

When I open the door to Dan, he leans in to kiss me in greeting. I sidestep quickly away from him but I'm already pleased about one thing. That he's rung the bell rather than used his key. This shows he's taking things seriously, not just assuming that because I've invited him for this meal, everything is back to normal and he can act as if he still lives here. He's going to have to work very hard to earn that right back – if he ever does.

He retracts from the almost-kiss and I usher him in. A storm is coming. The wind howls and gusts, banging the loose garage door, sending a flurry of leaves plummeting downwards from the ornamental cherry in the centre of the driveway. I push the door to and it slams itself shut. Though it's not cold, it's a wild night out there. This will be the first autumnal tempest. The weather forecasters predict it will be a big one. As we retreat down the hallway to the kitchen, I hear the rain starting, the gale flinging it aggressively against the windowpanes like handfuls of pebbles.

283

In the cosy safety of the kitchen, I offer Dan a glass of wine. He accepts and I discover that the first bottle, the one I opened earlier, is empty. I didn't think I'd drunk quite that much but what the hell? I uncork a second one. One only confronts one's lying, cheating husband once in a while, right? Might as well make it an occasion for indulgence.

'So,' Dan says, doing his best to look and sound contrite. Actually, he's managing both quite well. His face is drawn and pale. His hair is too long, giving him the look of a man trying, and failing, to preserve a lost youth. I'm pathetically and meanly glad that he doesn't look his normal devastatingly handsome self – and that it's not just me who's showing signs of being the wrong side of forty.

'So what?' I say, belligerently. 'So you've got some explaining to do, haven't you?' I'm not going to make this easy for him, however much he makes those puppy-dog eyes at me. Why should I? He's the one in the wrong. Even though the pain in my heart is tearing my chest apart, I won't let him walk all over me. He's done that for years. Enough already.

'Oh, Charlotte,' he says, staring into his wine glass as if that's who he's talking to. 'I'm sorry. Please believe that I'm sorry.' He looks up and meets my eyes. 'In all honesty, what happened is that for a moment – just one stupid, thoughtless moment – I gave up on you. I thought you were lost to me, that you didn't want me in your life anymore. I mean, well, we weren't … we hadn't had sex in so long … You went off to Corsica and you didn't seem to care that I wouldn't be there. You were content to be on your own with the boys. There seemed to be no place for me …'

His voice peters out after this string of petty excuses.

'What I'm hearing is you bleating that you're sorry and then going on to explain how it's all my fault.'

My voice sounds hard and uncompromising. That's OK. Right now, it's how I feel.

'No!' he protests. 'That's not what I'm saying. It's not what I think or mean. When I say I'm sorry, that's how I really feel. I want to make it up to you, Charlotte. What we had in Corsica ... that was like it used to be, wasn't it? That shows us we can be good again.'

I listen to all this with scepticism. But then he smiles, a meek, apologetic smile and it's the same smile Sam has when he's knocked the heads off my delphiniums with his football or scraped holes in the toes of his new school shoes doing tricks on his BMX bike. I sigh.

'OK, I accept that you're sorry, remorseful, regretful, whatever. But how do you expect me to just accept that you've betrayed me? Again.'

'Don't accept it. But at least try to understand it.'

I have to think about this for a moment. Should I try to understand? I think about my little problem and realise that, as I so desperately need Dan to reciprocate in understanding how that all came to pass, I probably should.

As if reading my mind, Dan says, 'And you've been so distracted ...' His forehead furrows as if he's trying to calculate something. 'I was going to say lately, but actually I think it's been for a long, long time. Hasn't it?'

I shrug. I'm not ready to be drawn on this quite yet. He needs to expiate his sins before I'll do mine.

'You've broken my heart, Dan,' I tell him. 'Ripped it out of my chest and trampled on it with hobnailed boots.' Suddenly, it's all too much. 'Why would you do that to me?' I wail, no longer able to keep the calm demeanour I had planned on. 'Why would you want to hurt me like that? And what if the children found out? What would they think of you then? How would you explain yourself to them?'

Dan doesn't answer. He looks as if he's about to cry. I can't feel sorry about that. He's brought it entirely on himself.

We talk for an hour or more, polishing off the second bottle of wine and opening a third. Sometimes I feel that we're getting somewhere, and then Dan says something that makes me think we're back at square one. Eventually I realise that if I don't eat something I'll fall over.

The casserole dish has been in the oven warming since before Dan got here and the rice is ready to cook. It only takes ten minutes to have everything on the table. I'm ravenous and load my plate with rice, naan, and several poppadoms. Dan raises his eyebrows but says nothing. I only take a little of the curry, two or three pieces of the lamb and a tiny bit of sauce. My earlier taste, when you delivered it, convinced me that a little goes a long way – unless you have a passionate love of chilli, as Dan does, but I don't. I pass him the spoon so that he can help himself. He looks thinner, reduced somehow, as if hotel food and solitary living have diminished him. It doesn't suit him, being exiled. He piles his plate high, as if he hasn't eaten for a week.

'Go easy,' I say jokily, trying to dissipate some of the tension that's been building between us. 'I've tried it and it's pretty fiery.'

We start the meal and Dan tucks in. I pick at some meat but don't finish it. Instead, I concentrate on crunching through the pile of poppadums. Soon Dan has finished. He reaches out to get seconds and I place my hand on the serving spoon to stop him. Stress and worry have always had a tendency to push him towards overindulgence. I've learnt over the years when to urge restraint. Now is one of those times. He'll give himself a stomach ache if he eats too much of that fiery concoction. I only allow him a small spoonful more.

When we've finished, we move to the sofa. I've had enough to drink now. More than enough. I feel a bit sick, dizzy and lightheaded. I pour Dan more wine but take a large glass of water for myself. We start to talk again but it feels like we are rehashing old ground, going over and over the same stuff. At one point, we both fall silent, as if there's nothing more to say and nowhere else to go.

'What was going on when I called yesterday?'

Dan's question, when it breaks the silence, is both unexpected and inevitable. I knew he wouldn't forget. Well, it's not exactly something anyone would just brush off as insignificant, is it? Someone hollering down the phone at you, swearing and talking about money being paid.

If it looks suspicious, sounds suspicious, smells suspicious ... it probably *is* suspicious.

I steel myself, breathing in deeply and taking a big slug of water to clear my head before beginning.

'It's something I should have told you ages ago,' I begin. 'Years ago. And I know it's wrong and I know you have every right to be really angry with me but ... but, well, it's not like sleeping with someone else. It's not betrayal like that. I would never do that.'

As if in agreement, the wind howls outside, catching at a dustbin lid in the refuse store and sending it slapping and banging like a macabre accompaniment to my confession. Rain pelts down, drumming on the glass roof of the extension, obliterating the view of the moon and stars.

Dan nods. He looks odd somehow, as if he's slightly out of it, on drugs or heavy painkillers. I assume it's the effect of a huge meal and a lot of alcohol.

'So what is it? Are you about to confess to being a contract killer or a pole dancer? Or something in between?'

He doesn't have a clue. All these years and he hasn't noticed anything. I could still retract, could still decide not to go ahead with telling him the truth. But now I've started, I mustn't stop; I must keep going until I've owned up to it all. And then maybe this whole damn business will be over and I will be able to live freely again, unburdened from the weight of terror.

'It started in Hong Kong,' I say, hesitant and nervous. Revealing something that's been hidden and covert for so long is harder than you might think. 'It began the first time we were there, and then, well, it never really stopped. In America, it just got worse. At least in Hong Kong it's illegal – apart from at the racetrack. But in America, it's everywhere. Absolutely everywhere, and the more I did it, the more addicted I became and the more I had to keep on doing it to try to make good what I'd lost. As time went on, the internet made it easier than ever ...'

Dan is staring at me, his eyes glassy, unblinking.

'You're talking in riddles. I don't understand.'

I can't prevaricate anymore, can't skirt around the issue and avoid facing up to it. He's my husband and for two decades I've been fleecing him to pay my debts.

'The thing is, Dan ...' I falter, then force myself to continue. 'I'm an addict. A gambling addict.'

There, the words are out. And now they're said, they don't seem quite so bad, quite so powerful.

'I've made and lost hundreds of thousands of pounds over the years, mostly online but also in syndicates. It was our second stint in Hong Kong when I got into real trouble. I had the *ayah* to look after the boys and you were working all the hours God sends. I was bored and I was lonely and my resistance was nil. I joined an illegal gambling den, playing cards and placing bets ... but these weren't nice people. Not nice people at all. I got in way out of my depth, I couldn't extricate myself, and I ended up owing tens of thousands ...'

My voice is droning on, the whole sorry tale pouring out now, no holds barred. I could understand if Dan hated me for it. If he despised the weakness and mendacity in me that could allow me to do things that were not only unwise but also against the law.

'I set up a payment plan with the syndicate.' I plough on, knowing I've got to get it all out. 'They allowed me that at least.'

What to tell and what not to tell? I got Dan to allocate me an allowance, paid straight into my bank account, money for myself, separate from the housekeeping and food budget. I told him I needed it. That he owed me an independent income when I had no paying job of my own. I used this to pay the debts. And, more recently, to pay for the help I've been getting from a private therapist to treat the addiction. Obviously I couldn't go to gamblers anonymous or whatever organisations exist for people like me because then I'd have had to explain my whereabouts.

I managed to keep a grip on it all for a while. A long while. But gradually things began to spiral out of control. I genuinely had to buy school uniform and pay for repairs to my car after I had a prang, things that Dan rightly expected me to cover, considering the exceptionally generous amount that landed in my bank account every month. I simply couldn't explain where it was all going if I constantly asked him for more. So I missed a payment or two. Well, quite a few actually. This is when I began to feel deep, visceral fear.

I was sure they would come after me.

These are not nice people. They don't have morals or scruples. They don't have limits. Wherever you are, people like this can find you. I still don't know if they've been casing the joint, stalking me. But I do know that, if they wanted to, they could.

I'm relaying the story, on and on, like someone has wound me up and now I can't stop, when I suddenly realise that Dan looks very unwell, really terrible. He's trembling and his pupils are huge, dilated as if he's taken a shedload of drugs. He shifts position on the sofa – or rather, he tries to – but only his upper body moves, not his legs.

I stop dead, staring at him, horror overtaking me, causing

my blood to run cold and my hands to tremble. I've never seen him ill, not really ill – he's the healthiest, most robust person I know. This was never part of the plan, that he'd come over for dinner and get sick.

'What's the matter? Dan, for God's sake, what's the matter?'

He tries to move, to get up, but he can't. It's as if he's paralysed, his limbs not working.

'Charl, I can't move. My legs aren't working. And I don't feel too good at all. My heart … racing …' His words dry up as if speaking is too much effort.

I feel paralysed myself, with fear and dread and desperation. I look at Dan, my handsome, charismatic, successful, much-coveted husband, suddenly, inexplicably, rendered incapable, incapacitated, and I don't know what to do.

'What's wrong? Is it too much to drink? Are you ill?'

The questions fire out of me as if there's any way he will have an answer. He's had a stroke, I think. He's going to be an invalid for life. And I've just been droning on about myself. I feel nauseous at the thought.

'The curry,' he says. His diction is completely clear even while it's obvious that his body is shutting down. 'Maybe the meat was bad …'

He shuts his eyes.

I hadn't imagined any of this.

When I asked him over, I'd thought it would be a chance to articulate our differences, to clear the air. Perhaps make him think – really think – about what he's done to me and how he's made me feel. But this has gone too far.

I press my fingers to his wrist and detect the faintest whisper of a pulse. I lean my ear against his mouth and cannot be sure if it is tickled by the weakest breath. I don't know what to do. I'm frantic with worry, with horror and terror. He cannot die before my eyes. Whatever he's done, I cannot lose him.

I grab the phone and dial 999. As I'm asking for an ambulance I'm wondering if this is the right decision. It will take them ages to get here, to find the place. The ambulance person is asking for symptoms and I'm trying to explain. That it started with paralysis and laboured breathing though he was conscious and talking. That now I'm not sure if he's doing any of those things.

The ambulance handler says the crew are on their way, but there have been reports of trees down on the side roads, and the rain is making driving conditions treacherous. I imagine the vehicle, lights flashing, sirens blaring, making its way towards us at a snail's pace, unable to pick up speed in the terrible weather. It'll never get here in time.

I stop giving the address and scream down the phone, telling the handler not to bother. Dan is fading fast; I'm going to drive him. It will be quicker and anyway, I can't stand the inaction. I can't sit here waiting. Watching him die.

Pulling him from behind his arms, I somehow manage to get him the short distance to the back door. My car is parked outside; I often leave it there rather than at the front or in the garage, in order to make a quick getaway if my mystery caller comes back. It's lucky I did so today. And that I filled the tank yesterday.

Even though he's definitely lost weight, Dan is still much bigger and heavier than me. But years of physio and Pilates to strengthen my back, plus fat-busting weight-training, mean that I am strong. Somehow – I have no idea how – I get him out of the door and into the car, willing my back not to give out on me now. I'm talking to him whenever I can, whenever I have enough breath, in between the monumental bursts of effort involved in lifting and man-handling him, trying to soothe him, comfort him. Keep him conscious.

His arms still work and, as I pull and haul, he helps me by dragging himself into the back seat where he lies prone, his legs stuffed in any old how.

'I don't think it can be the food,' I say, as I start the ignition and drive, desperately trying to keep my words reassuring, my voice even. 'It was made fresh today and they've been serving it in the cafe. Susannah made it. She said it went down like a house on fire. Everyone was ordering it. Fire is about the right word though, isn't it? It was very hot ...'

My voice trails away. I don't feel too great myself. My legs are heavy and I'm having to concentrate to make them work, to depress and release the pedals, to brake into and accelerate out of the bends, to change gears. I will myself to function, to keep going, to overcome the seeping lethargy that's engulfing me.

'Charlotte,' his voice is still audible, still Dan. 'I'm sorry. And I love you.'

And then the realisation comes to me, as I tear through the darkened lanes, barely heeding the surroundings, skidding slightly on a rain-slicked incline, like a religious epiphany. The true awareness of how much I love him and always will. We've been through so much together, me and him, over so many years. I couldn't live without him, and I don't want to.

I want us to be together forever – as long as he'll have me, after my confession.

Whatever I texted to you in a moment of madness, I don't want him to die.

I've never really wanted that.

# *Chapter 38*

## *Susannah*

Dan and Charlotte will be having their cosy date-night reconciliation, their let's-forget-all-about-it evening right now.

All I can do is wait.

I waited before, for weeks; the waiting for the sentencing seemed to go on forever, though of course it would have been even longer if I had not pleaded guilty and my case had gone to trial. I knew what was going to happen – it was painstakingly explained to me by my solicitor on several occasions and, every time, I sat and listened and nodded and made out that I was following everything she was saying. But in reality, I wasn't. Mainly, I couldn't actually believe any of it really related to me. It was as if there was another Susannah somewhere, lingering in the wings, and it was she who would be brought to the dock to face the judge's decision.

My parents oscillated between stony, pursed-lip silences, tirades of anger – 'How on earth could you possibly do this to us? Do you know what you've done to our reputations?'

– and anguished hand-wringing about how much time I might have to do at Her Majesty's pleasure and how often they would be allowed to visit.

I was impassive throughout. What I had done had occurred during a period of lunacy – diminished responsibility? – during which I couldn't see anything straight, could only feel. Feel the pain of Charlie's desertion, his lack of care or concern, his unceremonious dismissal of me and everything we had had together.

But, as my solicitor repeatedly told me, my actions had been premeditated. It had taken courage and planning and a type of low cunning that is apparently judged particularly harshly to buy the thermometers and the chocolates, to liberate the miscellaneous accessories from the work supplies cupboard.

On the other hand, it was also utterly incompetent. Laughably so. Who could have imagined that tampering with a box of chocolates would not be noticed? That the needle holes would be ignored?

Being a criminal is bad enough. Being a stupid one, worst of all.

But, I sometimes wanted to counter, the idiotic, simple-minded, tiny-brained, mini-skirted Josephine had not only picked up the chocolates from the doorstep, left by God only knows who, but she had taken them inside, opened them, and put one in her stupid, pouty mouth. So my work had fooled one person, albeit the thickest person on the planet.

I didn't say it, though. Even I could see that this would not help my case.

# Chapter 39

## *Charlotte*

We get to the hospital.

Even before I've stopped outside A&E, I've got the window down and I'm screaming for help. An ambulance has just discharged a patient and there's a paramedic waiting to close the doors. Seeing me hollering as if hell has boiled over, he runs over through the pelting rain. Within minutes, a whole team is there, assessing the situation, getting Dan onto a stretcher. I don't care what anyone says about the NHS, these people are amazing. Inside the building, out of the wind and wet, equipment is wielded, lines inserted, urgent instructions issued and commands followed.

Only Dan is oblivious to all the activity, unconscious now, his inert body long and lean. Lifeless.

My hand moves to his cheek, still gently caressing. I cannot stop touching him. His eyes flicker open.

'Sus,' he says. 'It was ... it was ... I slept with ...'

He stops. Mustering all the life left in him, he utters one last word.

297

'Susannah.'

Your name is like the blade of a knife slicing through my heart.

Dan's confession. His deathbed confession? I can't bear to think that is the case. Of course, he has no idea that I know already, that I have known for days.

In retrospect, I understand that your interest in my holiday in Corsica, in when I was going and how long I'd be staying, was never about me. It was about when Dan would be alone and open to your tender ministrations. I think of how you promised to 'keep an eye on Naomi', assuring me that you'd make sure she didn't get her hands on Dan when in fact it's your grubby mitts that have been all over him.

You've always been consumed by envy, have never been able to bear the sight of me and my family, with our money and status and position in the village, our beautiful home, our perfect life.

You've always wanted to destroy me. And I know what you've done in your efforts to achieve it.

Poison.

Our food, that you made out was to facilitate our reconciliation, was laden with poison. I suppose you must have wanted us both to go under. It's difficult to think that you intended our children to be orphans, but, as they say, hell hath no fury …

They're moving Dan's trolley again, towards bright lights that shine like beacons. The operating theatre? The doors open wider and Dan is borne away from me by a uniformed phalanx of nurses, doctors, consultants, anaesthetists. In my befuddled state, I don't know who or what they all are.

But I know what you are.

You are a bitch, a man stealer, a prize cow who thought she could take my precious husband right from under my nose. But you're out of luck.

Dan's not going to die, whatever's happened to him – he's far too strong. And when – not if – he overcomes this crisis, he has money to pay for any treatment, any medicine, whatever is needed. Surely his money will be enough?

At this thought, my legs give way beneath me and I'm on the floor, the tiles in front of my eyes not so white this close up, but spotted with colours of cream and beige and studded with particles of mud and dirt. As I'm scooped up by more of the uniforms, I swear one thing to myself. That I'm not going to die, either.

I need to survive so that I see you in prison.

# Chapter 40

## *Susannah*

Dan is in hospital, in intensive care.

The story goes around the village like wildfire, spreading from one gossip to another, changing and morphing with each retelling. He tried to commit suicide, Charlotte attacked him with a knife, he's paralysed for life from the neck down, he's made a miraculous and unexpected recovery, an intruder stabbed him, they had a car accident because of the terrible weather, he'll definitely die, he'll definitely survive, he's on the mend, he's six feet under ...

I try to call Charlotte, ostensibly to offer my sympathy, but in reality to ascertain the truth. To find out if Dan is all right, if he's alive, what the prognosis is. I'm frantic with worry, fretting and fussing around the cafe, muddling orders, dropping things. Whatever's gone wrong between us, I truly believed myself in love with him, I truly believed that we had a future together. Feelings like that don't just disappear in a puff of smoke.

But Charlotte doesn't pick up.

Naomi's devastated, too.

'Who would have thought it? Dan, of all people? My beautiful boy, my Dan?' she keeps saying, as if she'd given birth to him and then fallen in love with him. Weird. 'I never could have imagined something like this ...'

The question is, like what? Because we don't know but while we are ignorant, the imagination – and the gossips – conjure up all sorts of unpleasant options.

Finally, on the Tuesday morning after the Saturday night, Miriam turns up in the cafe with the whole story, which she proceeds to lay before us both, Naomi and I, the rapt and attentive audience she always longs for.

Apparently, Dan was taken ill during the course of the reconciliation meeting with Charlotte, after they had eaten. By the time she got him to hospital, choosing to drive him there herself through the raging storm rather than wait for the ambulance, he was at death's door. Miriam says that Charlotte wasn't feeling too clever herself, and ended up on a ward for the night, but that she was nowhere near as bad as Dan.

'But what was it?' presses Naomi, insistently. 'What could possibly have made them both so ill?'

Miriam pauses for maximum effect.

'Poison.'

All the breath is knocked out of my body as if I've been thumped in the solar plexus.

'Wh-what do you mean?' I can hardly articulate the words, am struggling to make sense of what she has said.

'Hemlock poisoning, so they're saying. There's no antidote but they pumped his stomach and did all the things you can do and by some enormous good fortune, Dan survived. Charlotte, too, though she was only minimally affected. Her life was never in danger.'

For once, Miriam is not speaking in exclamations.

'Hemlock,' I repeat, my voice wavering.

'The very same!'

The exclamations are back. In some strange way, it's reassuring.

'What the ancient Greeks did for Socrates with. And what the killer used in Agatha Christie's *Five Little Pigs*!'

It's almost incomprehensible. Almost, but not quite.

Because poison has long been a weapon of choice for would-be murderers especially, for some reason, female ones. I should know, I did it myself. And my idea to use mercury on Charlie and Josephine came from an Agatha Christie book. But though I knew how angry you were, I still never thought you'd take it this far. Then I remember the text you sent and it all makes sense.

When the police come calling, I'm glad I've still got it to show to them. They're glad too, finding it very interesting.

Sadly, I know from prior experience that however clever one thinks one is being, one always makes mistakes, leaves a trail, provides clues. That is bound to be as true for you as it is for anyone.

# *Chapter 41*

## *Charlotte*

It was a long, long night, the longest I've ever known. But Dan made it through those bleak hours of darkness, bravely battling the poison in his system as the wind and rain battled each other outside. My own suffering was not nearly as bad, just a little nausea. It was lucky I ate so little of the curry. Providence looked down on me when I decided to throw my no-carbs rule out for the night. I was so busy stuffing bread and rice and poppadoms into my mouth – tastes I haven't had for so long I could hardly remember how good they were – that I only had room for a tiny taste of the massaman. Which was far too hot anyway. Everyone knows I hate spicy food.

He and I have been back home for a few days now, recovering physically. Mentally, I'm not so sure. Well, how quickly would anyone get over being poisoned? Not the actual toxins themselves but the toxic realisation that someone wants to kill you, that someone will do anything to get what they want.

And when I say 'someone', of course I mean you. The investigative tests have confirmed poisoning by hemlock. I think of when you inadvertently discovered the hemlock patch. I showed you how to identify it, warned you to be careful. You know exactly where it is, and it doesn't take much of a brain to find out how to use it. A few internet searches and you're sorted. You masked the mousy scent and bitter taste with the super-spiciness of that curry you cooked. I bet you thought you were being so clever.

Still reeling from the whole event, I haven't even begun to think about what happens next. Dan's already given a full statement to the police, as have I. I've told them everything, all the lengths you went to so that you could get your hands on my husband. How you invented all sorts of ways to spend time alone with him, to beguile him with your blondeness, your sycophantic flattery, your sympathetic ear.

At some point, it's all going to come out in the local papers, isn't it? I've already heard that reporters have been sniffing round. So far, just the ones from the provincial rag, the kind of low-calibre journalists who have to cover everything from the cat rescue centre's annual fundraiser to the arguments over parking charges in the parish council meeting. But I'm sure it's only a matter of time until the big boys come calling. This is the kind of story the tabloids kill for. A jilted divorcee. A wronged wife. A love triangle.

Perfectly correctly, the doctors kept stumm on the amount of alcohol in my system. It was quite clear we'd been through enough, Dan and I, and turning me in for drunk driving would have been in nobody's interest. One, I didn't crash so no harm done on the roads and two, I saved a man's life getting him to hospital so quickly. So the hacks and journos haven't been able to get their grubby mitts on that. Though even if they did, everyone would be on my side. There are occasions when breaching a taboo is necessary and correct – and this was one of them.

Likewise, no one seems to have picked up on the gambling so far. And Dan has already paid off my remaining debt in one fell swoop – £150K, more or less. Those terrible people have nothing over me now. That's the power of money. A problem gone in the click of the fingers, a press of a button that transfers funds via Western Union to an anonymous recipient.

It's been difficult to know what to tell the boys. For now, I've just said that rich and powerful men like Daddy make enemies because people are jealous and they don't like the fact that he has more than they do. Those enemies sometimes do stupid, reckless, dangerous things and this is what has happened. But Daddy is stronger than all of them, he's pulled through, and together, we'll make sure that justice is done.

The boys seem to have fallen for that without too much awkward questioning. The only thing they've been really worried about is whether Dad is going to be all right. And me, of course. Which we are.

You're the one who's going to have to watch your back from now on. When I see you in the village, I can't keep in my rage any longer.

# Chapter 42

## Susannah

'Shame on you!'

The words, so clearly directed at me, induce an immediate rush of nausea. A hot flush suffuses my face. I want to remain cool, calm, and collected. But Charlotte's fury is so great it cows me completely.

Resolutely, I put my head down and continue walking. I'm on my way back from the school pick-up so I have Luke in tow. I can't bear for him to be involved. If I ignore her, she might go away.

Some hope.

'Susannah, stop right now and look me in the eye,' Charlotte demands, 'and tell me since when it became OK to betray your best friend by sleeping with her husband.'

I didn't know that she knew it was me. All the time since she's been back from Corsica, there's been no change in our relationship. That's why I assumed it was Dan who returned the necklace – there were no signs that Charlotte knew. But she obviously does. It dawns on me that Dan must have told

309

her. Unless she recognised it ... in which case, she's the best actress ever, not letting on in all this time.

She's paused after the first onslaught, but now she opens her mouth again and what comes out is delivered in a dreadful, hideous high-pitched shriek like a banshee's howl. 'And then to try to kill us both with poison!'

The words hit me so hard it's as if I've been winded. I gasp and struggle to breathe.

Luke tugs on my hand. 'What's she talking about Mum?' he asks plaintively, pleadingly. I think I might vomit.

Thrusting my hand into my pocket, I pull out a £10 note. 'Pop into the shop and get me some milk,' I instruct, thinking on my feet. 'And you can choose anything you want for yourself – a magazine, sweets, whatever.'

Too late I realise that this bribe will make Luke even more alarmed. The boys are never allowed magazines – too expensive – or sweets midweek. Looking scared and doubtful, he slips away towards the shop's doorway.

'So?' demands Charlotte. 'What have you got to say for yourself, you two-faced bitch.'

Her face is twisted into an expression as ugly as her language and she spits the words out as if they're bullets.

I say nothing. Hot sweat suffuses my body and I can feel the stickiness of my armpits.

'Susannah, you need to understand that Dan feels nothing for you, he never did, and he never will. Your cheap, underhand attempt to destroy my marriage was never going to work. And if you think you're going to get away with trying to kill us both ... how stupid are you? You're nothing but a pathetic little worm who can't keep hold of her own men so tries to steal other people's. No wonder Justin left you, and Charlie. Anyone would walk out on such a worthless piece of shit as you.'

I muster all my courage and self-possession. 'Charlotte, please let's not do this now, in public, in front of a child.' I flick my eyes towards the shop where Luke is presumably making his choice. 'The fact of the matter is that Dan invited me back to your house where he proceeded to seduce me, all of his own free will. If you're OK with that, and you're able to convince yourself that it meant nothing, and to believe him when he says the same, well, good luck to you. And as for … for poisoning you both, if you think that you must be even crazier and more insane than you seem.'

Out of the corner of my eye, I see Luke emerge with a blue plastic bag dangling from his hand.

'Now, this conversation is over and I'd appreciate it if you'd leave me alone.'

With that, I seize Luke's free hand and march towards our house, tears pouring down my cheeks and despair plucking at my heart. I'm shaking and trembling with anger and misery and embarrassment, and when I look down, I see Luke's little face, white with concern, gazing up at me.

'It's fine,' I say, feigning a conviction I don't feel, and even I can tell that I don't sound convincing. But I can't do anything more right now, not even to mollify my child. 'Don't worry.' I have to stop there because my voice is wavering and I can't stop crying and this will only frighten Luke even more than he is already.

I'm facing up to the fact that it's over with Dan, if it ever even began. I was stupid and gullible and I've been taught a lesson, big time.

But I didn't poison them. I wouldn't make that mistake twice.

# Chapter 43

## Charlotte

You walk off, leaving me standing on the road outside the shop, seething with undiluted fury.

The only satisfying thing about the whole exchange is that several people overheard. People who know who I am, and probably who you are, too. I'm not proud of my language – that was rather coarse and not the kind of image I like to portray of myself. But desperate times call for desperate measures and all that. I'm sure, once everyone knows the whole story, they'll understand my use of a few fruity phrases.

I walk back to the house, head held high in righteous belief that I am the injured party here. I trusted you. I confided in you. Most of all, I didn't see you for what you are and that is almost the worst of it. I always prided myself on being a good judge of character. Well, you've thrown that by the wayside good and proper.

At home, Dan is blindsided by the whole episode. He still can't believe that anyone would want to poison him. That *you* would want to poison him. And he's horrified that you've still got the gall to show your face around the village. We hunker down in the kitchen, me making chicken soup to aid his recovery, Dan in an armchair beside the Aga, wrapped in a blanket whilst making phone calls and hammering out emails. Not even a brush with death can keep Dan away from work for more than forty-eight hours.

'I didn't see it in her,' he tells me again, as he has done many times already. 'I just didn't see it. She always seemed so nice, so kind, so ...' He falters, presumably aware that showering you with compliments is hardly the right approach right now. But I know what he means. It's not just Dan. No one would have taken you for a murderer.

'I'm so sorry, Charlotte,' he says, for the umpteenth time.

I pause in my stirring of the pan and turn to him. 'Forget it,' I say, light-heartedly. 'That's what I want to do, and I recommend you do too.'

Of course this isn't possible. There'll be more questioning by the police, I'm sure, and then of course giving evidence at the trial. However much I wish it would all be over, that's not going to happen for a while. In the meantime, I want to concentrate on me and Dan, on our marriage and our relationship. As if to seal this commitment, I bend forward to kiss his forehead.

The staccato ring of the doorbell makes us both jump. For a second, the fear washes over me and then I remember. Remember that it's all sorted now, that there's no one out to get me any longer, if there ever was. Quickly washing my hands and brushing them dry on my apron, I go to the front door and open it. Two police officers stand on the doorstep, one man and one woman. I smile at them and greet them warmly, inviting them in. They must need more information, confirmation of the details we've already given.

'Don't mind your shoes,' I say indulgently, as if they are rare and favoured visitors, as I lead them down the hallway. I hesitate for a moment between taking them into the kitchen or the drawing room. In a split-second decision, I opt for the former; it's homelier, cosier. It will plainly reveal to these officers of the law that we are a loving family that someone – you – has callously attempted to rip apart.

Pausing beside the door, I stand aside and gesture for them to go in. I smile, a bigger, more emphatic one now as their lack of response has begun to bother me. They don't return the friendliness.

Typical police, I think, can't reveal anything, can't show any emotion, can't indicate in any way whatsoever whose side they're on.

In the kitchen, Dan's armchair is empty. He's clearly made a hasty getaway through the other door, presumably wanting to leave the coast clear for me to tell what I know. I imagine it's not too nice for him to hear, over and over again, that the woman who threw herself at him, when rejected, tried to kill him.

'Please sit down,' I say, pointing at the chairs around the large table. That seems more suitable than asking them to sit at the island breakfast bar. The male officer is large, the female one even larger. An image of them perched on high stools and swinging round and round the way the boys sometimes do to annoy me pops into my mind. I look away whilst I suppress the smirk.

*Alex Day*

When I turn back, the residual smile slowly wanes away as I register their expressions.

'Mrs Hegarty,' begins the woman, sounding self-consciously and irritatingly officious. 'I am arresting you on suspicion of attempted murder. You do not have to say anything ...'

# Chapter 44

## *Susannah*

Charlotte has been charged with attempted murder.

I am devastated, obviously. That anyone could have tried to kill Dan, that he nearly died – and that it seems that his own wife, my erstwhile friend, was responsible. But in another way, why should it matter to me? He's sloughed me off like an old, outgrown outfit he has no use for anymore. Even before the 'incident', he'd been about to move back in with her – or at least, that's the word she put about in the short period before her arrest, what she said the two of them had agreed during their curry-fuelled soiree.

His words to me as he seduced me – *Charlotte doesn't understand me, I can talk to you in a way I can't to her* – were as saccharine and hollow as a cheap child's Easter egg. There was nothing to them, no substance at all. And yet, whilst I hate him, I also still love him. Most of all, I don't know what to do without him. And though I know that all the evidence points towards him dropping me entirely, there's a part of me that clings to hope. Charlotte is on course to be convicted of attempted murder. Surely Dan won't stand by her when he is forced to confront the fact that she tried to kill him.

When I hear that Charlotte has been let out on police bail, I'm terrified. I can't stand to meet her again, can't even begin to contemplate what else she might accuse me of. I know from bitter experience how long it can take for the wheels of justice to turn. Investigations drag on and prosecutions take forever to see the light of day. I remember from all those years ago how the time between being charged and going to court seems never-ending. So it does again now, as I wait with bated breath for Charlotte's trial to begin.

But eventually, D-day arrives.

Charlotte has pleaded not guilty and I am called for questioning by her team. Though I am pure and innocent as the driven snow, it's still mind-numbingly terrifying to be in the witness box. I force myself to keep calm, to answer clearly and concisely, to make sure my body language is that of a guiltless, though spurned, woman.

'Ms Carr,' intones the barrister. 'You had an affair with Mrs Hegarty's husband. You slept with him in Mrs Hegarty's house, in her bedroom, in her bed. Is that correct?'

I swallow hard. This line of questioning is close to the wire. The jury will not look kindly on someone they will all too easily put into the category of brazen hussy. I survey their intent faces: seven women and five men. Women always judge other women more harshly; that's seen time and time again in this kind of situation.

I do my best to look demure, to make them see that I was

shamelessly exploited by a powerful and entitled man – which is in any case a version of the actual truth.

'Yes,' I say, my voice wavering with emotion, tears close to the surface. 'I did. But only because he told me his relationship with his wife was over, that their marriage was loveless, that it was going nowhere. I thought that he and I had a future together and therefore it wasn't, in my mind, an affair. For me, it was ...' I pause before completing the sentence, 'it was love.'

I conclude with the most important word of all and then fold my hands in my lap and wait, eyes cast decorously downwards.

'So you profess that you were – I put it to the court that you still are – in love with Mr Hegarty. And that you were planning a new life with him, once he had rid himself of the wife who got in your way.'

The words these lawyers use are so loaded, full of pernicious undercurrents.

The barrister continues. 'And yet, when you hear that they are having a meeting in order to effect a reconciliation, you offer not only to make the food but also to deliver it to their door.'

His artful use of the present tense makes my actions seem immediate, on-going. He looks around the courtroom, a magician playing to the crowd. 'A veritable one-woman Uber Eats, so to speak!'

He pauses for the ripple of laughter that drifts across rows of seating, his expression one of self-satisfied self-congratulation. It's all about self with these people, even though they're supposed to be working on behalf of their client. For them it's nothing more than a show, an opportunity to demonstrate how terribly clever they are.

I struggle to maintain a suitably humble demeanour. He's starting to annoy me, but I know I mustn't show this. I must play this absolutely right in order to make sure Charlotte gets her just desserts, i.e. a long period behind bars.

'Charlotte had been my friend,' I state, clearly and simply. 'I wanted to assuage my guilt about what had happened and help her and Dan to make the right decision. Taking round the homemade curry was a way to make amends for the wrong I'd done. It was never an affair between me and Dan. As I said, I thought it was love. Only in hindsight can I see how he exploited me, that in fact it was a misguided and misjudged one-night stand brought on by loneliness and too much alcohol, never to be repeated.'

I study the jurors again as I explain this, reading their body language. I see from their sympathetic smiles and gentle nods that they understand. Everyone makes mistakes; the better people try to atone for them.

But the barrister isn't finished yet.

'When you took the curry to Mrs Hegarty, how would you describe her state of mind?'

This comes from nowhere to take me by surprise; I don't know why it's relevant. Are they angling for a plea of mitigation, trying to establish diminished responsibility?

'She was ... distracted, I guess,' I answer, honestly. 'A bit all over the place, mess everywhere, no make-up on, halfway through ironing her outfit for the evening, that kind of thing. This struck me as unusual – she was always immaculately turned out and she was accustomed to hosting lunches and dinner parties for up to twenty people so she wouldn't normally be phased by a meal for two. Though she had given the housekeeper the day off so I suppose she was having to tackle the kind of menial chores – like laying the table and ironing her own clothes – that she usually left to others.'

I see various members of the jury frown, their foreheads creased, their mouths pulled into disapproving grimaces. It's only the absolute truth, which I vowed to tell when I swore my oath, but of course most ordinary people are either outraged by, or condemnatory of, the idea of having full-time live-in servants to wait on one hand and foot.

'And in her distraction,' continues the barrister, 'what did she do when you handed over the casserole dish which contained the ... lamb massaman?'

He enunciates the last two words so precisely and deliberately, emphasising the plosive 'b' and the sibilant 's' sounds; it's as if he's tasting them. And finding them wanting. I'm still not sure where he's heading with this line of enquiry, and that makes me nervous. But I do everything I can to hide my disquiet.

'She tasted it,' I say calmly. 'She found it very hot, as in spicy, but she knew that I'd made it that way because it's how Dan likes it. But she suffered no ill-effects, which proves that she added the poison after I'd gone.'

'And what happened next, that evening, after Mrs Hegarty tested the dish?'

I narrow my eyes as I try to remember accurately. 'I left pretty much straightaway.'

321

'Hmm.' The barrister sniffs and nods his head as if weighing up what I've said. 'Straightaway,' he repeats. 'You're sure about that, Ms Carr?'

I work hard to keep my face expressionless. 'Yes. Absolutely sure.'

'Really?' His voice is laden with disbelief. 'So you judged Mrs Hegarty to be distraught and distracted, as well she might be when what lay ahead of her was a meeting crucial to the saving of her twenty-five year marriage.'

*Twenty-five years.* The number hits me like a cosh. The jury will be beguiled by such a long-lasting union, censorious about the person who threatened it.

'Yes,' I repeat. What is his point? When he next speaks, I find out.

'So she was in enough of a muddled state that, when she turned away from you to finish ironing her blouse or to put something on the table, she wouldn't have noticed you slipping the poison hemlock into the curry?'

*Her blouse.* How old is he? Doesn't he know that women wear shirts these days, just like men? I hope this will show the jury how out of touch with reality this man is.

'Because that's what happened, isn't it, Ms Carr?' he continues. 'You set the whole thing up to frame Mrs Hegarty and you hoped her unsettled frame of mind would allow you to get away with it.'

'No,' I state, calmly but insistently. 'Categorically no. I did not poison the curry.'

'No further questions, m'lord,' says the barrister.

I step down from the box feeling a mixture of relief and

confusion. I'm not sure what was achieved during that questioning. But I have a lingering sense of something unfinished. None of it seems to be as clear cut as it should be – and that worries me.

However, as the case progresses I begin to relax.

There are plenty of other factors that add up against Charlotte, that leave her hung out to dry. Naomi tells the court about the 'welcome' meal Charlotte invited her to shortly after her arrival in the village, how she'd been very ill after eating mushrooms Charlotte had foraged. Crucially, it was another instance where more than one person ate the same meal but only one of them suffered symptoms.

If it sounds suspicious, looks suspicious, and smells suspicious …

Everything conspires against her. Why did she eat so little herself? She doesn't like curry, she explains. She hates spicy, chilli-laden food. But she also doesn't normally eat carbs and yet on this night, had a mountain of rice, naan and poppadoms on her plate – as testified to by Dan – a calorie-fest her body hasn't seen since about 1999.

The jurors stare intently. No one fidgets. No one loses concentration for a moment.

In addition to the mushroom story, Naomi uses her time in court to lay it all on the line – all the petty insults Charlotte has fired in her direction over the years, all the jealousy she's displayed towards the poor, sweet, buxom waitress her husband had befriended. Charlotte's barrister is good but he hasn't prepared for her to lose the sympathy of the court and once she has, it seems there is no way back.

By this stage, there may still have been a grain of hope for her. A soupçon, a gram. But then the fatal text message is read. I had to hand it over; it's a crime to withhold evidence. As the words are enunciated, everyone knows it is the moment that changes everything. It's an admission of intent, and laden with profanities, which never go down well with a jury. Especially not coming from a posh woman who should know better.

*I wish I could just get rid of him. For ever. I feel like fucking poisoning the bastard. In fact, I think I will. I'll kill the motherfucker for what he's done to me.*

There's only one thing I don't tell the court, and it doesn't involve a lie. They don't ask me. So I don't have to admit that I left the necklace on purpose, that I broke the chain and put it under the bed. I did it after Dan delivered his bombshell, popping upstairs on the pretext of fetching my cardigan. It was the only thing I could think of that might ensure Charlotte found out that Dan had slept with someone while she was away which, I believed, would bring their marriage to an end.

It was my only hope.

# Chapter 45

## Susannah

Eventually, just as spring was turning to summer and the leaves on the trees were thick and green, the date for my sentencing arrived. The press came out in force; it could hardly have been a better story.

The jilted girlfriend, the French temptress, the handsome, talented man caught between two beautiful women – precisely the stuff newspapers, particularly the tabloids, thrive on. The public gallery was full to bursting point.

Because of my guilty plea there was no need for anyone to give evidence, so there would be no weeping Josephine in the dock, relating how she nearly died (she didn't), no steely eyed Charlie recalling the fear I instilled in him (he wasn't, ever, frightened).

Only I would be there.

The judge, a kindly old man who smiled broadly at me when I was led in, gave a brief summing up of the case as he saw it. He explained how I had been so poorly treated by Charlie that I had been left in a state of utter despair, and that I had clearly suffered inordinately by being abandoned in favour of another woman. He understood that I obviously still loved Charlie very much and this had clouded my reason and made me act in a way that was completely out of character.

My unblemished record hitherto, my creditable exam results, my solid, middle-class upbringing, were all cited in my favour. Finally, explained the judge, I had already lost everything that mattered to me – my partner, my degree, my home. I had acted in an ill-advised and imprudent way but I had had no serious intent to maim or kill and, in his opinion, I had endured enough. He painted me as an ingenue who should be pitied, not punished.

In light of all of this, he let me off virtually scot-free. No penalty, just a suspended sentence. And, of course, a criminal record.

It was a better outcome than I could possibly have expected and no one could believe it, least of all me. But, when I had recovered enough from the shock to think about it more deeply, it was obvious what had happened. The judge had fallen for my youth, my pretty face. Perhaps I reminded him of his own daughter, or niece, or a family friend. The silly old fool clearly couldn't bear to see me carted away in a van, forced to endure the deprivations and degradations of life in a women's prison. I just wasn't that sort of criminal.

Thanks to that judge's old-fashioned attitude and susceptibility to a young girl's good looks, I walked from the Old Bailey, the scales of justice glittering in the pale autumn sun, a free woman.

Charlotte doesn't look as if she'll be as lucky as I was. I'm sure it would be the same if I were in her position. For a start, we're middle-aged women now, no longer able to hide behind the recklessness of youth, to use it as an excuse for foolish and impetuous behaviour. More importantly, we're no longer fresh-faced, dewy-skinned, doe-eyed beauties – not like twenty-year-olds are, anyway. So I suppose it's hardly surprising that the jury is not all that sympathetic.

Lacing a curry with poison hemlock, leaves that perhaps she gathered from the patch we had visited all those months ago when I had first got involved with her foraging club, is never going to be explained away as an accident, an inadvertent mistake. The fact that she used her wholesome, happy-clappy hobby to nearly kill her own spouse ... well, any courtroom would view that with the horrified disdain it deserves.

The gossips in the village have gone mad for this story, as one might imagine. Of course it's not just the poisoning that has set tongues wagging. It's the juicy details, now fully out in the open, about me and Dan, combined with Charlotte's incandescent rage, her quest for retribution.

Miriam has been wearing a stunned, disbelieving expression for weeks now; every time she sees me her jaw drops an inch or two further. I don't know if she's more incredulous that Charlotte is a would-be murderer or that I, the poor church mouse, managed to attract the village superhero. She's clearly having difficulty with the concept of taking Charlotte and Dan off the pedestal she's kept them on ever since they first pitched up in the village, Mr and Mrs Nobody from Nowhere masquerading as the squire and his wife.

The press is having a field day, just as they did all those years ago when it was me in the dock.

'Murderous mother vowed revenge' blares the headline of the local free sheet. Jealousy is an emotion that everyone can understand so it's no great surprise when the theory put forward is that Charlotte arranged the meal with Dan, pretending she was looking for reconciliation, whilst in fact secretly planning to murder him in the most terrible way. She accepted my offer of the curry to cover her tracks; if I had made it, it could not be her who was responsible for the poisoning, I suppose must have been her rationale – though of course, in court she denies it.

I'm so sorry for her boys, and there's a part of me that feels pity for Charlotte, too. When I gave chocolates injected with mercury to Charlie and Josephine, I was propelled by heartbreak and devastation. For Charlotte, as far as I can see, it was pure base anger, a desire for revenge, a determination to make sure that Dan never went with anyone behind her back again.

There's one thing I do feel bad about, that I sincerely regret. I should have told her about me and Dan. I should have been the one to tell her truth – though not of course that I deliberately planted the necklace. No, let her think that had been an accident, a silver chain broken unnoticed in the throes of passion. Once she and Dan were back from Corsica I had ruminated about confessing, going over and over it so many times, the pros and cons, whether I should or whether I shouldn't. In the end, I left it too late.

So instead I decided to say sorry. I went back to see

Charlotte, that evening after I'd dropped off the curry. But I wavered as I approached her front door, remembering her verbal attack on me when we met in the village. My resolve deserted me and I slunk back home. Jamie was still at his cinema party and Luke and Sam were so engrossed in whatever they were watching that they didn't even notice I'd gone out, so I never told anyone.

I read in the papers that it came out in court that Charlotte had recognised my necklace quite early on, that she was the one who had returned it to me, and also that Dan had confessed only when stricken with the poison – the last revelations of the dying man.

Except he didn't die.

Which is fortunate because it means she is not facing an actual murder charge. They say he'll be fine now; if it doesn't kill stone dead at the time, there are no lasting effects of hemlock poisoning. Charlotte played it so cleverly by pretending she shared in the poisoned meal, even though she actually barely touched it.

Anything other than a guilty verdict seems unlikely. If I had been to prison myself all those years ago I'd be in a position to give her advice – what not to do and say once she's behind bars, how to survive such a hostile environment. But mine was merely an act of folly that I got away with, whereas hers ... she had intended to take a man's life.

Once the jury gives their verdict, Charlotte won't be able to deny it anymore.

# Chapter 46

## Charlotte

During the trial, the hours in that courtroom, bland and sterile and windowless, there is nothing to look at but the intent faces of the jurors, trying to seem intelligent and as if they understand what is going on when they are clearly far too stupid to do so, the peacocking barristers, so full of themselves in their pretentious wigs and gowns, and the court reporters, pencils flying across shorthand notepads. And you.

Preening yourself, so pleased that you'd set up your attack on Dan so cleverly that it is I who is taking the blame. You would probably say that I made myself vulnerable by making so many mistakes and maybe I did. But that's often what happens to the innocent, isn't it? They fall foul of their own guilelessness. Their inability to foresee that their best friend might sleep with their husband and then, when told that it's going nowhere and that he really loves his wife, try to kill him. If you couldn't have him, you didn't want anyone to have him, did you? Least of all me, his lawful spouse.

When you put the hemlock in the curry, you cared nothing

for either Dan nor me; our lives were yours to take to make yourself feel better. Did you even think of my boys, orphaned so young? And what, really, were you going to gain from it? It's not as if you would benefit in any way. On the other hand, maybe you planned for only me to die, thinking that someone smaller and lighter might succumb more easily, leaving you free to close in on Dan, bereaved and suffering. To think that I am the one who warned you off the hemlock when we found it in that place we were foraging. If I'd said nothing you'd probably never have thought of such a vile plan.

All of these crazy thoughts tumble through my head as I sit in court or in my cell after I've given my evidence and wait for what is starting to seem inevitable.

The text message clinches it. Damn that stupid message. Damn that I sent it to you. Damn that you made sure you carefully preserved it. Handed it over at the first possible opportunity.

When the case collapses, at first I think it's a joke, a mistake, a cruel prank.

But it's not.

Non-disclosure of information. New facts. And then the words I'd hoped, but never truly believed I'd hear: 'You're free to go.'

These must be the sweetest words in the English language, the sound of justice being done.

# Chapter 47

## Susannah

I remember so clearly how I felt the day the judge set me free. A strange mixture of relief, disbelief, and aimlessness, as if now there was nothing left to fight for because all the fight had left me. I drifted for days, weeks, months. My parents tried to get me to restart my course, to contact the university and ask them if I could re-do the year. But my heart was no longer in it.

Anyone who's ever spent the night in a police cell, alone and afraid, with no idea what is going to happen, will understand that the experience never leaves you. If one has pleaded not guilty and therefore been to trial, undergone cross-examination and hostile questioning in the way Charlotte has over these past weeks, it must be even worse.

But now, against all the odds, inexplicably, unbelievably, she has got away with it.

I can't believe it. I didn't attend the trial, other than for my own time in the witness box. I thought it would come across as voyeuristic. There are plenty of people in the village who went along, populating the public gallery like so many febrile mediaeval spectators at a public hanging or burning. I had no intention of being one of their number. And anyway, I had to go to work and take care of my boys. I simply couldn't spare the time.

The papers filled in the gaps, reporting in infinitesimal detail the batting to and fro of the lawyers' statements and questions. It all seemed like a done deal. Until it wasn't. Until the day of the knock at the door.

It's early and I'm bundling Jamie out of the house to catch the bus to secondary school. Luke, in his last year at primary, is now allowed to walk there on his own but can leave twenty minutes later than his brother.

I see the patrol car approaching down the street and passing our door. I wonder what it's doing here. Probably there's been some trouble with the kids from the housing estate, I muse. There has been some vandalism lately, the swings in the children's playground have been destroyed and a litter bin set on fire. That's the problem with the country. There's absolutely nothing for these youths to do, no club, no sport, no activities. *The devil finds work for idle hands*, as Marjorie would say and, much as I hate to agree with her, it's true.

I pull the door closed behind Jamie and go back to trying to locate Luke's coat which has not been hung on the peg in the hallway as it should have been. I try to suppress my annoyance at his carelessness, whilst at the same time gently reminding him that it's his responsibility to look after his stuff and to know where it is for when it's needed.

The knock on the door comes as Luke is whining, 'Well, it's

not my fault,' and I am saying, in that voice of barely hidden irritation that all mothers will recognise, 'Well, whose fault is it then?' Telling him he needs to go and look again in his bedroom, the bathroom, the sitting room – in every room in the house, essentially – I go to answer the knock. I'm not even looking at who is on the doorstep as I open the door, but back at him to check he is actually following my instruction and not ducking back into the kitchen to retrieve his phone and play some more of whatever mindless game he's currently wasting his time on.

When I turn my head and see them, my heart skips a beat and my pulse starts racing.

'What ... what's the matter?'

Police officers on the door always spark terror. It reminds me of that time they came in answer to Charlie's accusations, but they're not just frightening for that reason. Immediately, I think the worst, that someone is harmed, that something awful has happened. It can't be Jamie, as he only just left. Justin? Has he done something stupid? No, he wouldn't; he'd never leave the boys without a father. But perhaps he's been knocked off his bike, injured, killed even? I'm probably still the person listed as next of kin on his documents ...

But it's not that. They're not here because of Justin, or Jamie.

'Ms Carr,' says the burly, tall one. 'We are arresting you for the attempted murder of Mr Daniel Hegarty and Mrs Charlotte Hegarty. You do not have to say anything ...'

Gradually, it dawns on me, the terrible, irrefutable, cataclysmic truth of what is happening.

That the person replacing Charlotte in the dock is me.

# *Chapter 48*

## *Charlotte*

I can't work out whether it's ironic that Miriam is the one I have to thank for how things changed. If it were, the irony would come from the fact that Miriam has been gossiping about me for years. Not in a bad way, you understand. Just that kind of tittle-tattle about someone that sets the tattler up as a friend and confidante, as someone special, someone with privileged access to the sanctified inner circle. With Miriam, it's all about her serf-like obsession with those richer, more beautiful, and infinitely higher in status than her.

The way she's always tried to inveigle herself into my good books through sheer, blatant sycophancy ended up being my saviour. The story, as I understand it, goes like this. Miriam is in the pub one night, after the parish council meeting. A young man joins the councillors at their table and says he's looking for someone, an old friend, who he believes lives in the village. Her name is Sue Birch, though she may have a married surname these days.

Miriam thinks there's something familiar about the name

but she can't quite place it, so she takes the young man's number and promises to call him if anything occurs to her. A day or so later, it does. She remembers exactly where she has come across the name Sue Birch. Written inside a book she'd seen in your living room, a tome on toxicology that you've kept all the years since university. You must have called yourself Sue rather than Susannah back in those days, and Birch is presumably your maiden name.

Miriam phones the young man and passes on the information. But the idea that he is a friend has started to seem strange. Surely he'd have looked online or on social media to find you if this were the case? Or enquired through mutual acquaintances?

Anyhow, armed with the address and phone number he needs, the young man clearly feels able to divulge more than he has before. He turns out to be a TV researcher, working on a documentary on female poisoners. Which, so it seems, is what you are. You once tried to kill your ex-boyfriend and his new partner with chocolates contaminated with mercury. Who would have thought that dear, sweet, unassuming Susannah could contain such evil intent within her? Truly, it's astonishing.

With that revelation, darling Miriam, always loyal, always on my side, endlessly held in thrall to my exalted position, my power of patronage in this small village, contacts my defence team. It's the spur they need to insist that the CPS pass on all of your phone and laptop records. The police have taken everything but not gone through it all, and not put any of your many incriminating internet searches, downloaded documents and phone calls forwards as evidence.

Once my lawyers discover your numerous delvings into foraging websites, asking questions about how much hemlock would be required to kill, how long it would take, if there is an antidote, your fate is sealed. You use the paedophile's excuse that it's all just research for your 'book' (the idea for which you scammed off me in the first place) but fortunately not even the police are stupid enough to fall for that one.

Interviewed under caution for the first time, Miriam comes up with her second gem. She had seen you, in the late afternoon, approaching my house via the back gate that leads to a path between the stable block and the walled garden, and thence to the kitchen door. Miriam herself had been in the lane searching for blackberries, which grow there in abundance. She had been concealed behind rampant tangles of brambles and, intent on her task, she had not called out to you. She had been surprised when you emerged only five minutes later but assumed you'd just dropped by on a whim and that I was out and therefore hadn't answered your knock.

Even after all this, once we get back into court, your defence team still tries to pin it on me.

'Mrs Hegarty, you are maintaining that, unbeknownst to you, Ms Carr entered your house, your kitchen, and put hemlock in the curry that you had already tasted. Do you really expect us to believe that she could have done this without you noticing, in the few minutes she had available to her? Those minutes that we know numbered no more than five as we have Miss Whitehead's testimony on this.'

I can see how it looks. A massive coincidence that in those five minutes, I was not in the kitchen or anywhere in the vicinity. But that's life, isn't it? Full of sliding doors moments – if this hadn't happened, then the next thing wouldn't have done and so on.

'Yes,' I reply. 'Susannah knew that when she dropped off the curry I still hadn't showered or done my hair. So she would have known that I would go off and do this at some point. And she also knew I wasn't my normal self, that I was all over the place. She took a lucky chance that I'd be elsewhere and it paid off. But she would have been able to see into the kitchen from outside and I suppose that, if she'd spotted that I was still in there, she'd just have gone away again and come back later. She didn't imagine that anyone would see her, so it wouldn't matter if she had to give it more than one try.'

'So we are supposed to believe, are we Mrs Hegarty, that in that grand house of yours, the biggest in the village, the manor no less, full of artworks and jewellery of considerable value and interest to thieves, you have no security devices against intruders? No alarms? No CCTV?'

The barrister flashes a conceited smile at the jury, as if to say, look at me, aren't I the bee's knees? Honestly, I thought having a woman against me would make it easier but actually I think they're worse than the men. Just as cocky and egotistical as the male of the species and utterly lacking in female solidarity.

'It may seem strange,' I respond, with complete equanimity, 'but you're right. We do have a burglar alarm but it's only used when the house is completely empty, which isn't very often with ...' I falter slightly as I realise that what I was going to say, 'with two live-in staff members, the housekeeper and the au pair we normally have' will not go down well with the twelve good men (and women) on the benches facing me. The last thing I need is for them to see me as a stuck-up rich bitch. 'With such a large family,' I resume, almost faultlessly, ending with a sweet, sad smile. 'We have never wanted our boys, our precious children, to feel like they're living in a fortress,' I continue, 'so we don't have CCTV. The fact of the matter is that there was nothing to stop Susannah walking right on in – and she knew it.'

Touché. I've done it. I've made us look humble and ordinary, no different, really, to any of the jury.

The barrister waffles on for a while, asking spurious questions that I easily bat back. When her questioning finishes, I allow myself a small, self-congratulatory smile. I think it went well.

Under cross-examination, Miriam helps out no end. She confirms that you were wearing your red trench coat. Not the obvious choice when slinking around trying to go unnoticed but, on the other hand, if you hadn't worn a coat at all it would have been odder. It was cold that day, rainy, the impending storm hanging heavy in the air. And everyone is used to seeing you in that scarlet garment – you might have drawn more attention without it.

Forensic tests add the final touch to the evidence. The right coat pocket, where it might be expected that a right-handed person would put things, bears traces of hemlock. Minuscule ones, but there nevertheless.

Incontrovertibly there.

# Chapter 49

## Susannah

Whilst the lawyers speak, we are only a few feet away from each other, Charlotte and I. We steadfastly ignore each other's gaze. The trial seems to last forever. My side has made a point of my good character, just as was the case all those years ago, my impeccable upbringing, my (mainly) private school education, my respectable position in society, my inherent decency ... They lay it on thick as treacle on a stack of pancakes.

Charlotte's side, on the other hand, has made a bad character application. There's an audible gasp when the details are put in front of the court.

That I have history. That I have form.

That I am a poisoner.

I'm hung out to dry, tarnished by a past that, to me, seems to belong to someone else. Unfortunately though, it is mine – and I can't escape it.

Eventually, it's time for the summing up. Nervously, I clasp my hands together and listen as if in a trance, unable to

343

connect to reality, my heart filled with a bitter, leaden dread.

'You poisoned Mr Hegarty because of your jealousy, hatred, and anger,' the prosecuting QC says, addressing the jurors, who are listening expectantly, eyes wide open, following his every gesture as he makes his statement. 'Over a sustained period of time, you did everything you could to try to win his heart, and to sour his relationship with his wife. You did this because you wanted him. His charm, his good looks, but above all his wealth, were things you coveted for yourself. But, though you seduced him and slept with him whilst Mrs Hegarty was away on a family holiday with her children, ultimately he turned you down. When you found out that the couple were trying to make up, to make a go of things, to rekindle their romance, you flipped. I put it to the court that you lost your mind and your anger – not for the first time in your life – became uncontrollable. You decided then and there to put a stop to it.'

The court is on tenterhooks, utterly silent, the weight of expectation hanging thick and heavy in the stuffy air.

'Mrs Hegarty never once suspected that you, the person who, though you had not known one another that long, had quickly become her best friend, was trying to steal her husband away from her. She could not possibly imagine what hatred lived within the depths of your heart, what cruelty you are capable of.'

'Objection!' My barrister's voice rings out. 'This is no time for melodrama and hyperbole.'

The judge nods. 'Please keep to the facts,' he says.

My legs are quivering, wobbling as if they might give way.

I don't understand what is happening, how they are making such a convincing case against me when it's all lies. No one realises that this is how justice works, that it hangs on who has the silkiest tongue, the most velvety words.

The QC's face is emotionless as he resumes. 'You poisoned their curry with hemlock you had gathered locally; you were well aware of where it grew and how toxic it is. Mr and Mrs Hegarty ate the curry.'

'No!' My voice is overly loud in the still, stifling air of the courtroom. 'No, it's not true.'

My defence team look towards me as one, horrified. The chief barrister makes a gesture that clearly says, 'Shut up.'

'Please could I request that all those in the courtroom are silent during the closing statements,' commands the judge, reprovingly.

The QC takes a deep breath and, with a flick of his gown, continues. 'Very soon the effects became apparent: a gradual paralysis of the limbs and the organs, but the victim remaining conscious to the last. Mr Hegarty was only saved by Mrs Hegarty's fearless journey through the stormy night to the hospital, and the prompt treatment he received once there from the paramedics, doctors, and nurses. Fortunately, Mrs Hegarty, who had barely eaten any of the curry herself, was minimally affected.'

The QC turns to me. I'm crying now, silent tears seeping from my eyes and down my cheeks. My head is in my hands, my blonde hair all awry, sodden strands sticking to my forehead and my face. I can sense the lack of sympathy in the stultifying air of the courtroom; it is like a thousand knives in my back. I rejoiced at this when it was aimed at Charlotte. Now pointed in my direction, it's a different matter altogether.

Pausing only for a moment, the QC directs his gaze back to the jurors. 'Hemlock, as many of us know, was the poison of choice of the ancients. It has not been used in a British poisoning case for many years, though another plant, a genus of wolfsbane, was used in a very similar crime in 2009. In that instance, the victim died.'

His voice, up to this point, has been measured, calm. Now it rises in volume and urgency as he addresses his comments directly to me. The theatricality of his actions is hard to ignore.

'Exactly what you hoped to achieve by what you did is unclear. As you have continued to protest your innocence, it is possible that we will never know. But the effects of what you have done will leave a lasting legacy on your victims for years to come.'

It won't. There are no lasting effects. You will be fine; so will Dan. It's all lies. Once more, I am silenced quickly when I start to shout this out.

A profound hush descends on the room. There is no possibility other than a guilty verdict.

# Chapter 50

## Charlotte

I read out my victim impact statement to the court. I have to take a few deep breaths to steady myself before I begin. My voice is strained and tight throughout. Frequent pauses occur whilst I forcibly suppress my tears. I conclude with the most powerful line of all: 'You tried to destroy our lives, but in the end, you destroyed your own.'

The judge gives a term of fourteen years. It's very reasonable, all things considered.

We leave the courtroom together, Dan and I, arm in arm. United. Everything you didn't want us to be. I manage to quash the urge to smile until we are out of sight of the cameras massed outside in the street. It wouldn't be good to be seen to be gloating, when the eyes of the world are upon us. Interest in the case has grown and grown, and it's built into a major story. Someone will probably turn it into a Hollywood movie. I wonder who will play me. Cate Blanchett would be good, but she's a little too old now, and too fair for me really. Anne Hathaway? So beautiful and talented, she'd be ideal. As for you, obviously Nicole Kidman leaps to mind. Fittingly blonde, and her character's cold pursuit of her aims by any means necessary in *To Die For* mirrors your manipulative murdering soul to perfection.

The whole business has done Dan no harm, either – he's busier, and richer, than ever. It'll make my book – nearly finished now – a bestseller. Shame yours will never see the light of day.

Back home, I wrap my arms around my husband.

'I'm cold,' I say. 'Let's have a sauna.'

Since Dan paid off my debts, I've rekindled my enjoyment in the sauna and we've recently had it upgraded, and a steam room complex installed. It helps both my back and Dan's stressed and work-sore limbs. I can really recommend it to anyone. It's worth every penny of the thirty thousand it's cost us. It doesn't remind me of my peccadilloes anymore, of my gambling. That's all in the past now, like so many things.

I go to the bedroom to take off my jewellery and my Dior jacket. I needed to look the part for court and I went for understated elegance. I think I pulled it off.

I take a piece of paper out of my pocket. I unfold it slowly and deliberately and scan my eyes over it. A slow smile spreads across my face. My 'alternative' victim statement. The one that is for my eyes only, that no one else will ever see or know existed.

# Epilogue

Well, Susannah, my erstwhile friend. What can I say? Walking away from the court when my case collapsed, I experienced the triumph that you probably felt when you got off more or less scot-free, all those years ago. It's a good feeling, isn't it?

You thought you were clever, that you could rob me of my husband. You pretended to be my best friend, but all the while you were plotting to take Dan from me. Unfortunately for you, though, I saw you coming. I've seen your ilk many times before. From the moment I first caught sight of you on the village green in your ridiculous scarlet coat, I knew the scarlet woman who lay beneath – and I knew that it was of the utmost importance that I keep close tabs on you. Keep your friends close and your enemies closer; it's the principle I always live by.

That 'accident' Luke had on the adventure playground? It was no such thing. I orchestrated it deliberately, knowing that yelling out would cause him or Jamie – hopefully both – to lose concentration and balance, leading to a fall. It was a surefire way to worm my way into your life, for us *to bond over a terrible tragedy that, by dint of some great good fortune, had been avoided. I needed to be close to you so that I would know what you were up to.*

*I have to say, though, that over time I did start to think that maybe my first impressions had been wrong. That you were, indeed, someone to be trusted. That you meant it when you said you'd look after Dan whilst I was in Corsica. Hindsight, as they say, is a wonderful thing and now I can't believe I was so stupid. Oh, you looked after him all right. Your treachery, in my opinion, was worse than his. Friends should stand up for each other, stick together. Have you never heard of sisterhood?*

*Of course I knew it was you who'd fucked my husband in my own bed. I suspected it even before I realised that the necklace was yours. When I remembered why it was familiar, that I'd seen the matching earrings in that photo that Miriam took of you and Dan outside the tennis club, I both could hardly believe it and knew it had always been inevitable. I saw that you had always been determined to get your hands on him. Was it arrogance, stupidity, or a bit of both that made you put the necklace straight back on again the day I returned it to you in the post? Did you do it deliberately to flaunt yourself? I wouldn't put it past you to have left it in my bedroom on purpose, some pathetic attempt to make sure I found out, to break Dan and I up. If that was the case, how little you know me – and him.*

*Even now, after all that's happened, I can hardly believe you're in prison, serving fourteen years for trying to kill my husband, Dan, the man you professed to love. Things got a bit sticky when I was arrested instead of you. I've got to admit, that was a tricky moment. It was so obvious to anyone with half a brain that you – the spurned lover, the discarded other woman – were the culprit. But for a moment there, I have to be honest, Susannah, I wondered if I'd completely blown it.*

*I'll grant you that what I did was risky. I had to take a chance – a big chance – that the hemlock I used to garnish the curry you made wouldn't kill him – or me. Planting the leaves in that ridiculous red coat of yours when you dropped off the curry and collected Sam for the sleepover was easily done. I knew that you had stashed leaves away in your pockets before and therefore wouldn't be surprised to find little bits and pieces of greenery still in there. The police, on the other hand, would be most interested in this evidence. Especially when forensic tests identified it as the very same substance that had been used to taint the dish that you prepared, supposedly so lovingly.*

*In the end, I managed the poisoning bit with admirable precision and accuracy. You should have been the only one ever to be in the frame. But Naomi blethered on about those bloody mushrooms, which were a genuine mistake, genuine, I tell you, and before I knew it I was in the dock. Everyone knew I had the knowledge from my foraging expertise and one thing led to another and … well, things nearly went very wrong for me.*

*Thank goodness for Miriam, faithful to the last, and always, always on the lookout for gossip. When she met that researcher in the pub she quickly put two and two together and made four, realising who he was seeking: you. Finding out that he was trying to track you down to take part in a TV documentary about female poisoners was a gift to my defence and therefore to me.*

*It was complete coincidence that I chose poison as the way to set you up. Absolute serendipity. I didn't know then that you had form in the poisoning area. But I did know that you would be able to find the hemlock patch again and that you knew how dangerous it was. Not only I, but any of the foragers who were with us that day, would be able to testify to that. When it came out that you had done it before, that you had tried to harm the man and woman who had thwarted you in your desires, it all fell into place. Your shameless offer to make the curry for my reunion with Dan bore so many similarities to adulterating that box of chocolates that you had given to your boyfriend and his lover, the woman he preferred over you.*

*From the moment all this information was out in the open my plan, which had for a while been under such threat, fell back into place again. I had made sure to taste the curry when you brought it round, but to take only such a tiny amount that it couldn't possibly have an adverse effects. That was important because at first I thought the allegation would be that you'd already poisoned it when you deposited it at my house. Miriam's eye-witness account of seeing you outside later on, in the early evening, changed all that. You'd come back to do the dirty deed, so my earlier tasting became irrelevant. I could hardly believe the gift I'd been given – such stupidity on your part, such luck for me!*

# The Best of Friends

When I look back now, I can appreciate that there were more than a few delicate moments. On the night itself I didn't bargain on the storm, nor on quite how much Dan would eat. But once a gambler, always a gambler – and this time, the risk paid off.

Now you're in prison and Dan's eternally grateful to me for what I did, driving through the relentless weather, the tree-felling storm, to get him to the hospital in time to save his life, even when my own was also in jeopardy. For snatching him away from your disingenuous clutches.

He'll never stray again.

You didn't ever really understand what kind of person I am, how far I'll go to protect me and mine. Though you knew that, when it comes to my kids, I'm a mother bear defending her cubs to my last breath, you failed to see that this would extend to my husband, too. You thought I'd just give him up to you. That I'd let him go and wish him well. How could you be so foolish? Like Icarus, you flew too close to the sun on flimsy wings of lust and deceit and inevitably you crashed and burned.

If you're feeling down, look at it this way. You haven't done so badly. With the sentence you've been given, you'll be out in under ten years, probably even less if you behave nicely. Don't come back to the village, though. You won't be welcome here, ever again.

Sorry-not-sorry, Susannah Carr – or should I call you Sue Birch? But nobody touches my husband, threatens my family, my lifestyle, my future and gets away with it.

I hope you know that now.

353

When I've finished reading, a smile of quiet and simple satisfaction upon my face, I tear the letter into tiny pieces, scrunch them up in my hand and put them back in my pocket. I leave them there until the afternoon, when we troop out to the green to take part in the first of the season's paper chases. 'We', today, means me and Dan and Sam. Toby is still at school, the twins on their gap year in South America. They had to postpone it because of the court case but they're back on track now and will be off to university in the autumn. It was hard for all of them to come to terms with the attempted assassination of their father, but over time we've helped them to understand and in the end it's actually brought us all closer together, the Hegartys against the world, snug and safe in our – extremely well-heeled – little unit. Even my baby, Sam, is over the worst of it now and positively revelling in all the attention that comes to the last one left at home.

Your Jamie and Luke have moved back to London to live with their father for the duration. Poor kids. But it's best for them to be away from your suffocating care; they were in danger of becoming terrible mummy's boys. All women deny that they criticise other mothers' parenting but they all do it. And with you, there is – was – a lot to criticise.

Leaving Dan and Sam talking strategies – it's lovely to see how much greater a part Dan is playing in the boys' lives these days – I wander a little way away, following the paper trail. I pull the remains of the letter out of my pocket and open my hand, allowing the wind to grab the pieces and disperse them into those already lying on the frost-hard ground. At first they seem conspicuous, so white amidst the colours of red, blue and green. But soon the eye becomes accustomed to differences and stops noticing them and so it is now. I pause for a moment, considering the irony of making my letter part of the very game that first brought us together, two years ago on Toby's birthday.

That day was the start of the competition between us, the tussle to win the heart and mind of Dan. And I've ended up where I always knew I would.

The winner.

A gust of wind stirs the paper pieces and then subsides, leaving the trail intact, stretching into the distance. A whistle sounds and the race starts. The boys stream past. My husband, on the sidelines, cheers them on.

This time, my Sam is in the lead.

# *Acknowledgements*

Like many authors, my writing takes place around the demands of an extremely taxing job so I must thank everyone who puts up with me taking notes, editing documents, and getting lost in thought in the middle of a conversation when an idea strikes me. My time to write is so limited that it has to be an ongoing process – there's no opportunity to wait for the muse to arrive, it's a question of making the most of every spare minute.

That said, in the midst of all my other commitments, this book has taken quite a few iterations to get right. I am eternally grateful to my agent, Megan Carroll at Watson, Little, for carefully, patiently and painstakingly helping me get the story right. It took a bit of time, but we got there in the end! Thank you also to Kathryn Cheshire at HarperCollins who greeted the manuscript so enthusiastically – that was a real boost at the end of a long-drawn out writing process.

Thank you, finally, to everyone who reads *The Best of Friends* – I hope you enjoy reading it as much as I – eventually! – enjoyed writing it.

Enjoyed *The Best of Friends?* Make sure
you've read *The Missing Twin* ...

**A missing girl ... a secret to be
uncovered.**

Edie and her identical twin
Laura have always been
best friends. So when
Laura surprises Edie at the
Mediterranean holiday resort
where she's working,
Edie can't wait for the partying to
start! But then,
Laura vanishes without a trace ...

At the same time, in a country on the other side
of the sea, Fatima and her twin daughters set out
on a harrowing journey that only the strongest
– and luckiest – survive.

Edie and Fatima's lives are worlds apart,
but now, their paths are set to collide, with
devastating consequences. When Fatima hovers
on the brink of survival, Edie must risk her
own life to save her, and finally discover the
truth about her missing sister.